When **Virginia Heath** was a little girl it took her ages to fall asleep, so she made up stories in her head to help pass the time while she was staring at the ceiling. As she got older the stories became more complicated—sometimes taking weeks to get to their happy ending. One day she decided to embrace her insomnia and start writing them down. Virginia lives in Essex, with her wonderful husband and two teenagers. It still takes her for ever to fall asleep…

A WARRINER TO SEDUCE HER

Virginia Heath

MILLS & BOON

First published in Great Britain 2018
by Mills & Boon, an imprint of HarperCollins*Publishers*
1 London Bridge Street, London, SE1 9GF

Large Print edition 2018

© 2018 Susan Merritt

ISBN: 978-0-263-07495-6

MIX
Paper from
responsible sources
FSC
www.fsc.org
FSC C007454

This book is produced from independently certified
FSC™ paper to ensure responsible forest management. For
more information visit www.harpercollins.co.uk/green.

Printed and bound in Great Britain
by CPI Group (UK) Ltd, Croydon, CR0 4YY

For Dave.

Welcome to our crazy family!

Prologue

Markham Manor—February 1803

'**W**hy don't we go and walk in the orchard, Mama?' He tugged her hand, hoping she would cease staring at the river. While her distant mood and melancholy were nothing new, and nor was the route their daily walk had taken, the water was high and angry after the week of rain and the sight of it bothered him.

'When I was a young girl, Jake, we used to promenade along the River Thames at Putney. Sometimes my father would row us out onto the water, but more often than not we used to sit on the banks with a picnic. He used to love escaping the crowds of London and while away the hours on that pretty stretch of the river.' At least she was talking, albeit about the past again, which was a marked improvement on the painful silence he had endured for the last two hours.

But then it was always the same after his parents had been fighting, which they did with the same regularity as the sun rose in the mornings and set at night. His elder brothers Jack and Jamie always claimed it was best to leave them both be afterwards, and although he knew they were probably right, Jake's bedchamber was next to his mother's and the familiar sounds of his parents' explosive, poisonous relationship taunted him and haunted him in equal measure. Her angry shouts and spiteful words, his father's drunken slurring, the short and terrifying bouts of violence which they both participated in and then the odd silence, broken only by whispers, intimate laughter and the inevitable rhythmic creaking of the bed frame. When his father left her soon after, as he always did to find more brandy or whisky or whatever cheap grog he had managed to procure instead, there would be more cruel words followed by his mother's noisy tears. It was so very hard to sleep with all that wailing going on and his poor childish heart wished he could make her happy, even though Jake knew that was impossible, too. His mother's happiness remained in the past, well before she had met his father and stupidly married him.

If he had been Joe, he could have read to her. Mama liked that—sometimes—but although only one year separated him from his closest sibling, Jake had struggled to learn his letters and his mother became impatient when he stumbled over the words. Jamie earned her smiles by painting her beautiful pictures, although he did that less and less because he said she was selfish and self-indulgent and he had no time for either. His eldest brother saved her from the worst of their father's daytime violence, by absorbing the blows in her stead, and took on the main brunt of the parenting because neither she nor his father could be bothered. The only thing Jake excelled at was making her laugh or by being the ears which listened to her incessant ramblings about her old life, back when she had been happy and he could only do that by keeping her company.

'Tell me about London, Mama.'

As he'd hoped, the usually dead light flickered in her eyes. 'It's a grand place, Jake. So vibrant and exciting. Every night there is a different ball or party to attend and my dear papa made sure I had enough gowns for all of them. They were always in the first stare of fashion and the gossip columns frequently commented upon them. The dancing was my favourite. I was renowned for my grace as much as for my beauty…' She sighed and closed her eyes, picturing it all. 'It's the most wonderful feeling, Jake, swaying in time to the music and being adored by the lucky gentleman I had deigned to dance with…'

Jamie often said she was vain, too, preferring to spend hours having her hair dressed for dinner than spending any time with the sons she conveniently forgot existed. Jake secretly agreed, but felt guilty for agreeing, because she was always so sad he reasoned it had to be good that looking pretty pleased her.

'That's where I met your father. Without waiting for the proper introductions, he pencilled his name on my dance card. He was a wonderful dancer and so handsome.' Two of the few positive things anyone could say about him.

Her eyes fluttered open and she noticed Jake for the first time in an hour. Her hand came up and cupped his cheek. A rare and precious moment of parental affection in a home devoid of any. 'You're the most like him, you know. You have his smile and his way with words.' As his father's words were always slurred or nonsensical from inebriation that comparison didn't particularly please him, but Jake didn't move or speak because at least she saw him. 'He was a charmer, too, just like you are... I dare say you'll grow up to be identical as well. His bad blood runs the strongest through you.' Her hand slipped back to her side and her expression soured. Because he reminded her so much of his father she looked away in disgust. That cold, dead stare out to nothingness reserved wholly for him for disappointing her so. How he hated that look.

'Go fetch him, Jake.'

'Not now Mama. It's still early.' Two in the afternoon was practically dawn by his father's standards. 'Let him sleep it off a bit longer. Tell me more about your picnics in Putney.'

'No, Jacob! Fetch him now.'

He never understood how it was possible for her to simultaneously loathe and love his horrid father at the same time. How could those opposing emotions exist together? He loved his brothers, sometimes they irritated him, but Jake never hated them. Joe reckoned this was because the love between men and women was entirely different from brotherly love. If that was true, then he wanted no part in that destructive other kind of love. Jake hated arguments. And bad moods. He preferred fun and laughter to tears and tantrums.

'Let's walk in the orchard instead.' Away from the dangerous, angry water which she seemed intent on staring at.

'I don't want to. I want my husband. Bring him to me! Tell him I will throw myself in the river if he doesn't come!'

And there it was, the usual threat. Mama was always threatening to end her life in whichever violent way was closest to hand to get her own way. Yesterday, she had threatened to stab her heart with her embroidery scissors, last week she was going to fling herself under a carriage. She never once tried, but his father still came running, after Jake had borne the brunt of his drunken temper at being awoken when his head still pounded. He would haul his dissolute carcass from his pit, dash to his woman and the pair of them would go at it again like vicious cats with their claws bared until they disappeared into her bedchamber.

With the threat of the customary angry punch from his hateful father and the petulant, dramatic whining he would hear from his mother if he refused, Jake nodded. Resisting was futile. This was the way of things. His parents hated each other and were addicted to each other at the same time. The emotions so powerful they blotted out and excluded everyone and everything from the personal hell they preferred to share together.

With heavy feet he trudged back towards the house and tried to fill his head with happy thoughts instead. Purposefully light and cheerful things which he would one day enjoy, but which did not exist in his miserable childhood. Parties, balls, dancing ladies in beautiful gowns, rowing boats and sunny picnics...

Instead of fetching his father he sat down to daydream, waiting long enough to ensure she believed his lie that dear Papa couldn't be woken. Another habit which earned him censure from both his parents. Sometimes that worked and she would march back to the house in a temper to give him what for. Other times, she scowled at Jake and called him useless like his father, then ordered him straight back, but at least he had delayed the inevitable.

It was always inevitable.

With a sigh he stood and headed back to where he'd left her. As soon as he emerged from around the trees she turned and smiled, then promptly launched herself off the bank into the swirling water.

At first he stood frozen to the spot, but then realised the gravity of the situation. She had carried out her threat and he'd failed to fetch his father. His father might well be a roaring drunk, but he was a strong one and could save her. Now all she had was Jake, the smallest and most useless Warriner.

He sprinted towards the river bank calling to her, dropping to his belly at the edge and stretching out his arm. 'Mama! Grab my hand!' But she was too far away from his childish arms to reach, clinging to overhanging branches of the bare weeping willow as the river foamed and rolled around her, coughing violently as water splattered into her lungs.

He ran to the tree, screaming for help. 'Jack! Jamie! Come quick!'

His elder brothers were in the field somewhere, working because most of the labourers had left long ago. He had no idea where Joe was, but willed him here, too. Joe was cleverer than Jake and his quick brain would find the solution, although anyone else would be better than just him. In desperation, he clung to the sturdy trunk and leaned out as far as he dared, knowing that if he tumbled in then the raging river would take him and they would both be dead.

'You need to grab my hand, Mama!' Hot tears were streaming down his face. Tears of guilt and terror, of shame at not being good enough and too selfish to sacrifice himself. 'Please!'

Her heavy winter coat and long skirts were weighing her down like an anchor. Jake could see that as well as he could see the fear in his mother's eyes just before her head plunged beneath the water. It bobbed up, but barely. Only her face was visible as she gulped for air, but her eyes locked with his and beneath her fear he saw the disappointment that he had failed her just as his father had so many times. In that moment, he realised she had never meant to die.

'Grab my hand…please!' Her chilled fingers were losing their grip on the slippery fronds, the fast current was greedily flowing around her, each new surge ebbing higher and higher as she struggled to stay afloat. Soon her fingers, then her face disappeared beneath the water and all Jake could see was the tangled whirl of her green skirts trailing like river weed among the branches of the willow.

He couldn't tear his gaze away from the dreadful sight, even for the thumping sound of racing feet behind him, watching powerless as his two eldest brothers selflessly risked their own lives to correct his mistake. Joe arrived soon after and was stood frozen behind, his face white and terrified. Like a statue, he was so still.

In his daze, the tragedy unfolded.

Jack, his eldest brother, waist deep in the water, holding Jamie's hand tightly on the bank as he tried to grasp her.

Jack carrying his mother's limp and bedraggled body towards the bank.

Jamie laying her out on the ground, pumping her chest. The eerie gurgle of water trickling from her mouth with each push. Painful minutes ticking by before pressing his ear to her chest. Shaking his head.

Joe's pleading voice. 'We have to save her. There must be something we can do?'

His eldest brother's arms went around his shoulder. He didn't offer platitudes or false hope, simply his strength, and Jake leaned on him.

'This is all my fault.'

'No, it isn't. You did all you could.'

Which was never enough.

His mother's lifeless eyes as she gazed up from the mud. That final cold, dead stare out to nothingness. Disappointed for evermore.

Chapter One

Lord Fennimore's Mayfair study, on a very wet night in February 1820

Thanks to the splendid port, the cosy heat from the fire and a distinct lack of sleep the night before Jake would soon need a pair of matchsticks to prop open his eyes. Viscount Linford was droning on about the latest numbers of confiscated barrels of brandy in every coastal county the length and breadth of the entire British Isles, or at least he had been before Jake's mind had wandered off to greener pastures while listening to the man's soporific voice.

As always, the Viscount measured success in numbers, seemingly oblivious to the fact it made no difference how many cargoes the blockade men had seized this month compared to last. Those dull statistics were a drop in the ocean—albeit the English Channel—compared to the massive cargoes which slipped past them daily. For a small pile of coin, most people could be relied upon to be resourceful. But smugglers weren't most people, the piles they wanted weren't small and their resources far outstripped those of the rag-tag disorganisation of the Board of Excise. Whoever the mysterious Boss was, his toxic network was proving near impossible to infiltrate. Crowbars wouldn't budge the terrified sealed lips of the few crews they had arrested and for every ship they seized another twenty sailed right past.

'All well and good, but can we trace any of those barrels back to Crispin Rowley?' Lord Fennimore's curt tone suggested he was as bored by the Viscount's bean-counting as Jake was.

'Not exactly.'

'Not exactly? What sort of an answer is that? Either we have a traceable link to the bounder or we don't.'

Viscount Linford began to blink at the challenge. 'We know that a substantial amount of those barrels were destined for the capital.'

'And?' Fennimore was losing patience. 'We are in the midst of the Season, when I dare say London consumes more than its fair share of brandy.

Are Rowley or any of his associates transporting the goods further afield or selling the stuff in the capital?'

'Not that we can find. He's covered his tracks well. However, we all know he is the source.'

'Knowing it and proving it are two very different things. The Attorney General will sign no warrant for the man's arrest unless he has tangible evidence of Rowley's involvement.' Something they had failed to get in the six months since Crispin Rowley had come under the suspicion of the King's Elite, a small but highly skilled band of covert operatives created to infiltrate and take down the powerful, organised smuggling rings which threatened Britain's ailing economy.

Rowley was linked to a ring that they believed was funding the loyal last remnants of Napoleon's army, which was a great cause for concern. This group was intent on stealing the former French leader from his island prison and returning him to power, using funds raised from smuggled brandy on the shores of the very enemy that had brought him down, and at the helm was one man: the faceless, untraceable and powerful man known only as the Boss. As much as ten thousand gallons a month were finding their way into the public's glasses in the south-east, no duty paid and all profits heading directly back to the French rebels.

But this smuggling ring was not only supplying the capital. Every major city, the length and breadth of the British Isles, was benefitting from cheap spirits to such an extent the bottom had practically dropped out of the legitimate market. Most worrying was the persistent intelligence that hinted the group's tentacles were firmly embedded among the ranks of the British aristocracy. Men with the power, connections and means to distribute the goods widely. Lord Crispin Rowley was the first and only name from that dangerous list they had.

So far they only had the tenuous word of a French double agent, who up until recently had been completely loyal to Bonaparte. His sudden change of allegiance, combined with his hasty flight from France, did not instil a great deal of confidence in his intelligence. Not when the man had urgently needed asylum and was still too terrified to come out of the hiding place Lord Fennimore had provided him, lest his former comrades hunted him down and assassinated him as they had so many other informants.

As much as none of them trusted that man's

word, there was a great deal about Lord Crispin Rowley which did not ring true and had set the intuitive Lord Fennimore's alarm bells ringing. Three years ago Rowley had been on the brink of bankruptcy. The government contracts he had enjoyed during the war years to supply grain to the British army were cancelled after Waterloo and with no market for his corn and prices plummeting, as with many of the landed aristocracy, Rowley had suffered gravely and become disillusioned with the crown, blaming his collapse entirely on the government's lack of perceived loyalty to those who had helped England win the war.

Crispin Rowley wasn't the only peer of the realm who had turned on the government. Others also felt betrayed and were vocal in their criticism. While Jake had some sympathy for the way those men had been treated, he was also a realist. The world was changing rapidly and to survive the aristocracy had to learn to adapt. Land alone would not sustain a fortune any longer. Not with the mills, mines and colonies proving to be more lucrative for canny investors with ready coin to spend and cheap foreign grain pouring into England's ports.

Rowley, like so many of his ilk, had appeared to be doomed. His fields remained fallow, his labourers laid off and his creditors lining up at his scuffed and peeling front door. Then, for no discernible reason as far as anyone could tell, his fortunes miraculously turned around eighteen months ago. The huge debts he had racked up had been paid off in impressive lump sums and the formerly penniless peer was now positively lording it up all over the capital.

And he suddenly kept some impressive company. Bankers, shipping magnates, dukes and foreign princes all now enjoyed Rowley's extensive hospitality and, if their intelligence was to be believed—and Jake had no reason to doubt it—there appeared to be no ulterior motive to the man's benevolence at all. He didn't own businesses outright, preferring to dabble in stocks and shares like much of the new money. He was, to all intents and purposes, merely an investor—yet the double agent was adamant Rowley's fortune was intrinsically linked to the free traders as their main distributor in the south-east of England.

'So we've hit another dead end!' His friend, and former Cambridge classmate, Seb Leatham slumped back in his chair like a petulant child and shook his head. 'We keep throwing mud at the man and nothing sticks. Nothing! Surely there must be a chink in the fellow's armour somewhere?' He and his men had been watching Rowley's every movement in the last few months and Seb's legendary patience was wearing thin.

'Not that I've found.' Lord Peter Flint sighed from his place across the table. Being the heir to a barony and an enormous fortune, Flint had managed to inveigle his way into Rowley's vast inner circle and had spent months socialising with him in the hope of being allowed into the inner sanctum. 'I'm starting to wonder if we're barking up the wrong tree and he is not the man we are looking for. I've plied his closest cronies with drink and asked them all manner of subtle probing questions and nobody knows anything other than the fact he likes to speculate.'

'He must have secret associates. We have to keep digging. If we could get inside his house, watch the comings and goings, read his correspondence and private papers, we'll find something.'

Flint glared at his boss. 'I've searched his study. Repeatedly. There's nothing there.'

'Which is why we need ears inside that house. A

slippery eel like Rowley is hardly going to leave damning evidence lying about in Mayfair when he's invited guests in. If we can bribe a servant or get someone on the inside during the day to snoop around, I'll wager that's when we'll find his weakness.'

'I've offered huge bribes to as many minor servants as we dare. All have been refused. The others are too close to Rowley for me to risk approaching them. They will only tip him off.' Seb Leatham always sounded angry even when he wasn't. Unlike the suave Flint he worked best in the shadows and had a knack for blending in with the lowest of the low. 'And we already know the place is guarded like a fortress. Right now, he's confident enough to make mistakes. We daren't risk shaking that confidence by breaking in.'

'Then we'll need to be invited, won't we?' Fennimore smiled enigmatically. A sure sign he had dredged up something thus far undiscovered. Whatever it was Jake didn't care. He'd spent the last eight months infiltrating a gun-smuggling consortium running out of the East End docks and, now that the lynchpins were all sat in damp cells in Newgate awaiting trial, blissfully unaware of how their empire had crumbled, Jake was due a significant stretch of leave. Hell, he'd earned it. It had been a dangerous assignment and one he'd barely survived without a bullet between the eyes.

Tomorrow, he would head north to Markham Manor and see his brothers for the first time in almost a year. For some strange reason, he had a hankering for the north and for home in particular. Probably because he was tired. Leading a double life, a secret double life, was exhausting. In deepest, darkest, dankest Nottinghamshire he was just Jake. It would almost be as good to be that carefree young rapscallion again as it would to see his family. Three months of being himself, no hidden agendas, no danger, no responsibilities and no web of lies.

Except the one.

The rest of the Warriners had absolutely no idea the directionless rake of the family had worked for the British government since the day he left Cambridge, when Lord Fennimore had recognised he actually had some potential, albeit not potential which would ever serve a good purpose. Not strictly true. Jamie suspected. The questions he asked and the quiet assessing way he had about him suggested he was piecing together the hidden puzzle of Jake's life. Jamie hadn't vocalised his theory outright, because that was not his reticent elder brother's style, but he had abruptly stopped joining in with the litany of criticisms Jake had received about his lack of purpose on his last two visits home, which in turn had led to more guilt and made returning home harder. That and the desire to keep them all safe. His job was dangerous. The risk of inadvertently dragging some of that with him on a visit home kept him up at night, when he much preferred to sleep. And, of course, it meant he prolonged his absences further and made more excuses.

Five years of lying to the brothers he loved was driving a wedge between them because Jake was actively avoiding them. They knew him too well and saw too much. They had also all made great successes of their lives and despaired that he had not. He tried not to feel envious at it, knowing they deserved all the good things and more, but the sight of their lives blossoming was coming to make his own existence feel barren. Yet he missed them and every day he missed them more. At least now his last assignment was completed he could go home and relax, safe in the knowledge he was working on nothing else which might put them in danger, trip him up or force him to tell them another pack of lies which he doubted they truly believed.

He let his eyes wander around the stuffy study which served as the King's Elite secret headquarters until they fixed on the dancing flames in the fireplace and listened with less than half an ear.

Or at least he thought he did.

'Warriner!' His head snapped around to see Lord Fennimore's bushy grey eyebrows drawn together in a scowl. 'Have you listened to a damn word I just said?'

'Er…of course, sir…well, actually…no. Not really. My eyes glazed over somewhere between one thousand barrels in Sussex and Rowley's resistance to mud. Forgive me. I'm tired and as I'm about to go on leave I didn't think it mattered.'

'Your leave has been cancelled. I have a job for you.'

'But, sir…'

'No buts, Warriner. Only you can do this one. It's a seduction job, so right up your street.'

Leatham and Flint were grinning at him smugly, no doubt having sold his sorry carcass up the river to avoid spending hours, weeks and months charming information out of yet another empty-headed smuggler's mistress. 'Now hold on a minute sir, I'm due leave. Urgently due leave. You patted me on the back only last week and said so yourself. I've made plans.'

'Plans change. You can have your leave as soon as you've exhausted this new lead.' There was no point arguing further. Fennimore never budged when his mind was made up. Never. 'Given the lady's age and experience, I dare say you'll have done the deed in less than a fortnight and you can head north to rusticate then.'

Two weeks wasn't so bad, even if it did mean letting his family down again. Something he had done all too often in the last few years, to such an extent he could already picture his eldest brother Jack's irritated shake of the head and hear, crystal-clear, the blistering lecture he would receive as a result.

When are you going to do something with your life? Being a rake is not a career.

Jake was so caught up in the imaginary conversation with his responsible elder sibling it took a few moments for his superior's words to sink in.

'What do you mean *age*?'

'You really weren't listening, were you?' Lord Fennimore huffed and began to snatch up his papers, signalling the meeting was over. 'Crispin

Rowley has a niece. His deceased, much elder half-sister's child. The girl has been hidden away in a convent since she was orphaned, hence we haven't bothered with her before. However, her neglectful uncle has now decided he's going to give the chit a Season. My sources tell me he is doing so with the express intention of marrying her off by the end of it and to someone of stature. She's recently moved into his house in Mayfair. Her name is Miss Blunt.'

'She's fresh from the schoolroom?'

'One assumes.'

'What does that make her? Seventeen? Eighteen?' Please God, not sixteen.

'I suppose.'

'You want me to seduce a child!'

'Eighteen is not a child and you only need to actually seduce her if other methods of persuasion prove fruitless.'

'Why can't Flint seduce her?'

'I need Flint to keep chipping away on the other side. He's making headway into the bounder's inner circle and all that would be put in jeopardy if Rowley disapproves of him courting his niece. Your reputation makes you the perfect choice. Besides, I can hardly send Leatham.' All eyes instinctively travelled to the jagged and impressive scar down Seb Leatham's right cheek. Even without the scar, his friend resembled a bare-knuckle fighter and was painfully monosyllabic around the opposite sex. Jake was nicely trapped and Lord Fennimore knew it.

'The girl has spent most of her life with nuns, Warriner, isolated from the manipulative machinations of the world. In the full glow of your legendary charm, she'll probably confide all her secrets with a few flowery words. A simple brush of the cheek will likely render her a melted puddle at your feet. It won't take long to pry a list of her uncle's associates from her or his day-to-day schedule. Perhaps you can even convince the chit to steal away a few stray letters and such for a couple of hours so we can analyse them. I'm sure you'll work out how to get her to do your bidding without having to bed her. But if it comes to it, then I'll expect you to do your duty for King and country. You've never complained about that before.'

'That's because I've never been sent after a child before!'

'I dare say she's not a child. The young ladies mature so much faster than the young bucks and it's not unheard of for them to marry at seventeen or eighteen.'

'But you're not asking that I marry her, you're asking that I ruin her!'

'You're a resourceful fellow, I'm sure you can find a way to get what you need from Miss Blunt without having to lift her skirts. But the point is moot regardless. This is the first time we've had the chance of getting close to someone who lives *inside* Rowley's house. The fact she is also as green as grass and ripe for the picking makes it all the sweeter. It's a chance too good to miss.'

Incensed, Jake merely shook his head. 'And how, exactly, am I supposed to seduce this *child*? I hardly have the sort of reputation which allows me to frequent the type of sedate and proper soi-rées the fresh crop of debutantes do and, even if I do, the girl is bound to have a handler. A chaperon with a sharp eye for the wrong sort of suitor. Which I am. They won't let me within ten feet of her.'

Everyone including the bean-counter grinned, which didn't bode well. 'If you had been listening rather than wool-gathering, then you would know Lord Rowley has engaged the services of his great-aunts to act as chaperons.'

'The Sawyer sisters?' Two spinsters in their sixties, both highly connected but with a penchant for hard spirits and reputations as characters. Hardly the sort of women who would be up for the task. 'The *slurring* Sawyer sisters?'

'The very same.' Lord Fennimore looked rightly pleased with himself at Jake's obvious disbelief. 'I know. I can't quite believe our luck either, but with no wife or other suitable female relatives, Rowley could hardly use his mistresses to launch the girl and my sources tell me he is determined to have her married by spring. He's probably already got the groom in mind, hence the sudden haste to launch the girl. It makes a strange sort of sense to align the girl to the slurring sisters. Cressida and Daphne Sawyer are invited to everything.'

'Because they are guaranteed to make spectacles of themselves and the *ton* likes a laugh. I can't think of two worse chaperons for a girl as green as grass.'

Fennimore shrugged. 'Perhaps that's deliberate, too. If Rowley has set his sights on a particular future nephew-in-law, if all else fails his lackadaisical choice of chaperons might aid the process when the girl is inevitably compromised. I wouldn't put it past a slippery and conniving snake like Rowley to have factored that into his equations. Being with the Sawyers will certainly get the girl noticed and that's usually half the battle on the marriage mart. It also aids us. I doubt you'll find it overly difficult to make a move on the chit. Even more fortuitous, the timing is perfect. The chit is being presented tomorrow. At Almack's.'

'I'm banned from Almack's.' Something which had happened quite early in his career and of which Jake was inordinately proud. Only the worst sort of scoundrel was denied admission to Almack's and the ban had done wonders for his bad reputation.

'Not any more, you're not. The patronesses have had a sudden change of heart. Here are your vouchers.' He slid them across the table. 'To be on the safe side I got you a month's worth.'

The sea of people at Almack's swirled by in a pastel haze, thanks to Uncle Crispin's ridiculous insistence she leave her spectacles in the carriage. The unfamiliar place, the surging crowds and her short-sightedness made every step precarious. Already she had tripped up the short step into the high-ceilinged ballroom and nearly flattened a footman in the process.

'Keep your head straight and *glide*, Felicity!' Great-Aunt Daphne advised in her usual theatrical tone. 'A lady should walk like a wispy cloud, floating across the sky.' Or at least Fliss assumed it was her usual tone seeing that she had only met her aged relatives five days ago and, in truth, they weren't technically any relation to her at all. But they were nice old dears who meant well, even if they were a trifle eccentric, and they had been very sweet while attempting to train her in the art of being a lady.

Not that Fliss had any desire to be a lady of the *ton*. She was perfectly content with the manners she had already. Perhaps she could be a bit abrupt and had an acid tongue when the situation called for it, but those minor faults were actually quite perfect in her role as the schoolmistress of Sister Ursuline's School for Wayward Girls. Some of those young ladies required a firm hand and many more needed her guidance because they were prone to make poor choices—especially regarding men. Once this silly visit was over, those girls would need the Miss Blunt they relied upon.

Not some *improved* version who was required to walk like a 'wispy cloud', whatever that meant.

Although why it was considered essential for a lady to walk as if she had a book balanced on her cranium was beyond her. For the better part of two days, Daphne and Cressida had made her walk backwards and forward in Uncle Crispin's ostentatious Egyptian-themed drawing room, with a Mrs Radcliffe novel perched precariously on her head, while they instructed her on the subtle nuances of etiquette she had never had use of before. Who knew that curtsies were graduated, for instance, saving only the deepest and most grovelling for dukes and the monarchy? There had not been much cause for curtsying in Cumbria, thank goodness. Nor for the baffling array of cutlery deemed necessary for every meal when a knife, fork and spoon had always served her perfectly well before, thank you very much. Before she had been a wispy cloud, of course.

'And smile!' Aunt Cressida nudged her with such force she lurched a little sideways. 'Think of yourself as a swan, my dear. Graceful. Elegant. *Effortless.*'

There was no point enquiring as to where the cloud had gone, because Aunt Daphne and Aunt

Cressida rarely remembered what they had said five minutes before. However, she was sorely tempted to point out there was nothing effortless in gliding like a swan in a strange place *sans* spectacles, but Fliss smiled tightly and tried her best, holding her head so still it made her jaw ache. She was here for her mother. Uncle Crispin had apparently made her a solemn promise upon her deathbed to give his half-sister's daughter a Season and, while she was fundamentally too old to be launched into society, the guilt had made her agree to the offer—the guilt, Sister Ursuline's insistence Fliss needed to go and have an adventure, and the desire to do something for the mother she struggled to remember fully yet had missed keenly throughout her life. For her tragic real mother, and her incorrigible surrogate mother, she would attempt to be a cloud or a swan or whatever other nonsense her new great-great-aunts came out with in the next few weeks and she would do it with all the enthusiasm she couldn't be bothered to feel.

The new corset she had been trussed up in like a ham about to be boiled didn't help. While it did serve to keep her from slouching, because bending at the waist was now quite impossible, it also constricted every organ from her lungs to her bladder. It had also pushed her bosoms up in a most inappropriate manner so they threatened to spill out of the neckline of her new, form-fitting white-silk gown. Of course, she had protested the unsuitable dress and the corset, but her aunts insisted such fashions were all ladies wore in the *ton* and *de rigueur* at Almack's. And from the amount of foggy cleavages she could just about see all around her, presented like soft loaves on a baker's tray, her new great-great-aunts appeared to be right. The knowledge did not make Fliss feel any better about exposing her own bakery goods to the eyes of the world.

And Fliss had definitely been thrust into the window of the bakery, despite repeatedly insisting to both the aged women and her stand-offish Uncle Crispin that she had no desire to find a husband while in town. Never had and probably never would. After years of being on her own, and after watching her mother's disappointing marriage to her unreliable father, she could see no reason why she would want to relinquish her freedom to just anyone. If, by some miracle, she ever did find a man who wasn't controlling or unreliable, then perhaps she would reconsider. But if she did, it would be of her own choosing somewhere very far in the future. And finally, and this was completely unnegotiable, he had to absolutely adore her. She wouldn't settle for anything less. She had agreed to a Season, not to any matchmaking, therefore introducing her to all and sundry was pointless. Solid, dependable and trustworthy men would hardly waste their time in this crush. They would be far too sensible and nothing like the fops, dandies and pompous aristocratic versions here, so why her new aunts insisted on parading in a constant loop around the room was beyond her. Not only was she unlikely to remember the fifty different names of gentlemen thrown at her so far, without her spectacles, every one of the fifty faces resembled blurred pink blobs. Aside from the varying colours of hair or clothing, none of the many men she had met had any discerning features which she could recognise them by, should she need to.

Mind you, parading around the ballroom was better than standing near the refreshment table. Her aunts had a worrying penchant for the lemonade—which they mixed liberally with the brandy they hid in hip flasks in their reticules, while they regaled her with outrageous stories from their pasts—and had pressed so many glasses into Fliss's hand her head was beginning to spin. Thanks to the rigid corset, that wasn't the only side-effect.

'I think I need to visit the retiring room.'

Both old ladies sighed. 'How very tiresome. Ever since the *great* ball at Osterley we have trained ourselves to take no notice of such things. Isn't that right, Sister?'

Cressida nodded sagely. 'Indeed. And a very prudent decision it has turned out to be.'

They often talked in riddles, too, sharing knowing looks and wicked grins about experiences from their pasts which they frequently assumed she knew about. 'That is all well and good, but the retiring room?'

Daphne flapped her hand to the left. 'It's over there.'

'Aren't you coming with me?' Because Fliss didn't trust herself to get there unattended. Not when she wasn't entirely certain where 'over there' was. *With* her glasses she had a poor sense of direction. Without them she would be hopeless. 'I'm afraid I might get lost.' An understatement. It was almost guaranteed.

'As long as you have a tongue in your head,

Felicity, you will never be lost. Remember that, dear.' Daphne was also prone to issue random guiding words of wisdom at odd times. 'Head towards the alcove and you shall find it in the furthest corner.' The hand flapped ineffectually again. 'We shall wait for you by the refreshment table, won't we, Cressida?'

Of course they would. Because that was where the *lemonade* lived.

'Yes, indeed. Now that you mention it, I am a bit parched, Daphne.'

To Fliss's complete disgust, the older women immediately left her on their quest for yet more refreshment. She stood impotently and watched their ridiculously tall and elaborate feathered headdresses disappear into the sea of people and allowed her irritation to bubble.

How perfectly splendid. She'd been abandoned by the only two people she knew in the room. Yet another thing to sour her already dour mood. She was stuck miles from home at a ball she didn't want to be at, wearing a dress she feared she was spilling out of, trussed in a corset she couldn't breathe in and, to make the occasion all the more perturbing, she couldn't see more than two feet past her nose. As soon as she got back to Uncle

Crispin's soulless Mayfair house, she had every intention of penning a sternly worded letter to Sister Ursuline telling her the next time she had the urge to suggest Fliss have a *little adventure*, she could mind her own business.

Typically, within a few minutes of squeezing past the silk-clad throng she was hopelessly lost and it didn't feel polite to ask such personal directions of complete strangers. Aunt Daphne had said the ladies' retiring room was in a corner and Almack's was reassuringly rectangular. If she kept resolutely to the edge, she would doubtless find the dratted room eventually, even if that involved going around a few times. Retracing her steps to the refreshment table might be more problematic, but at least left to her own devices she was spared a few minutes of pointless parading, smiling and gliding like a wispy, blind swan. A slow smile bloomed on her face at the prospect. Suddenly, being lost held a great deal of appeal.

Chapter Two

In a secluded alcove in St James's

Jake was still sulking when he arrived at Almack's. Seducing an innocent, wide-eyed chit didn't sit right with him. And, if he was being entirely honest with himself, neither did flirting with one. While he was supremely confident in his ability to do both with exceptional finesse, he made it a point of principle never to dally with nice young ladies. Bawdy young ladies, experienced older ladies and anyone who ran the gamut between was fair game, but impressionable virgins had always been off limits.

For all the many notches on his bedpost, he had not been a single woman's first lover, nor had he ever wooed a woman who didn't know how the game of illicit courtship was played. He might well be a scandalous good-for-nothing scoundrel, but even scoundrels had standards. A line in the sand which they did not cross. Yet now he was being asked to cross it for King and country—another standard he held sacrosanct. Despite a whole day to ponder the moral dilemma he still wasn't entirely sure he was prepared to make an exception.

Lord Fennimore had no such reservations, but then Lord Fennimore was not the one who was going to be whispering sweet nothings into her inexperienced ear or trying to trick her tender heart into trusting a man who shouldn't be trusted. But if his gut instinct was correct, then her uncle deserved all that was coming to him. Aside from the French double agent, every single person who had brought them closer towards the dangerous smuggling ring had wound up dead. All in very believable circumstances, of course—a carriage accident, a nasty fall, drowning in the docks while roaring drunk—but all cases a little too convenient and too close to their investigation to be dismissed. It positively reeked of foul play and Rowley was at the heart of it. And they did have to stop him, the sooner the better, but Jake sincerely hoped not like this. The whole situation left a very bad taste in his mouth.

Careful to stay in the shadows in the alcove, he scanned the room for the latest crop of debutantes. Fortunately, they were easy to spot. They were all obscenely young, eager and clad in the palest silk gowns. They were also all wearing permanently awestruck expressions. With no clue as to what Miss Blunt looked like, he instead searched for the Sawyer sisters, a task which didn't take long. The two ladies were glued to the refreshment table, clearly enjoying their matching glasses of lemonade too much for the contents of their glasses to be purely lemon.

Lady Daphne was sporting what resembled a whole peacock's tail on her head, while Lady Cressida's coiffure sprouted ostrich plumes dyed pink to match her garish dress. The weight of both headdresses, and perhaps the hard spirits the two women had a legendary fondness for, was making the feathers list. Or perhaps it was the ladies who listed. From this distance, Jake couldn't be sure. He watched them closely for a full ten minutes before he could say for certain they had already misplaced their charge. With nothing else to do, he propped himself against a pillar and settled in for a long wait. With any luck, the chit would have already been waylaid by a handsome fellow who'd have already swept her off her juvenile feet, thus providing Jake with a ready excuse to throw in Fennimore's face when Jake failed in his unsavoury mission. Surely they could get to Rowley another way? He could work his way through the man's changing parade of mistresses, seduce a willing and lusty maid—hell, if it came to it, Jake was even prepared to whisper sweet nothings into the ears of Rowley's housekeeper as long as the woman was not a complete hag. Anyone, in fact, but an innocent child.

It was the perfume which distracted him first. The heady scent reminded Jake of fat summer roses, fresh air and sunshine. Nothing like the stuffy smell of Almack's. His nostrils twitched as they sought the source until his eyes located her.

Now this was more the kind of woman *he* would choose to seduce. Too bad *she* was not his assignment. He'd even go as far as admitting the tantalising vision that had just turned the corner would be pure pleasure, for once, rather than business. Thick honey hair, sultry almond eyes and the lushest pair of lips he'd seen in a long time. And the sensuous way she moved drew his eyes and imprisoned them. Her own had a faraway look in them as she hugged the wall, trailing the tips of her gloved fingers along the plaster as if she had all the time in the world and was in no hurry to go anywhere. He liked that about her.

Here in Almack's the ladies always had a higher purpose. To be seen. To be noticed. To make a good impression. To find a husband. This woman preferred the shadows and had no interest in the nonsense going on outside the alcove. Just like him.

She still hadn't noticed him, despite the fact he stood barely ten feet away, so Jake watched her gaze out towards the dancers and sigh. There was a distinctly dreamy look about her, as if she wished she was somewhere else, something he also empathised with. If he hadn't been working, he might have walked over and suggested they go elsewhere together. But alas, he was on a mission and needed to see it through as swiftly as possible no matter how distasteful he found it. Something which would not happen if he gave in to the overwhelming temptation to talk to her. Jake watched her scan the room again, this time with very narrowed eyes which made him wonder exactly what it was she suddenly disapproved of until she clearly saw something—or someone—

she didn't want to. She darted behind a pillar and straight into a potted palm.

The clumsy manoeuvre made him laugh out loud. Her head whipped around in alarm at the sound.

'Don't worry. I shan't tell whoever it is that you are hiding from them.'

'I am not hiding.' But she didn't move from the safety of the pillar. 'Oh, all right, I am. Have they gone?'

Jake scanned the area and nodded. 'There's nobody here but you and me. If it's any consolation, I'm hiding, too.' Hiding from the inevitable. 'What are you hiding from?'

'The gentlemen my chaperons appear intent on introducing me to. What are you hiding from?'

'Responsibility and duty.'

Those lush lips instantly turned up in a smile and she was prettier for it. 'You can't hide from those.'

'I can and I have for the better part of a decade. What's wrong with the men your chaperons are foisting upon you?'

'Nothing, I suppose, other than the fact they are being foisted upon me. I didn't come here to meet gentlemen.' That in itself set her apart from the sea of eager hopefuls in the ballroom.

'Then what did you come here for?'

She sighed and looked miserable. 'My mother. Apparently, it was her dearest wish that I visit Almack's—among other things. Although I fail to see the appeal of the place.'

'Such enthusiasm.'

'I have no enthusiasm.' The corners of those plump lips twitched again. There was the vaguest hint of the north in her accent, more northern than where he came from in Nottingham. Yorkshire, perhaps, or Lancashire? 'That is part of the problem. I got lost half an hour ago and I find myself surprisingly content with being lost and by default reluctant to be found again just yet.'

Intriguing. Much more intriguing than the onerous task he was meant to be doing. 'What is it about this quintessential society ritual which has forced you into hiding?'

Her nose wrinkled endearingly before she spoke. 'I find the whole thing pointless and a little shallow, if I am honest.' Something he had a feeling she always was. A northern trait. Brutal honesty and the inability to suffer fools or foolishness gladly.

'I can see how the attraction soon wears thin. Especially as Almack's has so many tiresome rules one has to obey. How many visits to this stifling establishment did it take for you to become so jaded?'

'Oh, this is my first. I was presented to the patronesses an hour ago.' She smiled a little shyly, but leaned a little closer than was proper, treating him to more of her delicious perfume, more alluring now that it was closer to her skin. 'I am being *launched* into society tonight. Rather reluctantly as I am sure you can see.'

She looked nothing like the traditional debutante. For a start, she had at least five years on most of them and lacked the dewy-eyed innocence prevalent all around them which Jake found so distasteful. 'This is your *come-out*?' Laughter threatened at the preposterousness. She had to be well past the age of majority, but, age aside, she was too canny a woman. Too comfortable in her own skin and mind when all around her were awed and awkward girls.

'I can see, sir, that you are as staggered by it as I am and are racking your brains for a polite way to say I am a bit too old to be coming out. Which I patently am.'

There was no point in denying it. 'How come a matron of such *advanced* years is only just being launched into society?' As he had hoped, she smiled at the sarcasm. He had no time for people who didn't understand it. Irony and sarcasm were two of his very best friends.

'I confess, I honestly have no idea. One minute I was happily enjoying my dotage in Keswick and then I was dragged here.'

Very north, then. The more she spoke the more he could hear it in the lilt of her voice. 'How awful for you. Were you dragged from the bosom of Cumbria against your will?'

'Not completely. When the invitation came, I'll admit to being intrigued. London is an adventure, I suppose, and I was due one. And I was curious about the city I was born in, but have no memory of. I wanted to visit some of the sights I've only read about. The Tower of London, the British Museum, St James's Palace...' She sighed dramatically to amuse him. 'But alas, my uncle expressly forbade any touring about until I was launched properly.'

Little flags raised in his mind. 'Your uncle?' Surely it was a coincidence?

'Yes. My mother's brother. I hardly know him

really, but he wrote to me saying he had promised my mother he would give me a Season and, apparently, dear Uncle Crispin only remembered that solemn promise this year. Hence, I am undoubtedly the *oldest* debutante anyone has ever seen and feel much like an old trout, rather than a common or garden fish out of water.'

'Hardly old.' It was difficult to sound nonchalant when his mind was already reeling, both at his good luck at naturally meeting the woman he had been sent here to seduce and his relief at finding her a grown woman rather than a child. 'What are you...three and twenty?'

'Save your polite London charm, sir, it's wasted on me. I am five and twenty and look it. And happy to be so. Although even when I was younger, I doubt I was ever quite as *young* as some of the girls I was presented with. They all seem so surprised and dazzled by everything. I've never met such a jittery crop of girls before in my life. Do they not let young ladies out here in the capital before they come out?'

There was an earthiness and healthy cynicism about her which felt familiar and made him oddly homesick. Jake had grown up around people who said what they thought without artifice. Here in

London, the true meaning of a person's words was often buried under layers of the polite façade they presented to the world. 'Of course not. Gently bred young ladies are practically locked up and kept well out of polite society to avoid them being corrupted.'

'Yet overprotecting them makes them all the riper for corruption.' She frowned as she said this, and shook her head. 'No wonder those girls all appear overwhelmed. They have lived such sheltered lives and then they are brought here. A place where its sole purpose, as far as I can ascertain, is for unattached young ladies to be tirelessly paraded around like farm stock on auction day in the hope someone will notice them, then deign to marry them. And they are grateful to be put up for the gavel. Listen to them all twittering like excited sparrows at the prospect.'

'You sound as if you disapprove, Miss...?' There was the slim chance there was more than one Uncle Crispin in town.

'Blunt. Blunt by name and blunt by nature, I'm afraid.' Thanking all his lucky stars she was the right woman, Jake was suddenly ridiculously grateful he had had his leave postponed. Of all the women to, quite literally, stumble into him he'd been blessed by Rowley's niece. Rowley's lovely, womanly and ripe-for-the-picking northern niece. Seducing this tart morsel wouldn't feel like work at all. This he would do for pure pleasure. 'I apologise if you find my frankness rude.'

'I am delighted to make your acquaintance, Miss Blunt.' He took her hand gently in his and kissed the back of it, confident she wouldn't care when he failed to let go. 'And I find your frankness refreshing. Like you I am from the north— deepest, darkest, dankest Nottinghamshire to be exact—my name is Jake Warriner and I loathe Almack's, too.'

She leaned closer again, her pretty face tilted to one side and her palm heating his through the thin fabric of her evening gloves. Awareness. Chemistry. Mutual attraction. Jake knew the signs too well to mistake them for anything else. He had the urge to kiss her. An urge which had nothing to do with Crispin Rowley and everything to do with his bewitching niece. 'Is it obvious I *loathe* it, Mr Warriner, only I have been trying exceedingly hard to appear as if I don't?'

'To me it is obvious, but then again, just like you I am loitering in the alcove and avoiding the sad crush. It hardly makes me a genius to have seen a kindred spirit.'

She gracefully disentangled his grip from hers. 'When you put it like that, I suppose it doesn't. Why do you loathe it?'

An easy question to answer with complete honesty for once. 'This place, the stifling, petty rules and the callous way an elite few decide who is worthy to be allowed in, grates on me. I hate the power those few have over the others. If they take to you, you are guaranteed the best invitations of the Season. If they don't, well...' He left the implication to settle. 'It all strikes me as grossly unfair.'

'Those poor sparrows will be devastated by the cut. Some might never get over it.'

'But I get the feeling you won't be devastated?' Jake had a talent for reading people. Each tiny nuance and expression told more truth than lips usually did and Miss Blunt did not look impressed with being here.

She sighed and shrugged again, something she did a great deal and which made his eyes want to wander down to where her neckline met flesh. Soft, perfumed, pert, female flesh. Jake resisted—but only just. 'Is it terrible that I hope they thoroughly disapprove of me, then I will be spared the effort of coming here again? Or of receiving the best invitations of the Season. I fear my uncle has lined up a whole host of *entertainments* for me to attend, none of which I suspect I shall find entertaining in the slightest.'

'Not every soirée is as dull and constrained as Almack's.'

'Perhaps. But being paraded around town like meat on the butcher's board is not what I had in mind when I agreed to this visit.'

'It's just a visit, then?' Clearly Miss Blunt was not aware of the fact Uncle Crispin was intent on marrying her off.

'Yes. A month. Then I shall return to Cumbria where I belong. Perhaps two at the most, although after tonight I sincerely doubt I'll manage two. It has been less than a week and I already find London society suffocating. I find I am fiercely wedded to my freedom, you see, while here it is stifled. At home, I can walk outdoors where and when I please, say what I think, do what I want.' Clearly Fennimore's intelligence was lacking, as Miss Blunt was even less of a convent miss than she was an eager debutante. 'Here I have chaperons and all these rules I have to adhere to.'

'Such as?'

'Where to start? How to dress, how to walk. The correct way to curtsy to a duchess, which is I now know quite different from the way one curtsies to a countess or a queen. Who I should speak to, who I shouldn't, how to behave when dancing.' Another put-upon sigh. 'I was promised I would have an adventure and so far it has been anything but. However, at least I was dragged here by my family and had no idea it would be this awful. What's your excuse? Seeing that you loathe the place.'

'I, too, was dragged here, in a manner of speaking.' To do his duty, a duty he was now very much looking forward to doing. He gave in to the urge to touch her again and scandalously allowed his thumb to caress the centre of her palm where it rested among the folds of her skirt. Her eyes dropped to the spot. Stared. When her lush lips parted slightly he raised her gloved hand almost to his lips. He gazed up at her with the hooded eyes women always found appealing, knowing the deep blue soulful depths were his best feature. 'Although now I am very pleased I was. Else I never would have met such a rare bird of paradise in this tiresome cage full of sparrows.'

If he said so himself, Jake was rather pleased

with the symbolism even if the words themselves were a tad triter than he would have liked. But a seduction was a seduction and there was no point in beating around the bush. The rakish smile he bestowed upon her was second nature. It suggested he had a poetic heart beneath the cynical irony she found so amusing. He had certainly amused her enough that she had happily confided in him. A total stranger. In his vast wealth of experience, the sensible ladies adored both a man who made them smile and one with romantic sensibilities who listened to them. A deadly combination which had served him well since the day he had turned sixteen. Being used to forthright and charmless northern men, she would doubtless find his easy, open manner disarming.

Her eyes locked with his.

Narrowed.

And before he could kiss her hand, she snatched it away.

'Are you flirting with me, Mr Warriner?'

'I would certainly like to, Miss Blunt.' His voice was low and silky, the practised tone in a timbre he knew to be his most seductive. 'Do you mind?'

'I most certainly do.' Both gloved hands came to rest imperiously on her hips, giving her more of the appearance of a schoolmistress than an intriguing temptress. 'I have remained lost these past thirty minutes to avoid such nonsense.'

'Ah—in the main here at Almack's it is reliably all nonsense, but that is because the gentlemen over at the auction block are all shamelessly on the market for a wife. It is contrived and insincere. Here in the alcove—like you—I was content to hide and had no plans to flirt with anyone until *fate* introduced us.' Had he not been here at Lord Fennimore's bequest and had she not been Miss Blunt, the woman he had been sent here to seduce, he still would have wanted to flirt with her without the interference of fate. There was something about her which called to him. 'Do you believe in fate, Miss Blunt?'

'Good lord! Did you really just say that?' Her brows furrowed. 'Do I look as green as grass, Mr Warriner?' She was positively glaring down her nose at him in bemused outrage. And if he was not mistaken it was tinged with real outrage rather than the feigned outrage he usually encountered when he turned on the charm. Her green eyes hardened; her honey brow furrowed slightly. Tiny, physical nuances that could not be faked. There was no hint of interest on her face—only disbelief. Making him feel like a fool for flirting. That made him uncomfortable because it was so…so…unheard of. He always flirted as a matter of course and had never once felt foolish in doing so. But Miss Blunt-by-Name-and-Nature seemed to see right through him to the hard kernel of insincerity buried deep in his chest which he had never noticed before. Now that he had— well, frankly, he felt queasy. At a loss for charming words for once, Jake simply stared at her and she began to giggle at his shocked expression.

'Do such hackneyed and slapdash endearments garner you much success with the ladies, Mr Warriner?'

'While the prose might have been slapdash, the sentiment was not.' He could save this. He was a master in the art of seduction. A maestro. 'But usually I am not so overawed by the beauty of my companion that my tongue becomes twisted.' Once again the rote phrases sounded hollow and unoriginal, making Jake want to wince at his own crassness. What the devil was wrong with him? 'In the few short minutes I have spent in your company, Miss Blunt, you have made a great impression on me and—'

'Oh, goodness.' She snorted and covered the

offending sound with her hand. 'I must give you credit for perseverance, but really...' She eyed him as if expecting him to finish her sentence. He schooled his features into a look of the utmost sincerity although his toes had begun to curl uncomfortably in his boots.

'I'm not sure I follow, Miss Blunt.'

'Oh, Mr Warriner! You are funny. Are London ladies so daft that they do not know a philanderer when they see one? Why, I saw it the moment I first encountered you, you have the look of one. And the manner.'

'The manner?' Jake usually enjoyed the sparring. It was part of the game and a part he loved. However, sparring with the blunt Miss Blunt was making him uncomfortable. Especially as she had his full measure and he didn't particularly like the label of philanderer. He was a rake. A proud one. Rakes were dashing and roguish. Philanderer sounded sordid. Cynical. Oily. Good grief! Was he oily? The urge to find a mirror and check he had not turned into a simpering toad made him self-conscious. 'And now I suppose you are an expert on philanderers?' Why didn't he correct her and say rake?

'Indeed I am. So much so I could probably write

a book on the subject. The self-assurance and smug satisfaction in your own allure was as plain as the nose on my face—although while you *weren't* practising your philandering on me I was prepared to overlook it.'

Blast—she *could* see right through him. He was confident in his allure. So confident he had made a career out of it. Obviously he had become too complacent. A new and worrying development Jake was ill prepared for. He must have slipped up somewhere. He had probably bared his hand too soon to this canny northern lass because he was too used to the relative ease of the pampered society ladies. He was tired. Desperately needed leave—and, if he was honest, he had rushed things because he was attracted to her. Very attracted to her. 'Forgive me. In my haste, perhaps I have overstepped the bounds.'

'There is no perhaps about it.'

'As I said, forgive me. When I see something I want, I am inclined to listen to my heart rather than my head.' He knew instantly he had laid the charm on too thick again, he didn't need to witness her exasperated eye-roll or to hear her amused snort to confirm it. What on earth was the matter with him? Jake wasn't usually this ham-fisted. He couldn't remember the last time he had run roughshod over a seduction and she had called it correctly. Tonight he was no better than a hackneyed philanderer. Maybe there was still time to fix it? And maybe the damage was done and was probably irreparable. He stopped himself trotting out more banalities because of the inevitable humiliation which would follow. Rowley's gorgeous niece was not the normal run-of-the-mill society miss. Judging from her incredulous scowl, he was in for another skewering for the *heart and head* claptrap. Miss Blunt didn't disappoint. Those playful, inviting eyes froze again.

'You are in danger of ruining a perfectly pleasant conversation with your contrived, insincere—and while I am being completely frank—tired, overt and practised attempts at seduction.'

That stung. Jake was the master of subtle. 'Hardly practised, Miss Blunt.'

'Oh, dear. I can see I have hurt your feelings and that was not my intention. I simply wanted you to be aware that I am more than accustomed with men of your ilk. You're not the first scoundrel to try your luck and I dare say you won't be the last. All the clues were there right from the outset. The oh-*so*-casual lingering hold of my hand.

The heated look. The purposefully intimate and sultry whispering. And do not get me started on the crass and *unspontaneous* way in which you tossed my own words back at me to try to convince me of your sincerity. Kindred spirits and birds of paradise indeed. What rot. I'm sure a handsome man like yourself is used to gullible women falling for your lies, but…'

'I don't lie.' Although Jake was internally wincing at the falsehood. He lied so much nowadays he had to keep a notebook of what he said and to whom to avoid tripping up. He even lied to his own family and had done for years. Nobody had called him on it before, that was all. Because usually he was damn good at it. He forced himself to smile. Forced himself to appear amused. 'When you walked into that palm I was charmed. I'm still charmed, despite your inaccurate and mean assassination of my character. But I can see I have inadvertently insulted you with my honest enthusiasm, which I never meant to do because the truth is…' The gloved hand appeared palm up near his face and the lush lips were grinning behind it.

'Let me save you from further embarrassment, Mr Warriner—I wasn't born yesterday. Save your insincere seductions for the silly girls in the ballroom. As undeniably attractive as you are, I have less interest in being seduced by a man of your ilk than I do for this cattle market. I am only sorry that all these young ladies are not as pragmatic about men as I am.' Her fingers went to the fan hanging from a ribbon on her wrist and for a moment Jake experienced the forlorn hope she might snap it open and use it to flirt over the top of in the customary manner he understood so well. However, she wielded it like a broadsword aimed directly at his ribcage.

'And for future reference should we collide again in the foreseeable future, if you are going to throw about bird analogies, I'm neither a feeble sparrow nor an exotic *bird of paradise*, Mr Warriner. If I am any bird, I am an owl. Wise. Older than the rest of these foolish girls and blessed with the ability to see danger coming from all angles. And you, sir, are a hawk, circling the sky for unsuspecting prey.' Her arms folded across her chest and the stance did wonders for her figure—just to taunt him further.

'You are a very charming hawk and I like you for it, but I am far too prudent to fall for your nonsense. Please, take my advice and heed it well. Never flirt with me again, Mr Warriner, else I will stop liking you and I would hate to do that. Now, if you will just point me in the direction of the refreshment table, I fear I have been lost long enough.'

Chapter Three

In a soulless bedchamber at Uncle Crispin's Mayfair town house

Somewhere in the distance a clock chimed the hour, reminding Fliss it was now three in the morning, but she was still nowhere near ready to sleep. How could she when her mind was still whirring with images of the evening? The provincial plays she had seen paled into insignificance when compared to the splendour of the opera. Everything about it had been breathtaking, from the sumptuous and vivid costumes to the aching purity of the soprano's beautiful voice. And watching the audience had been equally as thrilling. The Prime Minister had been there and so had the famous Duke of Wellington. Aunt Cressida had pointed out both men in their private boxes just a few feet away from Uncle Crispin's, although even if she hadn't, Fliss's eyes would have soon been drawn to the spots where everyone else was staring.

All around them had been a sea of people dressed in their finery and, thanks to the opera glasses she had been given upon entering the box, Fliss was able to see every tiny detail despite her lack of spectacles. Spectacles she had been politely banned from wearing in public by her stand-offish uncle and which her new maid, Kitty, had already *mislaid* twice the moment Fliss dared to put them down.

During the interval, she had drunk champagne for the first time. It had been brought to their box perfectly chilled and served in crystal glasses; the delicious bubbles tickled her nose and the alcohol went straight to her head, making everything sharper and brighter than before. She allowed herself a second glass. Her aunts smartly finished the second bottle while Uncle Crispin discussed business with an older gentleman who had joined them. The Earl of Redditch was a portly man who creaked when he moved, thanks to the corset he was squashed into beneath his evening coat. A coat which bore the stain of recently spilled food on one lapel. He had a profusion of wiry grey hair which grew at right angles out of his head and sprouted out of his ears. He also smelled a little musty and had a habit of spitting slighting each time he talked. Fliss was painfully aware of both things because he had been placed next to her during the first half, but as soon as the orchestra began to warm up, signalling the interval was over, she cleverly sandwiched herself between her aunts to watch the second act.

Just before the lights dimmed, she experienced the oddest sense someone was watching her and instinctively dropped her eyes to the stalls below where they locked with the intense blue gaze of Mr Jacob Warriner. There was a wry smile on his outrageously handsome face that did peculiar things to her insides. They heated. As did her flesh, while her tummy fizzed with unwanted bubbles of excitement which were surprisingly reminiscent of those in the heady champagne. Then the lights had faded, casting him in silhouette, and the odd yet special moment was gone.

As much as she adored the second half of the opera, she was constantly aware of him. Every time she glanced down, he was gazing back at her in the darkness. Flirting with his eyes in a more tempting way than he had with his practised words two nights before. She made a half-hearted attempt at ignoring him when the performance ended, but that stare drew her like a moth to a flame. A secret smile played at the corners of his mouth when their gazes briefly met and, before she could turn away, he pressed a kiss on the tips of his fingers and then blew it towards her. Thank goodness nobody else appeared to witness it in the melee exiting the theatre, nor did anyone comment on the ferocious blush which decided to bloom on her cheeks in response to his scandalous lack of propriety in a crowded public place.

After that, and to her great chagrin, Fliss had practically floated home. The carriage ride had been silent. Her aunts were softly snoring from the after-effects of all the champagne they had consumed and Uncle Crispin made no effort at engaging her in conversation, so she had stared out of the window up at the stars, trying and failing not to notice that they twinkled like Jacob Warriner's eyes. Now she was lying on her bed, recalling every nuance of the evening, more awake than she had ever been in the small hours of the morning.

Yet thinking about him was not constructive. Twinkling eyes aside, he was a rake through and through and Fliss was too savvy to be seduced by a handsome rogue. At Sister Ursuline's, she had seen the consequences of seduction first-hand. Ruined reputations, scandal, broken hearts, divided families and, on more occasions than she cared to count, inconvenient pregnancies. A succession of wayward girls had spent their confinement hidden at the convent and then were forced to say heart-wrenching goodbyes to those innocent babes when the girls were dragged back into society by their parents. Sister Ursuline always found those cherubs good, loving homes, but Fliss still thought each incident a tragedy and one that could have been easily avoided if the young lady had the wherewithal to resist the scoundrel in the first place.

While she knew that not all men were so inclined, regrettably all the male role models in her life were also scoundrels. Her father had been one through and through. He might have done the decent thing and married her mother when he had got her into trouble, but from the moment he had placed that ring on her finger he had abdicated all responsibility. Like all the men Fliss had encountered since, he was inherently untrustworthy and proved time and again to be an unreliable husband and father.

Fliss had spent her formative years with her mother growing up in his crumbling house in the country, while he frittered away all the money in town. The only benefit to that situation was her mother was happy when there were a significant number of miles between her and her wastrel husband. Fliss rarely saw him and they conversed little when they did. Much like her fledgling relationship with Uncle Crispin.

Perhaps one of these days she would meet a man who didn't fit the mould? A selfless man whom she could truly depend upon in the same way she could always depend upon Sister Ursuline, and before that her mother. A man who would always be there for her. One who put his family above his own selfish needs. A man who absolutely adored her...

And perhaps one day humans would fly. Both eventualities were as unlikely as the other. While she liked some men for their wit or their intelligence, found some interesting and wise, nothing would ever tempt her to want one all of her very own unless he measured up to the same exacting high standards of dependency Fliss set for herself. In most cases, experience had taught her the best you could hope for with a man was that he entertained you and had a back strong enough to lift heavy things. You didn't need to marry them for either.

Her uncle wasn't proving her theory wrong. Already, after some serious thought, Fliss had come to the regrettable conclusion she didn't like him at all. The only thing she had been able to truly ascertain was that he was dependably domineering and emotionless. She supposed the signs had been there all along, because she hadn't heard hide nor hair of the man in years, but it still didn't sit right to completely dislike the only blood relative she had in the world. Or half-blood at least. She had hoped to see bits of her mother in him, when in fact he behaved more like her uninterested and feckless father.

After her mother had died, *dear* Papa had found having a grieving and ever-so-precocious ten-year-old daughter taxing, so had parcelled her off to Sister Ursuline's School for Wayward Girls without so much as a backwards glance. She had never seen the man again.

However, for years her childish heart had secretly hoped one day her uncle would come to rescue her and she had assumed for the longest time he was prevented from doing so because her father was still alive. Even after the demise of her sire, she continued to kindle the tiny flame of hope with regular missives to remind him she was still alive and still hoping. Still praying that he might miraculously become someone she could depend upon.

It was only after she turned twenty-one that she stopped sending him an annual letter at Christmas, by which time she had embarked on her new life as a schoolmistress at the same school she had called home from eleven, and couldn't muster the enthusiasm to feel anything other than mild disappointment any longer. Anything more for a virtual stranger was self-indulgent and Fliss much preferred to march onwards and upwards rather than wistfully glance behind.

When his only letter finally came out of the blue, she had been surprised and dismissive. Something about it did not ring true and as she was well past the age of majority she was under no obligation to acquiesce to the odd request. She had been on the cusp of writing him a brief thank-you, but no-thank-you note when Sister Ursuline had intervened.

A perpetual romantic soul at heart, Sister Ursuline was prone to see the good in all. Including feckless men—an odd trait for a woman who dealt with unwed and abandoned mothers, scandalously ruined young ladies and the most precocious and troublesome girls society had to offer. What if her mother *had* tasked her uncle with giving her a Season? And what if the poor man had been so financially embarrassed he could not do so until now? She deserved some adventure and it was only right and proper she met her only kin. While a dose of healthy scepticism was necessary in a young woman, Fliss was in danger of being an outright cynic. What was the harm of spending one month with her relative to find out which of them was right?

It had only been a little over a week and she already had his measure. Uncle Crispin was detached, clearly didn't give two figs about his only niece and seemingly only cared about what others thought of him. His fancy and no doubt expensive box at the opera had been purchased only so that others could be impressed. He had less interest in the actual opera than he did in Fliss. A decidedly good thing, else he might have seen Jacob Warriner's scandalously blown kiss.

Oh, for goodness sake! Stop thinking about that man! Now there was an untrustworthy, undependable libertine if ever there was one. Eminently likeable, yet as dangerous to a young lady's virtue as it was possible to be. But it was too late. Her body was already misbehaving. The rapid heartbeat, the fluttering pulse, the overwhelming suffusion of heat...

Good lord, she was hot.

Fliss flung the covers off and threw out her arms and legs to cool them. After five minutes, during which time the unwelcome warmth did not subside, she flung her legs over the side of the mattress and padded over to her window. A bit of cold February air was exactly what she needed to banish all thoughts of the dark-haired, blue-eyed rake who had lodged himself in her mind and stalwartly refused to leave.

She cracked open the window and stood directly in the draught. The icy breeze was delightful, as were the goosebumps which instantly prickled her limbs. Anything that brought down her erratic temperature had to be a good thing. The trouble with living in a convent was there was a distinct shortage of young men. Fliss collided with them infrequently—at the assemblies or parties Sister Ursuline insisted all the girls attended to help them cope better with social situations—but not on a day-to-day basis. Therefore, it was difficult to make oneself completely immune to their charms. Familiarity breeds contempt, yet the opposite sparks interest. Her traitorous body was interested in the dashing Mr Warriner. Too interested. And that simply wouldn't do.

Somewhere below, she heard a door creak open, closely followed by the sound of the gravel crunching as someone walked down the garden path. More curious than scared, because everything about her uncle's house was still strange, Fliss hid her nightgown-clad body behind the heavy curtain and peeked out through the glass. There was a man walking around the edge of the lawn. It was difficult to make out much in the pitch-black darkness without her spectacles, but from his silhouette he appeared to be wearing what looked like shabby workmen's clothes.

'Wait—we're not done.' Her uncle appeared, probably from the same door, although she couldn't be certain. From his tone, he seemed angry. 'Next week is not good enough!'

The shabby man stopped in his tracks and slowly turned. Fliss squinted, but still could not discern his face. 'It's next week or not at all.' He had a London accent. A common one. His coarse diction matched his attire. 'I've other buyers, Rowley, and if you can't wait someone else will happily take your place.' He turned, but as Uncle Crispin came level with the Londoner, he grabbed the sleeve of his coat.

'Tell them I'll pay them double the usual. I need the goods now!'

'Double. Treble. Even if you quadruple it I doubt it'll make much difference. Dead men can't spend. And the boss won't like it if his cargo gets seized. He's lost enough already this month. There are many new eyes along the water. I told you, this is not the time for haste.'

'But you're in haste for my money! This costs me. It costs me dearly, damn it, every time a shipment is late.'

The man pulled his arm free with such force her uncle took several steps back, his posture wary. It made no difference, as the other man closed that distance quickly, grabbed his lapels and loomed over him menacingly.

'Don't get all brave on me, Rowley! If you don't like the boss's terms, then we've got plenty of others who'll happily step into your fancy shoes. If you're not *our* man...'

'I'm your man. You know I'm your man. I'm doing my best for you and the boss...just like you asked.' His voice came out a few octaves higher than usual and pathetically desperate. 'I didn't mean to complain... But I've made promises. People are relying on me. What am I supposed to do in the meantime?'

'You wait.' The Londoner slowly uncurled his fingers from her uncle's coat and made a great show of rearranging the lapels before he patted his head roughly. 'Like a good boy.' His gravelly voice sent involuntary chills though Fliss, her every instinct warning her he was a dangerous man. 'Be ready.' With that he left, disappearing into the shadows behind the shrubbery and into the night.

Her uncle watched him leave, the clenched fists at his side evidence his temper was barely controlled, then he stalked back towards the house and she heard the angry slam of the door in his wake.

It had been an odd exchange. She couldn't shake the feeling that it had been a bad one. Dangerous, even. If her relationship with her uncle had been better, she might have gone downstairs and asked what was happening, enquired if he was all right, but Fliss knew he wouldn't deign to confide in her. At best, he ignored her. If they spoke, he was curt and dismissive, or downright aloof. When she had first met him just a few short days ago, she had thought him a cold fish and he had done nothing in the time since to alter that opinion. If he was in trouble, then it was doubtless of his own making and therefore nothing to do with her. In a few weeks she'd be gone.

Besides, there was no point in allowing her vivid imagination to run away with itself. There was probably a perfectly reasonable explanation why Uncle Crispin had met with that man.

In secret.

In the dead of night.

Perhaps this was the way things were done in town? Having little experience of the world outside her sleepy part of Cumbria, much of the ways of the capital baffled her. And she was tired. It had been a long day. Why, only five minutes ago her silly mind had been conjuring up images of kisses with an untrustworthy rake, so clearly she wasn't thinking entirely logically. Sleep would put a different perspective on things. A problem was always best considered when the mind was at its sharpest and had one of her charges at the convent confessed to Fliss the same emotion Fliss was currently feeling, with no other proof than the peculiar disquiet she was experiencing, she knew she would scoff and be dismissive of unsubstantiated flights of fancy conjured during the witching hour. She would send the girl to bed, which was exactly what she should do herself. With an uneasy feeling, she silently closed the window and crept back under the covers, certain sleep was considerably further away now than it had been a few minutes ago.

'Rowley has recently bought shares in another small shipping company. The Excise Men have boarded every one of their boats in the last three weeks the moment they have docked in British ports and performed thorough searches. There is no contraband. The cargoes are all legitimate and all the taxes are paid.' Flint was pacing back and forth as he spoke, his frustration evident in every step. 'That's three merchant fleets he's directly involved in, yet all apparently clean.'

'He's bringing the stuff in somehow. Perhaps those ships are decoys? Perhaps he deliberately bought those shares to take us off the scent?' Lord Fennimore's reasoned tone did little to calm Flint's temper. 'There is a chance he is smuggling the goods in on other boats. The old way—in the dead of night and onto quiet beaches.'

That didn't make sense to Jake. This single band of smugglers had flooded the London market to such an extent they now dominated it. Both London and the entire south-east. 'The volumes of brandy alone make that impossible. Even if he were using rowing boats, transporting that many barrels of illegal French spirits across the country to the capital would be problematic. They would be seen. We've had men watching all the roads into the town for months. He's got to be bringing the stuff straight into London. By sea.'

'The Excise Men assure me they have searched every nook and cranny of every ship linked to Rowley. They've had the cargoes apart the moment they've off-loaded and found nought that hasn't been recorded on the ships' manifest. Those vessels are clean.'

'Too clean.' These were the first words Leatham had said in the hour they had been sat in Lord Fennimore's study. They all turned to look at him. He didn't say much, but what he did was always worth waiting for. 'In my experience, the best place to hide is in plain sight. I'll wager he's using those ships and bringing the goods right into London just as Jake said—right under the Excise Men's noses. They won't use the roads. Not when it makes sense to keep everything in the water. Quieter, darker and harder to stop.'

He had Lord Fennimore's attention. 'You think he's solely using the Thames?'

'I would.'

'The river police patrol those waters like hawks. He'd be taking a risk.'

Leatham shrugged. 'Maybe they offload the big ships well shy of London. Transfer the stuff onto local coasters or barges. There are thousands of smaller vessels which run those waters every day and never get challenged—just as generation after generation of Thames watermen have done in the past. If they can fool the Excise Men with legitimate loads like fish, bricks or hay, then I doubt a paltry few river police will worry them and that's assuming it stays on the Thames. There's also the Fleet, the Lee. Or the canals. There are hundreds of miles of canals, remember. There aren't enough river police to watch everywhere or to check every boat and everyone knows they focus on the big ships and the docks. The ones that cross the sea rather than the local waters.'

Lord Fennimore nodded thoughtfully. 'Smaller boats? There'd have to be a lot of them, a whole rotten network. Perfectly synchronised. But I suppose if they avoid the docks, once they are through the city they can move largely undetected and unchallenged throughout the country.' His bushy eyebrows drew together and he nodded decisively. 'Send some of your men to do some digging around the wharfs, Leatham, and see what you can find. Flint, see if Crispin Rowley, or any of his cronies, has any links in any canal companies or river hauliers. I'll arrange for the Excise Men to pay close attention to the Essex and Kent stretches of the Thames Estuary. Get them to covertly follow a few of the regular wherrymen. It can't hurt to explore the possibility further. Better safe than sorry, even if we are just shouting into the wind until we have credible intelligence on Rowley's *actual* business dealings.' At that, Fennimore's head turned to Jake. 'How are things going with the niece?'

'We've met.' That awkward introduction still grated.

'Met? It's been a week. Have you lost your touch, Warriner?'

'Miss Blunt is not the sort of woman one rushes.' Because she saw right through flannel. 'I flirted with her tonight at the opera.' Well, he'd gazed longingly at her. 'And thanks to subtle enquiries—' which involved flirting outrageously with several well-connected society ladies '—I've managed to piece together most of her engagements for the next few weeks. She will be attending the Renshaws' Ball on Friday.' Where he fully intended to sweep the pithy Miss Blunt off her canny northern feet.

'Engage her in conversation about Rowley's business interests. See if she's heard any mention of canals over the dinner table.'

Jake rolled his eyes. 'Yes, that ought to do it. Nothing says seduction like talk of barges.' Although with hindsight, that might have been better than waffling on about birds of paradise. Anything would have been better than waffling on about those damn birds. 'Leave Miss Blunt to me. By the time I'm finished wooing her, she'll sing like a canary.' Another crass bird analogy! Good lord, he was doomed.

If only he'd been able to stop thinking about the

delectable Miss Blunt, then Jake would be more on his game. But there was something about her which had got under his skin and, even when it shouldn't, his mind kept wandering back to her. It wasn't just her beauty which appealed, although there was no denying the physical attraction he felt. Tonight, he could barely take his eyes off her. From the moment she had appeared in Rowley's box, he had been transfixed.

She had looked stunning with all that honey-gold hair piled loosely on top of her clever head, outshining every other lady in the opera house. When the done thing was to appear bored, Miss Blunt had flown in the face of convention and been utterly charmed by the occasion. Openly smiling at the actors on the stage and swaying in time to the music. To do that when all around you were people behaving *properly* showed a tremendous amount of confidence. That confidence, that comfortable sense of self, made Miss Blunt very alluring indeed. The way she had closed her eyes in bliss at the taste of the champagne had done peculiar things to his nerve endings, creating all manner of unwelcome images of the vixen in the grip of pleasure. Images which resolutely refused to leave his mind now, when he was supposed to be concentrating.

Of course, it didn't help that the copper-silk gown had shown off her magnificent figure to perfection. Cut to sit off the shoulder, the acres of creamy peach skin had tormented him each time the lights went up and haunted him in the darkness. Skin he now knew blushed more beautifully than any skin had blushed before—and from something as simple as a cheeky blown kiss when nobody was looking. A kiss he had every intention of delivering properly, in person, at the first available opportunity. And not because he'd been told to.

Flint's fingers snapped in front of his face and Jake realised he'd missed an important part of the conversation. 'Sorry. I was...'

'Daydreaming about your conquest, if your expression was anything to go by.' Flint grinned. 'I *said* you might have some competition for Miss Blunt's affections, dear boy. The word among Rowley's crowd is he has her earmarked for Redditch.'

'The Earl of Redditch!' The very idea was disgusting. The man was in his sixties and smelled like feet. 'I sincerely doubt I'll have much competition from that quarter. Miss Blunt wouldn't entertain an obnoxious fellow like him.' Or at least he hoped she wouldn't. Not that imagining her in the throes of passion with the aged Earl was any more distasteful than imagining her in the throes of passion with any other man. The mere thought made him strangely jealous and, if he was entirely honest, a tad nauseous.

'Perhaps not—but her uncle is keen to make a match. I've heard he fetched her to town with the express intention of presenting her to the Earl. Redditch is recently out of mourning and has been quite vocal about his desire to marry again. His first marriage was barren, so it stands to reason he wants a wife young enough to give him heirs and he is as rich a Croesus. Despite his stinky disposition, he's still quite a catch and one Rowley seems intent on catching. Miss Blunt does make attractive bait.' Flint and Leatham shared a knowing, wholly masculine look which made Jake yearn to punch the pair of them for the heinous crime of having perceptive eyes.

'Miss Blunt is a woman with her own mind and well past the age of majority. I wish her uncle all the luck in the world trying to bring her around to his way of thinking.'

Lord Fennimore frowned. 'This is a dangerous and unforeseen complication.'

'Hardly.' Jake made a show of adjusting his cuffs. 'I'm easier on both the eyes and the nose, and much more appealing than the Earl of Redditch.'

'Not all women's heads can be turned by a handsome face, Warriner. In case it has escaped your notice, most of the *ton* marries for status and wealth. As an earl he has the status—and he certainly has the wealth. The girl has nothing aside from her beauty to recommend her and now that we know she has been on the shelf gathering dust you will need to act fast. An earl on the hook usurps a rake. Especially if Miss Blunt is as clever as you say.'

The words unsettled him far more than Jake was prepared to admit. 'She's too clever to settle for an old letch like Redditch.' Surely? Although she had told him she also had a pragmatic attitude towards men. A dyed-in-the-wool pragmatist might well see the benefits of marrying a rich old earl. She would outlive him, for a start, and enjoy the rest of her life as a very rich woman. Completely independent and free to do as she pleased. Maybe speed was of the essence after all.

Chapter Four

Bored, in Uncle Crispin's dining room before the Renshaw ball

This was the second night in a row that the Earl of Redditch had been invited to dine and the second Fliss had had the misfortune of being seated opposite him. Just as he had during yesterday's dinner, the Earl had slurped his soup, chewed with his mouth open and used his hand to cover said mouth only after one of his many belches had escaped. Meanwhile, her uncle fawned over the fellow as if he were visiting royalty, while Daphne and Cressida quaffed the wine like it was going out of fashion.

For the sake of family harmony and out of ingrained politeness, Fliss had put on a brave face and made a concerted effort to engage with the dull conversation about canals right up until her uncle had begun to extoll her virtues to the fusty old Earl in the same way one would list the attributes of a fine horse up for sale at Tattersall's. 'As you can see, my niece is a sensible girl. Well read and not prone to the silly behaviour many of the younger debutantes display. The extra few years of maturity set her apart from the rest.'

Why on earth was he giving her indirect compliments when he could barely tolerate to be in her presence most of the time? Unless he was attempting to project an aura of the doting uncle? Fliss pasted on a smile and tried to think of a suitable response. She was spared the effort by the Earl.

'I approve of sensible gals.' He said this with a spray of pastry crumbs from the apple tart he was in the process of demolishing. 'Can't be doing with chits who have no common sense.'

'Felicity has more common sense than most, my lord. She is also blessed with good health as well as a fine figure.'

Unless her ears deceived her, which she sincerely doubted as she had always enjoyed excellent hearing, she had a sneaking suspicion Uncle Crispin was doing a bit of matchmaking. Very unwelcome matchmaking. The Earl's eyes dropped to her bosom, another one of his odious habits which made her flesh crawl, and he leered.

'Yes, indeed. A very fine figure. So far, I find very little about Felicity which I do not approve of.'

'My name is *Miss Blunt* until I give you leave to call me otherwise, my lord, and while I appreciate your approval, it is wasted on me.'

'She's feisty too, Rowley.'

'Too feisty.' Her uncle shot her a warning look down the table.

'I like a feisty gal.' Now the old fool was positively ogling. To her horror his wrinkled face scrunched unattractively as he winked at her. This needed to be nipped in the bud.

'Sir, I sincerely hope you are not flirting with me. I take a very dim view of flirting at the best of times, but *you* are far too old to be engaging in such nonsense.'

'Remember your manners, Felicity.'

'My manners? Surely it is the height of bad manners to discuss a lady's figure at the table as if she were an item available to purchase from a shop?' She turned to the Earl and bestowed him with a sugary, insincere smile. 'Unfortunately, I am not for sale, my lord. Not now, not ever.'

'I like a woman with spirit.'

'And I prefer a man with all his own teeth.'

'Felicity…' her uncle practically growled as his cold, silver eyes bored into hers. 'Be *pleasant* to our guest.'

'A lady shouldn't drink spirits,' Aunt Daphne said, waving her wineglass in the air. 'They don't have the constitution for it. Could you pass that bottle of wine, please, Felicity?' Her aunt was blissfully ignorant of the tension between uncle and niece. 'I must say, Crispin, your staff are very lax at topping up the glasses. Guests shouldn't have to resort to serving themselves.'

'Nor should they be insulted by members of my family.' Uncle Crispin glared, then turned back to their guest. 'Perhaps now is the opportune moment for us to retire with our port and cigars. It will give my niece's hot temper a chance to cool down.'

Fliss grabbed hold of the bottle and considered smashing it over her uncle's head, before banging it down on the table in front of Daphne and biting back the angry words on the tip of her tongue while both men stood. She waited until they had closed the door behind them before venting her anger out loud.

'How dare he try to broker a match between me and that awful man!'

Aunt Cressida turned and blinked at her tone. 'What awful man, dear?'

'Weren't you listening? Uncle Crispin has decided upon the Earl of Redditch as a potential suitor.'

'Surely not. The man is old enough to be your grandfather. I was of the belief you didn't want to hunt for a husband.' Cressida appeared dumbfounded. Or wine-addled. Either way she was clearly not complicit in the matchmaking.

'I didn't come here to hunt for a husband! I'm quite capable of selecting my own suitors should the sudden urge appear. Uncle Crispin barely knows me, so what makes him think he will know what will make me happy or lure me to give up my position at the convent? I've told him as much, too. It hasn't deterred him.'

'Men always think they know what's best for us, dear—' this came from Daphne '—yet they rarely do. Ignore it.'

'Difficult to do when it is happening right in front of me and Uncle Crispin appears determined to be persistent. He knows my feelings on the subject and understands I will be returning to Cumbria as soon as the Season is done. I'm not sure what he thinks he's playing at. It's as if he hasn't listened to a single word I've said.'

'That's where you're going wrong.' Daphne sloshed more wine into her glass and over the tablecloth. 'You used words. Words are largely wasted on males and one should never try to reason with a stubborn man. They simply dig their heels in further. Men respond better to visual stimulus than anything audible. If he's selectively deaf, which Crispin most assuredly is, deliver the same message in other ways.'

'Are you suggesting I mime it, like charades?' Unfortunately, the only gestures she knew for *mind your own business* were those deemed too unsavoury for a gently bred lady to use, but she treated her incorrigible aunts to a few of them just the same.

Daphne cackled with delight. 'If only! You shall just have to be more devious in future. The key to manipulating the *simple* male mind is to appear to be compliant, but to behave in a manner quite the reverse. They soon get the message you are not to be trifled with. *Show* my supercilious nephew you cannot be swayed. Remember, Felicity, a lady's actions *always* speak louder than words.'

Surprisingly, it was a piece of advice sound enough to have come from the wise lips of Sister Ursuline and Fliss decided it did have some merit. So much so that when her uncle and the Earl returned she held her tongue in check and proudly *showed* her frosty indifference until she climbed in the carriage taking them to the ball.

Jake found himself a secluded nook in the alcove and watched the proceedings from a distance. The trouble with having to socialise while working meant you were denied the opportunity to arrive fashionably late in case something happened, which inevitably left lots of time to twiddle the thumbs. He was hiding out of necessity. There were several eager young ladies and several more mature ladies who were always desirous of his company, yet he could hardly be seen flirting with one of them when he had to seduce Rowley's niece. From his first impressions, she wasn't the type of woman who would accept playing second fiddle and would regard evidence of his obvious philandering in a very dim light after calling him one.

Not that he was in the mood to philander. Since he had first seen her at Almack's, the indomitable

Miss Blunt had rather taken over all his romantic thoughts and, until he had slaked the powerful desire he had for her, frankly no other woman would do. Normal rakish business would doubtless resume straight after. Jake's attention span for an affair was akin to a bumble bee's attraction to nectar. As a bee blithely buzzed from flower to flower, Jake hopped from bed to bed. He preferred things that way. No commitments, no expectations and definitely no complicated and messy feelings to contend with. Much calmer and less problematic all around.

While love had apparently worked out remarkably well for his three brothers, Jake knew in his heart it wasn't for him. The elder three Warriners deserved to find lasting happiness with the women of their dreams. They were good men. Worthy men. Men who had found the right path to travel and had marched down it with single-minded determination and all had reached the destination they had intended against all the odds. He admired them for that. Jake's path meandered, largely because he had no idea where he was going. Never had. Therefore, his dreams were filled with transient lovers and as he was never quite good enough, and had been that way since birth, it was probably for the best.

He excelled at ultimately disappointing everyone he came into contact with as a matter of course—from his parents, to his brothers, to all the women he had charmed. He was the reliably unreliable Warriner, yet quite comfortable in that skin. On the exterior at least. Inside, he wasn't as blasé about it, but then he knew bits about himself which, with hindsight, he would have changed had the die not been cast a long time ago. Once a disappointment, always a disappointment and rightly so...

Good lord, he was getting maudlin. Another irritating side effect of twiddling one's thumbs was excessive time for introspection. Something he staunchly refused doing for exactly this reason. It served no purpose. The clock could not be turned back, but he could do everything in his power to avoid becoming his father, even though those character traits were as imbedded in his body as firmly as his identical bright blue eyes and jet-black hair. He used those characteristics to do good rather than wreak havoc, although lying to women and using his innate charm to seduce information out of them was perhaps not the dictionary definition of good. But he was working with the limited arsenal of attributes God had given him. Attributes which would rapidly deteriorate with age. A depressing thought indeed.

At this rate, he would sour his mood, which would seriously impair his ability to be charming and seductive, two things he did excel at and always had. Two things he now used for the good of King and country to great effect. That thought cheered him slightly. Jake was about to risk a quick dash to the refreshment table, when the air in the ballroom shifted. That was the only way of explaining the peculiar sensation which directed him to turn to the staircase the very moment Miss Blunt sailed down it. And, by God, she looked stunning. So stunning he forgot to breathe until the air he had been holding in his lungs all came out at once.

Had that ever happened to him before?

Jake couldn't recall it if it had.

Miss Blunt was a vision in forest green. A dour choice for most women, but a statement on her. The plainness of the colour was lifted by the daringness of the cut. The bodice clung to her upper body and hung off her shoulders. One single, fat, jewelled pendant rested above the tantalising glimpse of cleavage on display. Once again, there was a faraway look in her eyes as she floated into the ballroom, almost as if she didn't care where she was or who was around her.

His throat clenched when he realised his wasn't the only head that had been turned. Every man she floated past gazed appreciatively at her, not that she appeared to notice, a few young bucks even going as far as nudging their companions and hungrily grinning at the sight. Jake wanted to throttle every one of them.

Her chaperons appeared at her elbow and then Crispin Rowley materialised and took up the rear as the party moved to a free spot in the furthest corner. Jake had to crane his head to keep watching, something a man trying to be inconspicuous shouldn't be seen doing, yet he did it anyway. He couldn't help himself. Jake could watch her all night and never get bored.

Rowley left to fetch the ladies' drinks. When he returned, he handed Miss Blunt a card along with her glass. Words were exchanged and her expression changed from faraway to annoyed. She went to say something to her uncle, but he marched away mid-sentence, leaving her glaring after him as he disappeared into the crowd. The Sawyer sisters appeared to sympathise. They patted her arm and tried to distract her, but for the next twenty minutes Jake was forced to suffer seeing her distressed when she should be smiling and he willed her to break free of her charges so he could seek her out and make it all better.

Being rebellious at heart, she eventually did slip away and backed herself into the opposite alcove and out of his eye line. Like a man possessed, his feet began to move instinctively and he found himself skirting the perimeter of the room to find her. She was hidden behind a pillar. Well hidden, yet his intuition pulled him to that exact spot without any trouble. Her back was turned away from him and she was staring intently at the card. His eyes devoured the expanse of golden skin on her back; the loose honeyed tendrils of hair which curled seductively at the nape of her neck. The rest of her glorious hair was casually piled on top of her head, giving him the distinct impression that the removal of one or two strategically placed pins would send it tumbling around her shoulders. Enjoying himself far too much to interrupt, Jake rested his own back against another pillar close by and savoured the beautiful sight.

She sensed him.

Turned around.

Then guiltily tore the spectacles from her face. Spectacles!

He hadn't been expecting those. Spectacles which did peculiar things to his nether regions.

'No. Leave them on. I rather like them.'

Good lord—now his obligatory nightly fantasy involving this Cumbrian temptress would include those spectacles…and nothing else.

'Mr Warriner, we've spoken about the flirting.'

'We have indeed, Miss Blunt, but I am incorrigible.' The knowing grin he shot her was all male arrogance. 'Stifling my natural instinct to flirt with a beguiling woman would be as futile as suggesting I give up breathing. You are going to have to suffer it, I'm afraid. Especially as you *are* beguiling and have a fortuitous habit of lurking in the same alcoves as I do.'

She stiffened her perfect shoulders and sniffed. 'I am not lurking, Mr Warriner. I am pondering. *You* are lurking.'

'Sounds important. What are you pondering?' He pushed himself away from the pillar and sauntered towards her. 'And might I suggest you ponder in those spectacles. There is something about a beautiful woman in spectacles. It gives her an air of the superior…the stern schoolmistress… the prim and proper governess…' He flicked his wrist as if tossing the flirting aside. 'But I digress. You are hiding again and I am intrigued to know why. It's a fault of mine. I need to know everything about everyone.'

'I am avoiding the Earl of Redditch.'

'A very sensible thing to be doing, if you want my opinion. The man is a dreadful bore.'

'He also smells like feet.'

He laughed at that wonderfully blunt summary which perfectly matched his own from just a few hours before, enjoying her brutal honesty and the half-smile she tried to cover. 'That he does. Has stinky Redditch taken a shine to you?'

She pulled a face of disgust and made a great show of shuddering. 'Unfortunately, yes. Even more unfortunate is my uncle's persistence in foisting the man upon me. He has even gone as far as pencilling the Earl's name on my dance card for the first waltz—' she waved it angrily in front of his face '—and I am currently in two minds about what to do about it.'

'And what are the two warring parts of your clever brain saying?'

'The cowardly half thinks I should remain hidden during that dance and then have it out with my uncle later. The rebellious half wants me to dance it out of spite—but with a partner of my own choosing—and then have it out with my uncle later.'

'My condolences to your uncle. Whichever you decide, he is in for it regardless.'

'Although I doubt he will listen. Uncle Crispin is stubbornly ignorant of my feelings. When I speak, I am convinced his ears fill with wool, because he always does what he thinks I want regardless of my repeated assertions to the contrary. Why do men do that, Mr Warriner?'

'I hope you are not tarring us all with the same brush, Miss Blunt? Some of us listen.'

'You certainly don't. I've asked you not to flirt and yet you still do it.'

'I'm not flirting now. I'm listening.' Although Jake wanted to flirt. Instead he lifted the dance card and leaned conspiratorially towards her. 'I wonder why he wants you to dance with Redditch? The man is rich and titled, to be sure, but no more so than half the men in this ballroom. Did he give you any idea as to his motive?'

'Aside from telling me to be *pleasant* to the old

fool I was not apprised of the purpose. My uncle is irritatingly sparse with his conversation.'

'Perhaps they are old friends?'

'I believe theirs is a business relationship. It is the main topic of conversation during the interminable dinners I have had to sit through.'

Jake's ears pricked up with interest. 'Who else was invited?'

'What difference does it make who else was there?'

Good lord, she was sharp and he was clumsy. 'It doesn't. As I just said, I'm simply a curious soul by nature. Was there any delicious gossip? I'll bet there was.'

She huffed and shook her head, the motion causing one stray gold ringlet to bounce enticingly by her cheek. 'If only… I'm afraid the conversation was as deadly dull as it always is. They talked of canals.'

Leatham had been right, then. 'Canals? Gracious, that does sound dull. Tell me, are you now an expert on the subject?'

'By default and quite unwillingly, yes—but I was brought up to believe it is the height of rudeness to snore at the dining table.'

'That it is.' He was on to something, but had to

tread carefully. 'Although I doubt it is *dull* enough to help me.'

She folded her arms across her chest, something which did wonders for her figure. 'Help you?'

'Indeed. I've been suffering through a bout of insomnia, Miss Blunt.' Largely caused because of her. 'And am in dire need of some mind-numbingly boring things to think about in the wee hours to alleviate the problem. Indulge me with your dull expertise on canals. It might come in useful later tonight when I am tossing and turning and wistfully yearning for you. Only the dullest facts, if you please.' Jake assumed a stance of a man ready to learn and it earned him another smile.

'The Regent's Canal will be almost nine miles long on completion later this year.'

'A painfully short canal, then. Hardly worth all the bother of building it. Go on.'

'Although painfully short, it will link the Grand Junction Canal with the docks in the east of the city.' Docks which sat on the Thames and flowed conveniently out to sea. Smuggling boats could bring their contraband right into the city and then transfer it to barges to send it inland. Smaller boats wouldn't even need to unload. They could sail on unencumbered by the Excise Men.

'That is dull.' Jake pretended to yawn. 'Go on.'

'The canal will have three tunnels, the longest of which is at Islington, which is already built, and runs to nine hundred and sixty yards, which I think you will agree is a very long tunnel indeed Mr Warriner.'

A lovely, long, dark subterranean place to unload unseen. Not that Rowley would even need the tunnels. The fetid stench of most canals meant people tended to avoid them. 'Long and *deathly* dull, Miss Blunt. I already sense a good night's sleep coming on. I shall probably regret asking, but feel that I must—why on earth are the pair of them discussing an unfinished, painfully short canal over their soup? Does one of them have shares in it?'

'I cannot tell you about *that*, Mr Warriner, as that is the most interesting part of the story and it might undo all of the good work we have done thus far to ease your sleeplessness.'

'Tell me anyway, because now you have me intrigued.'

'New investors had to be sought a few years ago when the promoter of the canal, a Mr Thomas

Homer, embezzled all the funds. The Earl of Redditch snapped up a significant stake in the venture for a steal, or so he says, and is very smug about his brilliance for he has a *magnificent* fleet of barges which he intends to use on that same canal.'

Transferring goods to and from the docks would be a lucrative business indeed for any canny investor. 'And your uncle has plans to invest in this venture?'

'Apparently, one cannot have enough barges, Mr Warriner, or so the stinky Earl of Feet claims. Uncle Crispin is one of three investors bidding to extend the fleet. So until the deal is sealed, he is doing his upmost to fawn over the old fool and I am expected to be *pleasant* to him and endure my uncle's flagrant attempts at matchmaking.'

'Does your uncle invest in other canals that you know of?'

Chapter Five

In the Renshaws' stuffy ballroom

'**W**hy do you care?' Because Fliss got the distinct impression he did for some strange reason. 'And what has this to do with either your insomnia or my uncle's matchmaking attempts?'

His expression changed. Briefly he appeared almost frustrated at her answer, harder, less flippant. Somehow more intelligent and, strangely, much more attractive. 'It's your fault. You promised me a dull story, then piqued my interest and now I want to know all the gory details. I'm fundamentally a nosy fellow, as you now know. All manner of things fascinate me.' He smiled again and the easy charm returned, making her wonder if she had imagined the glimpse at a very different man who lived within the same skin as the dashing rogue.

She probably had. And if she was brutally honest with herself, which of course she always was, she had likely done so because a tiny part of her wanted him to be more than a rogue. Aside from being the only person she'd had a decent conversation with since arriving in London, the female part of her was physically attracted to him. But attraction was a dangerous emotion which couldn't be trusted alone. Sister Ursuline's was filled with silly girls who had succumbed to the lure of attraction and then paid the ultimate price when the gentlemen concerned turned out not to be gentlemen at all. After their last meeting, Fliss had made some enquiries about Mr Jacob Warriner and her aunts had confirmed her initial assessment of his character.

He was a rake.

Handsome, charming. Hedonistic. A man who pursued pleasure with the same fervour a great scholar sought knowledge. She failed to acknowledge that the two old dears didn't seem to disapprove of his rakishness at all. Quite the opposite, in fact. Cressida had sighed wistfully and declared that rakes made the very best lovers and then the pair of them had waxed lyrical about the startling array of scandalous gentleman they had enjoyed relations with. More shocking was their ability to compare notes on quite a few of them, which caused even more wistful sighing as they relayed all the gory and fascinating details. Details which conjured up images of sinful blue eyes which Fliss had not needed at all. Attributing deeper layers to such a man led to nothing but folly, especially when she knew better. The only thing such a man could be depended on to be was the sort no sensible woman could afford to be charmed by.

'Their conversation was exceedingly dull, Mr Warriner. Tediously so. I spent most of the meal completely excluded from it, counting the fleurs-de-lys on the wallpaper.' She had reached one hundred and sixty before she had lost count as all the patterns began to merge into one. No mean feat when she had been callously separated from her spectacles again. Uncle Crispin took great issue with them and had briefly threatened to stamp on them if he saw them again on her face before smiling insincerely and reassuring her it was a joke. Regardless, she had taken to keeping them hidden, and always on her person, just in case he had instructed one of the servants to conveniently lose them.

'It was very rude of them to ignore you.'

'I thought so. I came to the conclusion my presence at the table was entirely decorative.' Fliss was stuffed into another new gown which was designed to show off her figure. While she much preferred the bold green silk from the insipid pastel frock she had been told to wear to Almack's, the neckline still displayed far more flesh than she was used to displaying. She had pulled it up as far as it would go the moment she had stepped into the alcove. The additional inch did nothing to cover her modesty. 'My uncle seems determined to find me a husband.'

'Which you are adamant you do not want. Why is that?' His dark head tilted to one side and for a moment Fliss found herself drowning in his deep blue assessing gaze before she remembered she was supposed to answer.

'I am used to living on my own and actually rather enjoy it. It is liberating to only have to depend on one's self, when others are nowhere near as reliable.'

'It sounds awfully lonely.'

'Not at all.' Although lately it had been. Most of her best friends had married and moved on. Now that they had their own families to look after, friends, even the very dearest ones, tended to come second. Seeing them happy and content, embracing motherhood and all that came with it, did make a part of her yearn for the same. Not enough of a part to lower her high standards, of course, but enough to make her stop and think from time to time. 'My life is phenomenally busy.' Fliss got to look after other people's children—an ever-changing, moving stream of girls went in and out of the convent's doors.

'There is a chance he is not really matchmaking. Have you considered the prospect he is using you as a distraction to lure Stinky Redditch into choosing him as a business partner?'

'Of course I've considered it and I still resent it. I have no desire to be a distraction either, Mr Warriner.'

'But you are Miss Blunt. Very distracting.'

As he appeared on the cusp of laughing at his own words she couldn't help smiling back at him. 'If you were me, Mr Warriner, what would you do? Hide in the alcove or rebel?'

'Wherever possible, I would rebel, Miss Blunt, but then I am a rebel, too, by nature. I wouldn't dream of counselling you on the correct course of action and nor should you actively seek it from

a man with my reputation. What does that intelligent, stubborn and vexing head of yours say?'

'I am erring on the side of rebellion.' Even after
all these years, the precociousness still surfaced
occasionally. 'It sends a warning shot over the
bow to Uncle Crispin stating I am not to be trifled
with.' Saying it out loud cemented her determination. Politeness had made her closed-mouthed
about her clothes and spectacles up to now, but
her uncle kept taking liberties. Now that she was
secure in her growing dislike for her overbearing,
cold and calculated only relative, there seemed
little point in playing happy families any longer.
Actions spoke louder than words. 'I shall dance
the waltz—but not with the aged and fusty Earl
of Redditch.'

'That's the spirit.'

All Fliss needed was another man to waltz with.
A man who was the exact opposite to the one
who had been foisted on her. Someone young and
handsome. One whom her uncle would heartily
disapprove of. One she could nab quickly as, according to her dance card, the dratted waltz was
imminent. 'Mr Warriner, I don't suppose you
would dance with me?'

The sinful grin spread up his face slowly. 'I

thought you would never ask, Miss Blunt.' His eyes were twinkling with mischief. Outrageously blue eyes. Beautiful even. No wonder the ladies fell for him in their droves.

'Don't get any funny ideas. It is just a dance.'

'It's not *just* a dance. It's the waltz, Miss Blunt. Renowned as the dance of *love.*' He held out his arm and she took it, unprepared for the way the simple gesture would alter the dynamic between them. Jake was solid. Much taller up close than she had realised. Although patently not, against him she felt petite and because he smelled as gorgeous as he looked, she had the urge to lean closer and inhale him. Sensibly, she moved away instead. Just a few inches, but he was having none of it. He curled one warm hand over hers where it rested in the crook of his elbow, anchoring her gently but effectively at his side. It was a solicitous, possessive motion other men had done many, many times before, yet none of those had felt quite as significant.

Fliss had never been so bothered by a man before. And she was bothered. Jacob Warriner was infinitely more dangerous to all her senses, if her rapid heartbeat was any indication. Even her tightly laced corset seemed suddenly tighter now that their hands touched. He dipped his head and whispered in her ear and her whole scalp tingled. Ripples of awareness shimmered down all her nerve endings the moment his hot breath caressed her cheek. 'You should probably be warned I am devilishly good at waltzing. Barricade your heart now, Miss Blunt, else you'll fall head over heels in love with me before we have twirled a complete circuit of the room.'

'Oh, I can assure you there is no danger of that happening. I would never be so foolish as to fall in love with a rake, no matter how dashing and charming he is reported to be. Dashing and charming are not dependable and I'll never fall head over heels for anything less.' She made the mistake of slanting a glance up and into his intoxicating eyes. They must have contained magnets or something, as once his eyes locked with hers, hers were powerless to look away.

'Never say never, Miss Blunt. Remember, even the mighty Achilles had a heel.'

Had Jake not been a little overawed by the intensity of the moment and his reaction to her, he would have patted himself on the back for the return of his smooth, subtle and effective charm. This time, it had been more successful, although he suspected there was a long way to go before he had the delightful Miss Blunt eating out of his hand. Thanks to their enlightening conversation, he was also making headway on his mission. There was dirt to be uncovered on Rowley, mud that perhaps they might make stick this time if they could prove a direct link to him and the smuggling ring. Investment in a new canal was not evidence enough to secure an arrest warrant. The Attorney General would need more before he set the King's lawyers on a wealthy member of the aristocracy. So much more. A very good reason to keep his wits about him with Rowley's clever niece. Unfortunately, his wits were currently scrambled and had been since the first moment she had touched him.

Oddly nervous, he turned her towards him and slipped her hand in his, trying to ignore the excitement building within his body at the prospect of holding her close. Thinking calming thoughts weren't helping, so he tore his eyes away from hers and scanned the edges of the dance floor. There was no sign, as yet, of either the Earl of

Redditch or Crispin Rowley, but Flint was there. A half-smile on his face and a quick wink towards Jake; a stark reminder that he had come here with a job to do. That focused him.

Sort of.

'Aside from your uncle, I know nothing about the rest of your family, Miss Blunt.'

'There is nothing else to know, Mr Warriner. For a long time there has been just me and my elusive uncle.'

'I take it you didn't see him often growing up.'

'See him?' She laughed. 'I believe that would have been far too much trouble for him. Until last week, I'd never so much as heard from him.'

Interesting—if sad—and he felt sorry for her. The first notes from the orchestra filled the room as he slipped his hand around her waist and tried not to think about the lovely way it curved beneath his palm. 'Surely you corresponded?'

'I did. He didn't. But then I suppose he was busy as important men are prone to be.' Her tone told him she didn't particularly like Rowley, but was trying to be tactful with the truth.

'I doubt he was busy for the entire fifteen years you've lived in Cumbria.'

'How do you know I've been in Cumbria for

exactly fifteen years?' Good heavens, she was sharp.

'You've caught me out. I have been asking about you.'

'I shan't ask why in case you use it as an excuse to flirt.' She stepped on his foot.

'Is that a warning?'

Her lovely green eyes lifted towards his and quickly dipped again as a rosy blush stained her cheeks. 'Actually…this is technically my first ever real waltz. I never learned it in Cumbria. Aunt Daphne has been teaching me, but as she is so often—' She clamped her mouth shut and those bewitching eyes widened slightly, and Jake just knew she was going to say the word *drunk,* but stopped herself.

'She is so often what, Miss Blunt?' The corners of his mouth were already twitching and as one they both glanced towards the refreshment table. True to form, both the slurring Sawyer sisters appeared to be already the worse for wear. Cressida's silk turban had fallen so far forward it almost covered her eyes and Daphne's whole body was definitely listing on the scuppers.

'Shall we change the subject?'

'Probably safest.' His thigh brushed hers and

sent ripples of awareness directly to his groin. 'What would you like to talk about?'

'Why don't we talk about you, Mr Warriner?'

Did that mean she was interested in him? Jake certainly hoped so. 'What would you like to know?' She was staring at his face intently, a little too close than was proper. Now that he knew she needed spectacles to see, the close proximity made perfect sense, yet only a fool would fail to enjoy it. 'Did your obvious enquiries about me turn up anything intriguing?'

She didn't deny making them, which he also took as a good sign. 'I think I have the measure of the man you are now, Mr Warriner, but I am curious about how you came to be so. Tell me about your background—*before* you were a rake.'

'I have always been a rake.' She was an atrocious dancer. Delightfully atrocious to the extent Jake would have to take his handkerchief to his boots to remove all the dusty footprints she was leaving on them. She almost tripped over them again and he used it as an excuse to hold her closer. Relieved to be supported, she gripped his shoulder tighter and gazed up into his face with an expression of intense concentration.

'Nobody is born a rake, Mr Warriner. Rakes

are made. We are all nurtured by circumstance. There is probably some pivotal moment in your past which shaped your future.'

There was, not that he'd ever tell her. 'Do you really think a person's character can be altered by circumstances?' He was trying to distract her from probing further, but typically she refused to be swayed.

'Of course. It has certainly shaped mine. I doubt I'd be as stubborn and vexing if I hadn't spent fifteen years on my own. There has to be something in your past. A significant occurrence which set you on the wrong path. Why don't we start with your family?'

'Well, up until very recently they were a very bad lot, so perhaps we should blame them for the shocking way I turned out. At home in Nottinghamshire we are known as the Wild Warriners—a title which was earned thoroughly by every generation of my forebears going back to Tudor times. We are a rotten lot. Very bad blood.'

Rather than shocked, she seemed interested. 'How bad?'

'The worst. My father was a violent drunkard, my grandfather was little more than a trickster and my great-grandfather was exiled from the *ton* for all manner of nefarious shenanigans too awful to sully a young lady's ears with. The earlier ones were no better. I come from a long line of ne'er-do-wells and, if the family stories are true, a couple of out-and-out traitors. The family seat is built like a fortress. There is a twenty-foot wall surrounding the house, enormous impenetrable gates and even a priest hole, although I doubt it ever held any priests. Sir Hugo, a Warriner from way, way back, had it made to hide his own sorry carcass in when angry people came looking for him. That says it all. So you see, I was doomed to be a rotten egg long before I was hatched.' Jake spun her in a quick set of turns straight past her fuming uncle and the bristling Earl of Redditch, and she shot them both a defiant smile as they twirled away.

Slightly and attractively breathless, she then picked up the conversation exactly where they had left it. 'I do not subscribe to the belief of bad blood. My own father was a wastrel, yet I have turned out all right. But then I had a good mother to see me through my formative years. Tell me about your mother.' Like a dog with a bone, she was determined to get to the root of his problem and she had inadvertently found his tangled roots straight away.

'I barely remember her.' A lie. 'She died when I was very young.' Because he hadn't fetched his father when she'd asked. 'My eldest brother Jack brought me up.'

'You smiled as you said his name. Are you close to your brother?'

'Brothers,' he corrected with a grin, 'There are four of us. I'm the baby of the family.' Fearing for his feet, Jake manoeuvred them back towards the alcove rather than back to her chaperons as was customary at the end of a dance. He both needed and wanted to talk to her more. She didn't seem to mind and allowed him to lead her to their secluded spot in the corner.

'Tell me about them.'

Thankfully, this was much safer ground so he happily complied by keeping things superficial. 'We are all the spitting image of our father, who despite being a scoundrel was devilishly handsome, but obviously, I am the most handsome Warriner by far.' She rolled her eyes, but was smiling and that smile warmed his heart. 'We also all have the same initials—J.L. Warriner— why I cannot say, but it makes receiving letters at home very confusing. I open my eldest brother's bills and he receives all the adoring love letters sent from all the women who desperately want to marry me. His name is Jack. He's the responsible Warriner. He looks after everything and everyone. Did I mention he is an earl? We might be wild, but at least there is a title lurking in the background, although Jack doesn't like to use it. Too much bad history is associated with it and he's trying to rise above it. You would like him, he's very *dependable*.' She acknowledged this with a grin that made his chest swell to have caused it. 'Then there's Jamie. He's the brave Warriner. He enlisted in the army and fought against Napoleon, but now he's an artist who illustrates children's books for a living. And he's doing very well at it, too. The clever Warriner is Joe. He's a doctor. A very good doctor who recently got married to an equally scholarly woman. He and his bride are nauseatingly happy. All my brothers are nauseatingly happily married and settled. Jack has three sons and Jamie has four daughters and I dare say Joe will have a family soon enough. A new niece or nephew might be pending, but alas, I am a bit behind on the latest family news.' The numerous exchanged letters weren't the same.

'You miss them.'

'I do, but their life is in Nottinghamshire and mine is here.' Suddenly the pull of home was stronger than it had ever been. He missed his brothers and their noisy families, missed being part of that noise. More than anything he missed being him. Just Jake rather than the rake-cum-spy—or was it spy-cum-rake? He didn't know any more and he was suddenly tired of it. 'Would you like me to get you a drink?' Over which he would quiz her some more about her uncle's business interests to avoid getting maudlin and homesick.

'No. I'd best go back before Uncle Crispin or my aunts come and fetch me. I can't spend all night in the company of a rake. No matter how diverting that company is, Mr Warriner.' She smiled somewhat reluctantly. 'Thank you for struggling through the waltz with me. I hope I didn't crush your toes with my clumsy big feet. No doubt I shall see you in another alcove in the very near future.'

Jake would have tried to convince her to stay a while, but he could already see a furious Rowley elbowing his way across the crowded dance floor to get to her. 'No doubt you will, Felicity, but alas, the cavalry is on its way to rescue you from my wicked charms.' He winked as he bent to kiss her gloved hand. 'By the way, most ladies call me Jake, because I am dashing. Like a pirate.'

She grinned and shook her head at his return to shameless flirting. 'Most enlightening, but I am not as susceptible to dashing pirates as most ladies. For the record, I prefer Fliss to Felicity, but you can continue to call me Miss Blunt as is proper. Especially when one is conversing with a pirate. Goodnight, *Mr* Warriner.' She slowly walked three steps away before turning back. 'Responsible…brave *and* clever?'

'I'm sorry?'

'An interesting choice of adjectives to use for your three brothers. Hardly *wild*-sounding Warriners at all. In turn you called them responsible, brave and clever. Admirable qualities. Noble. *Dependable*. Which beggars the question—if they are the responsible, brave and clever Warriners, what does that make you?'

For a moment, he wished he was more like his brothers and less like his father. Worthier. Admirable. But alas, fate had chosen this path for him and both King and country needed him to stay on it. He covered the uneasy well of longing with his most rakish smile. 'Why, that's easy, *Fliss*.' The sound of her name was like heaven on his lips. 'I'm the *disappointment*. Somebody has to look after the family legacy.'

Chapter Six

Seething in Uncle Crispin's phaeton

'If you don't mind, Felicity?'

Her uncle shot her his *get out of the carriage and give us some privacy* look. Fliss knew this because he had already left her twiddling her thumbs as she stood idly waiting for him to conclude his business three times already.

'Actually, I do mind. This is not at all how I thought I would be spending the day.' This morning she had awoken early because her uncle had promised she could finally visit the Menagerie at the Tower of London, a place she had been dying to see for as long as she could remember.

'I have a little bit of business to attend to, Felicity. We'll be on our way shortly and I promise my little surprise will be worth the delay. I am just waiting for one more thing and then I shall take you to Gunther's.' He said this as if she should be impressed.

'What is Gunther's?'

'The home of the finest ice cream in all of London.'

'You want to feed me ice in February?' Thanks to the sedate pace and lack of exercise, Fliss's fingers were already frozen inside her thick gloves.

'You might sound a little more grateful. Gunther's is *the* place to be seen.'

I don't want to be seen, I want to see the lions! Or the Elgin Marbles or the Changing of the Guard. In fact, almost anything which did not involve the rest of the fashionable residents of Mayfair.

Fliss bit back the angry retort because her uncle's business associate had pulled his curricle alongside and was doing his best to appear as if he couldn't hear their taut conversation. Uncle Crispin nodded to the man, then turned back to glare at her. 'Now if you will excuse us, Felicity, I shall be but a few minutes.'

For the fourth time she reluctantly lowered herself on to the path and took herself a few feet away. For good measure, she folded her arms and positively seethed at him, not that it had any effect.

Behind her she heard the snort of a swan and turned to watch it floating across the Serpentine, instead. For such beautiful birds, they had the ugliest sound. They didn't quack or tweet. The best way to describe the noise of a swan was a cross between a snort and an asthmatic cough. Nature's way of reminding the bird it wasn't perfect. Nothing ever was. Today was certainly turning out to be a thorough disappointment. Even though Fliss had awoken in a perfectly lovely mood, her uncle had spoiled it straight after breakfast and she was already regretting the compromise she had made in the spirit of family harmony.

Last night, after the Renshaws' ball, he had promised faithfully she could begin seeing the sights of the capital, decreed that she could take the carriage and her great-great-aunts to visit the Tower with his blessing and Fliss had started the day believing him. With hindsight, she should have realised something was wrong when her maid had laid out a wholly inappropriate and showy outfit for her to wear. Kitty had been most insistent she wear it and Fliss had been equally as insistent that she didn't.

She'd rejected the thin silk ensemble specially designed for her by Madame Devy because clearly the modiste had never ventured outside in winter. To the maid's vocal consternation, Fliss had rifled through her own wardrobe for something more suited to a cold February morning of exploring. That flimsy pelisse and those thin-soled slippers would have left her hideously exposed to the elements and ruined her feet. Instead, Fliss had dug out the sensible navy-wool walking dress she had brought with her from Cumbria, complete with its matching thick coat, and paired it with her sturdy yet comfortably worn boots. Garments much better suited to traipsing around a damp castle and climbing up its ancient battlements. But when she reached the hallway to meet her aunts, she met her uncle instead.

'There has been a change of plan.' Her uncle was dressed in his expensive riding clothes and the smile which materialised on his face was not echoed in his cold, flat, grey stare. 'It occurred to me last night that we have not spent enough time together, Felicity. I wish to remedy that and I hope you will indulge me in my quest to get better acquainted with my only niece by asking you to accompany me this morning on a little adventure.'

She'd had an adventure planned, one which blessedly had not included him and the unnecessary restrictions he placed upon her. 'I don't ride and I want to see the lions.' The churlish response was the best Fliss could manage in the wake of the disappointment. Yet another day would pass and she would still be denied the opportunity of seeing the places she had specifically wanted to see.

'I have something more exciting planned and you do not need to ride. I shall drive my phaeton and take you to see a part of this fine city which is much more interesting than the Tower. You will be diverted. I promise.'

His jaw was tight and his gaze was frosty and Fliss was well and truly trapped. It would be unforgivably rude to turn down her host's invitation even though she sincerely doubted he really wanted them to become better acquainted. He was up to something. She knew that in her bones. 'If you insist, Uncle Crispin, then I shall postpone my excursion.'

'That outfit is a little plain for what I have planned.' His eyes rested on the spectacles sat on her nose and narrowed. 'I'm sure your maid can quickly find you more suitable attire.'

How splendid. Another battle of wills and directly after breakfast. The food had already begun to curdle in her stomach. 'Uncle, it is February and freezing outside. If I am going out in a phaeton, then I shall do so wearing wool or not at all.'

'Will you at least take off those ugly spectacles?'

'I thought you were taking me to *see* something special. If I take off my spectacles, then it's hardly worth going as I shan't see whatever it is you are so *eager* for me to see at all.' As she had intended, he couldn't argue with sound logic and they walked to the phaeton in a silence so brittle, the merest puff of the cold February air would likely shatter it.

Since then, Fliss had been largely invisible to him. Uncle Crispin's apparent idea of a treat not to be missed was to join the fashionable crowd in parading up and down Rotten Row. A pointless exercise in her opinion if ever there was one. So far they had spent an hour either saying hello to people they had said goodbye to only a few hours before or, like now, he was discussing business and she was excluded. She had a good mind to take herself off to the Tower as a mark of protest, but with her atrocious sense of direction, going alone would doubtless end in disaster. There was no telling where she'd end up if she attempted the trip by herself on foot. Kent, probably. Or worse.

It would be typical, for her useless nose would take her to one of the less salubrious parts of the capital where she'd end up accosted by footpads or garrotted in an alleyway.

Much as she loathed taking the coward's way out, a solitary expedition to the Tower of London was out of the question. With a sigh, she stared out over the lake and smiled at the sight of a solitary rowing boat drifting across the middle. Only here, in London, where people ate ice cream in February, would a person be daft enough to row across a freezing lake for pleasure. The gentleman in charge of the oars appeared to be flagging under the exertion, while the lady passenger was hunched inside her highly ineffectual but highly fashionable coat as if her life depended on it. It was a pretty coat, made in the exact shade of blue as the eyes of a certain rake of Fliss's acquaintance. A rake she had dreamed about last night despite her better judgement and one she rather liked. For all his faults, Jake Warriner had rescued her at the ball and asked nothing in return.

And they had waltzed.

Even now her body warmed at the thought of it.

His arms been firmly wrapped around her body. They had needed to be to hold her up and to prevent her from seriously damaging his poor toes, yet he'd not mentioned her embarrassing clumsiness once, despite the fact she had stepped on his foot repeatedly. Although not all those footwork mistakes had been caused by her ineptitude with the waltz. At least two mishaps had occurred from being so close to him while staring into his beautiful bright blue eyes. Or perhaps it had been the solid feel of his shoulder under her palm which had made her pulse quicken and her feet fail? Thanks to Jake's raw masculinity Fliss had experienced a bit of a moment worryingly akin to swooning.

He smelled sinfully delicious, too, which was indeed a bonus when she considered what she could have been forced to sniff on that dance floor at that particular time. Whatever cologne he had applied before dressing must have contained some sort of magical ingredient, because it was more intoxicating the closer her nose got to it. At one point, during a dizzying set of fast spins, the urge to press her nostrils against his Adam's apple had been fairly difficult to ignore, but she'd struggled on. Valiantly. Making do with seductive wafts which emanated from his exceedingly fine person and chastising herself for being weak. Waltzing with the rakish Mr Warriner had not been a chore at all. It had been, she was prepared to admit only to herself, the highlight of her week.

He'd hardly even flirted and yet still she had been charmed. Charmed and intrigued in equal measure because the more she got to know him, the more she began to suspect he wasn't quite as superficial as he seemed.

Jake did have a way of looking at a woman as if she was the *only* woman in the room, which had made her feel very special. She had also spied a few jealous glances from the other young ladies as he had twirled her around the floor; young ladies who would have given their eye teeth to have been in his strong and capable arms in her stead. Fliss was just vain enough to be flattered by this and rather liked being the frivolous centre of attention for once, rather than the responsible Miss Blunt who always set an example to her students. The former wayward girl made good. An inspiration to aspire to. Sometimes all that made her feel old and dull.

With Jake, for a few short minutes, she had been vivacious and gloriously young. That waltz had been an adventure in itself. Shameless flirting aside, he was also good company. Interesting.

Interested.

He listened to everything she said, whether it be her bemoaning of her uncle's persistent and irritating attempts at matchmaking or recounting boring details about canal tunnels. He had called himself a nosy fellow and that he was, but Jake also paid attention and knew how to make a lady feel special. And his name suited him. Piratical and dashing.

Of course, he was still a shocking rake and liking him didn't mean Fliss was less mindful of his wiles. One of the benefits of living among a succession of wayward girls was one became an expert on the sort of men who waylaid them. Fliss had trained herself to be adept at ignoring her body's natural reaction to men like him. She wasn't a man-hater after all. A great many males were exceedingly tolerable, Fliss just knew their limitations. Some men were dictatorial. Some men were unreliable. Most men, however, were fundamentally untrustworthy. It was embedded in their nature, like the female urge to mother, and they really couldn't help it. One could still thoroughly enjoy the company of a rake without succumbing to his charms. Like all successful rakes, Jake had all the attributes to make a female body yearn. Such things were down to biology, not logic, and she would never allow herself to be a slave to something as base and savage. Logic made him wholly unsuitable. Not that she was in the market for a man at the moment. If she were he would be the very last sort to settle down with. Still, she was grateful he had stepped up to help her in her moment of need. That had been noble of him. It was too bad he was untrustworthy, else she might have been tempted.

To keep her mind from being further seduced by his presence, Fliss had asked him questions about his past. Although his answers had been glib, she could tell they were purposefully so. Another benefit of living among wayward girls was one became an expert in the art of lying. Her students knew she was a master at uncovering deceptions. At Sister Ursuline's, her ability to spot a lie at ten yards was legendary, although how she could spot one was a trick she kept entirely to herself in case the girls got wise to it and tried to camouflage the clues.

However, the simple truth was it wasn't really a trick, it was mere observation. There were little, almost minute physical tells which always gave the lies away. Each unique to the person, yet obvious to a master at reading them. To most people, Jake's casual and seemingly open answers would have sufficed, but Fliss wasn't most people and Jake's tell happened to be in those spectacular eyes which had a habit of taking her breath away. And by golly it was tiny. Had she not been staring wistfully up into them she would have missed it. But she had been, so she'd spotted it.

His pupils constricted.

In fact, they had constricted three times.

Once when he had blithely denounced his father as a violent drunk, suggesting he was making light of something which had not been in any way light at all. The second had been stronger, his black pupils constricting to a pinpoint for less than a second, and it had been in a throwaway sentence about his mother. The woman who had died when he was so young he *barely remembered her.* Fliss would wager all her savings on the fact he didn't *barely* remember her. That was a tactic to avoid talking about her and one Fliss sometimes used when new acquaintances inadvertently probed a sore spot. Like her, he remembered his mother keenly. Too keenly and it hurt.

So much so, she had taken pity on him and allowed him to direct the conversation to his brothers where he felt comfortable. Something she empathised with. Despite outwardly projecting otherwise, the rejection of her father when she had needed him the most still cut deep if she allowed herself to dwell upon it. All those years of loneliness and of feeling abandoned. Rejected. Not quite good enough to warrant even the tiniest place in his life. That pivotal moment in her past had shaped her and left her wary of all men, just in case another broke her heart quite so thoroughly and this time the wound would never heal.

What Sister Ursuline called cynicism was the necessary fortress that protected that tender organ from further damage. It was easier to not challenge the comfort of her carefully constructed status quo than subject herself to the risk of further pain. Once upon a time it had been enough, the walls of the fortress impenetrable, yet as the years had marched on Fliss was honest enough with herself to acknowledge those same walls which protected her also imprisoned her as well. This unexpected trip away from the sanctuary of normality had weakened those defences. Heightened the disquiet which had taken root without her noticing and had made her increasingly dissatisfied with her life. Made her yearn to climb a ladder to peek over the battlements at the possibilities beyond. The possibilities Jake presented.

Of all the men to be attracted to, her foolish heart had selected a rake.

Perhaps Jake had constructed a new persona to protect him from history repeating itself, just as she had? And perhaps Fliss was frantically hoping that there were deeper layers to him simply as a means to justify her continued fascination with a man her instincts screamed was wholly unreliable.

Or was he? It was obvious he adored all three of his brothers as his face lit with pride as he described them. Responsible, brave and clever. And then those brilliant, vibrant irises had constricted again when he had called himself the disappointment. In that instant she learned it was a label he wore openly, almost like a shield like her cynicism, but hated it nevertheless. It was on the tip of her tongue to question him about it, but her uncle had come and claimed her, and by the time they parted ways, the flirtatious look was back in his eyes and the peculiarly telling moment and the opportunity to explore it was gone.

Much as the foolhardy rower and his lady friend were now. Gone to freeze in another part of the Serpentine on their quest *to be seen*. With nothing better to do, Fliss went back to watching the swans and wishing she was somewhere, anywhere, else. Trying to ignore the image of twinkling blue eyes which constantly invaded her daydreams.

Chapter Seven

Laboriously plodding along Rotten Row

Jake had always enjoyed riding. Dashing across an open meadow, racing between steeples or simply meandering aimlessly along the open road at a leisurely trot never failed to lighten his mood. However, there was no joy to be had jostling his poor horse through the well-heeled crowds at Rotten Row at a speed little faster than the average arthritic octogenarian could achieve going uphill. He'd never understood the point of this aristocratic ritual, where the horses served as pedestals for the *ton* to display themselves. But Crispin Rowley was guaranteed to be here preening, because he always came here preening, which meant his fetching niece might be here, too. Or so he hoped.

He turned his horse towards where the congested gravel path arced around the Serpentine and plodded on, forcing himself to return the smiles of the many young ladies who made no secret of the fact they had their eye on him. However, for the first time in as long as he could remember, not one of them caught *his* eye.

That was odd.

Usually, at least one tempting damsel would lure him into furthering the acquaintance. The ladies loved a naughty boy, but while Jake had worked hard to become one of society's naughtiest boys for King and country, earning that reputation had hardly been a chore. He liked women. Really liked women, usually much preferring their company to men. Women, in all their shapes and sizes, intrigued him and distracted him in equal measure. The way they saw life quite differently from men, the calming influence they had, their resilience and intelligence, the way they smelled, moved, laughed. He was a healthy, virile, gloriously unattached man in the prime of his life. Why shouldn't he enjoy them if the opportunity presented itself?

Most knew he was not marriage material, accepted it and enjoyed him all the more as a result. The neglected wives, young widows and the occasional scandalous debutante who had been happily waylaid many times before he had arrived in their lives were immediately drawn to him for their fun and he was fine with that, too. Both parties got exactly what they wanted and had a great deal of fun in the getting. No matter whether he was bedding them for business or for pleasure, Jake treated all types of paramour the same and hopped cheerfully from one lover to the next like a bumble bee in a summer garden full of flowers.

At the first sniff of awkward feelings, Jake usually made his excuses and ran, because he was an honest rake beneath it all and didn't want anyone wasting their love on him when he wasn't prepared to take the risk of offering it in return. They might come to rely on him and nothing good could ever come of that, although fortunately he was so successful at being a rake that few of his conquests were silly enough to truly try. They knew he was superficial and transient, which was half of the fun of the dalliance in the first place. For them he was forbidden fruit. For him, each new lover was a tempting diversion from the gnawing empty, growing void in his life and the guilt which quickly turned him maudlin if he allowed himself to remember the cause of it. Therefore, it stood to reason that as long as Jake kept lining up potential diversions, then everything in his disappointing garden was as rosy as it could possibly be and he could flit through life without accruing fresh guilt to add to his burden. Therefore, he always had his wandering eye open for the next welcome diversion and Rotten Row had always been a particularly fertile hunting ground.

Except there was only one diversion currently lined up in his sights right now. Fliss. The only woman he truly wanted to dally with was the one he had fortuitously been tasked with seducing. A unique situation he had not found himself in before.

That vexing woman was taking up too much space in his head and, if he wasn't careful, when this mission was completed he would have nobody ready to fill her clumsy dancing shoes and would be left all on his lonesome to contemplate his failings. Something which wouldn't do at all.

It was worrying, but clearly not enough for his fixated mind to wander from its chosen route. Since the opera, he had done nothing but think about her and her alone—or rather his overwhelming reaction to her. Not a single other lady had occupied his thoughts or tempted his body in all that time, something unheard of and ex-

tremely unsettling. The damn woman had be-
witched him almost as thoroughly as she appeared
to see straight through him and he wasn't entirely
comfortable with that either. Yes, she was still a
diversion and, yes, he desperately wanted to seduce her, but there was an irritating and nagging
part of him which wanted more from the canny
Miss Blunt-by-Name-and-Nature than good sense
dictated.

Bizarrely, for a man who purported not to care
one jot what others thought of him, Jake wanted
her respect as much as he wanted to make her
smile. He wanted to kiss her senseless *and* talk
to her for hours on end. He wanted to spend time
with her. Lots of time. Considerably more than
the few accumulated hours he usually allowed
himself and to hell with messy, complicated feelings. Truth be told, he suspected he wanted her
to have messy and complicated feelings for him.
He wanted to matter to her as much as he now
suddenly wanted to be a better man than the one
he was whenever he was around her. A man with
the admirable characteristics of his three brothers. The sort of dependable man she had set her
heart on. More than anything, he wanted Fliss *not*
to be a mission to be accomplished for King and

country. A ridiculous notion he couldn't seem to dismiss. What was that all about?

There had been a moment before they had parted ways at the dance, when she had turned around and simply stared at him as if she was assessing him and all he had just said, and for the briefest moment Jake swore he saw her recognise the real him. The man riddled with guilt and plagued with self-doubt. As ludicrous as that terrifying thought was, he had struggled to shake it off for the rest of the evening because he couldn't help wondering what she had made of the real him. He doubted there was a hope in hell she'd want to take a chance on the reliably unreliable Warriner any more than he wanted to risk opening himself up to the unpalatable complications which came with romantic love. Except for the first time, he was sorely tempted by those complications and that bothered him.

To add insult to injury, he had even dreamed about her again last night and what a dream it had been. Jake had awoken hot and hard and so blasted frustrated he'd washed in ice water straight from the pump just to cool his ardour. Ardour which flagrantly refused to be cooled and still plagued him now. Ardour which could have been readily spent elsewhere. Why was he torturing himself with abstinence when she was his mission and he'd never been loyal to a single woman—business or pleasure—in his entire life? Misplaced fidelity wasn't rakish behaviour.

But then, he was tired. That probably had something to do with his uncharacteristic confused state. And he was supposed to be enjoying his well-earned leave. Casanova himself must have been exhausted from time to time and thus less inclined to woo willy-nilly. The simple truth was Jake needed to be home. In Nottinghamshire, sleeping. Not here traipsing up and down Rotten Row, so it was hardly a surprise his libido had gone into hibernation or that every female face and form seemed to merge into one and none of them piqued his interest. It wasn't the vexing Miss Blunt who had rendered him ruined for all these other women. It was tiredness. Pure and simple.

Nothing to worry about.

'Why, *hello*, Mr Warriner.' The sultry redhead and he had been exchanging smouldering looks for months. 'Fancy bumping into you here?'

Come on, Jakey-boy. Make some effort. 'Why, *hel-lo* to you, too.' He reached for her proffered gloved hand, easy to do when she had brought her pony directly level with his, and placed a lingering kiss on the back of it. A kiss that did nothing to fire the loins which had been ablaze a few scant days ago. 'How are you on this fine morning?'

'Very bored, Mr Warriner. I am in dire need of some *excitement*.' A blatant invitation to sin if ever he'd heard one, yet still nothing stirred in his breeches.

'I'm sorry to hear that. A beautiful young lady should never be bored.' The back of his neck prickled.

Awareness.

Jake turned his head slightly and saw her. Her dress was as plain as the grey February sky. Her hair was simply styled. Her bonnet austere by Rotten Row standards and she was wearing those spectacles which had haunted his dreams last night. Spectacles, which by rights should lessen her attractiveness—yet his gaze had never beheld anything so lovely and every drop of blood he possessed suddenly rushed to his groin, the overly friendly redhead already forgotten.

'What do you suggest I do, Mr Warriner?' Reluctantly he tore his gaze away from his canny northern lass and gazed back at the sultry vixen next to him. A woman who plainly wanted him naked and soon.

Nothing.

The fiery lust he had for Fliss fizzled out the instant he had turned back to look at the other woman. Clearly Jake really was doomed. He could already feel the powerful pull of whatever it was only she possessed.

'I really couldn't say…if you will excuse me.' He tugged the reins and angled his horse to trail after Crispin Rowley's phaeton and the golden-haired passenger his heart was suddenly beating loudly for, keeping enough of a distance that he remained unnoticed in the crowds, but close enough that he could watch her.

She didn't appear to be very comfortable sat next to her uncle. There was a stiffness about her posture which suggested she wasn't very happy with him, her eyes and body angled away. When Rowley slowed the carriage to greet a group of people, Jake lingered behind a tree. Her eyes drifted away from the people her uncle was chatting to and towards the banks of the Serpentine. After another few minutes, those people drifted away and an unfamiliar man walked towards the carriage. Rowley and his perplexing niece exchanged what appeared to be terse words, then she climbed out of the carriage to stand with ill-disguised impatience on the path.

Jake knew he should be watching the men, but his eyes followed her as she began to walk towards the lake and his shady vantage point. Making a snap decision he hoped he would not regret, Jake decided to forget about Rowley and his acquaintance. He quickly dismounted, secured his horse to a branch, then sauntered towards her.

Fliss had her back to him as she watched some swans close to the edge of the water. Her neck curved gracefully, much like those of the swans. Something he would rather die than mention as it was yet another trite bird analogy, but he suddenly had the urge to place a kiss on the exposed slash of skin between her bonnet and collar. He didn't, knowing full well it would probably be the last liberty she ever afforded him and because he was here on the King's shilling. Jake had a job to do and needed to stop being waylaid from the purpose of his quest by swanlike necks and spectacles and tiredness-induced yearnings.

Chapter Eight

On the chilly banks of the Serpentine

'Hiding again, Fliss? We must stop meeting like this.'

To her credit she didn't jump or startle, despite the fact he had crept up on her unawares, making him hope that she had experienced the same early awareness of him as he did her. Instead she slanted him a glance and gifted him with a smile which lifted the dullness of the day in much the same way a beautiful sunrise would. 'Good morning, *Mr* Warriner... Even though it is not morning by any sensible standards in the rest of England, but here in the capital it apparently still is.'

'I see you have escaped the clutches of your evil uncle.'

She frowned slightly, her perfect brows wrinkling for a split second before they smoothed and she appeared bored. 'Evil? Why did you choose that word?' The way she studied his face intently, waiting for his answer, gave him pause. Did she know or suspect something about Rowley's activities?

'Merely that he tried to force the Earl of Redditch on you at the ball. Why? Has he done more dastardly deeds I should be aware of?'

'I don't think so.' She stared back at the water, her expressive brows furrowed briefly again. Not a *no*, then. Interesting. 'But he has dragged me here, as far as I can ascertain, just to ignore me, although he claims we are going to get ice cream. In February.' Her eyebrows said all the things she stopped herself telling him. Now they were slightly raised. Not amused.

'People do odd things like that here in town. It takes a while to get used to their peculiar ways. Why are you stood here all alone?' They both gazed back at the intense conversation going on between Rowley and a man Jake was sure he recognised, but could not place.

'I have been dismissed while my uncle talks business. Again.'

'How rude of him.' Jake offered his arm. 'Would

you care to take a little turn about the lake, Fliss? To help pass the time?'

She briefly flicked her gaze back to her uncle's phaeton, saw he was still engrossed in whatever social discourse he was embroiled in and nodded curtly. 'I do believe I would, Mr Warriner. Are you going to flirt?'

'Most assuredly.'

'How tiresome.' But she smiled as she took his arm and Jake purposely led her along the bank and away from both her uncle and prying eyes. He allowed the companionable silence to hang for a minute, quietly enjoying the way her undulating hips intermittently brushed against his as they walked.

'Forgive me if I am speaking out of turn, but I get the distinct impression all is not right between you and your uncle this morning.'

'Is it that obvious?'

'To me it is. Every time I see you with him, your expression always tells me you want to be somewhere else.'

'I am trying to enjoy my visit here. It's just...' She sighed and shook her head. 'Why do I keep confiding in you, Mr Warriner?'

'Perhaps because I ask the right questions?'

'You do have a canny knack of hitting the nail on the head.'

'It's a northern trait. Like you, I say things as I see them and here that is a rare treat.'

She paused, then laughed. It was a throaty, earthy sound. Unpractised and without any artifice. Jake made the mistake of turning to look at her and when their eyes met he lost himself for a moment.

'It *is* a treat. I never thought I would miss northern honesty. It can be brutal at times. But I do. I miss saying what I think without first checking myself.'

'Then I am glad I came along to fill the void. Be brutally blunt, Miss Blunt. You know you want to. Unburden yourself by listing all the things you are not enjoying about your visit. Cry on my attractively broad shoulders.'

She stopped for a second, assessing him with amusement, before tugging gently on his arm to signal she was ready to walk again. 'I had hoped to see the sights today. The interesting sights like the lions at the Tower or museums and such, but instead I have been ambushed yet again by my uncle's personal agenda. Since I arrived, I have done everything he has wanted and nothing of mine.

I've been dragged to Almack's and *launched*. I've made a tiresome number of morning calls on strangers I do not know and have no desire to, eaten numerous dull dinners in the company of the awful Earl of Redditch, where I am forced to listen to dreary conversation about barges or have to suffer the old fool's unwelcome attentions. I'm coerced into coming here to Hyde Park rather than visiting the Menagerie as I had planned. Soon I shall be fed ice cream because Gunther's is apparently *the* place to be seen. But I don't want to be *seen*, Mr Warriner. I am desperate to *see* things before I run out of time and have to go home.'

His mission dictated he should press her about the dinner conversations, but her eyes were suddenly sad and he wanted to make her smile. 'No wonder you are at odds with your uncle.'

'I think I am doomed always to be at odds with my uncle. His matchmaking aside, we have nothing in common. All he cares about are appearances and business. Uncharitably, I am starting to believe the only reason he hauled me away from Cumbria was to give that stinky Earl someone to fawn over, for all my uncle cares about is how I look. Which is never quite good enough.'

'I can't think why. You look splendid.'

She shook her head at his rakish grin. It made a stray tendril of hair float in the faint breeze enticingly against the rim of her bonnet. If she had been any other woman he had been ordered to seduce, Jake would have given in to the urge to touch it and tuck it back where it belonged, knowing that brief intimacy would create a *frisson* between them. For some reason, although desperate, too, he kept his itching fingers to himself.

'We have already had words about my dour appearance today. He thoroughly disapproves of my choice of outfit this morning. Who knew that warm wool was not suitable for a cold ride in Hyde Park? Clearly I am expected to freeze to death in one of the frivolous silk concoctions he has had made for me.'

Jake couldn't help sweeping his eyes down the length of her. The dress and her winter coat might well be sensible, but she filled them spectacularly. The way the wool clung to her pert bosom and trim waist made his mouth water. The dark navy was the perfect showcase for her golden hair and English rose complexion. She was beautiful, breathtakingly so. 'Your uncle clearly also needs spectacles if he thinks you look dour. That is a very lovely outfit despite being less draughty than silk.'

For some reason, she blushed slightly and her fingers went to her spectacles. Without looking at him she slipped them off and stared at them in her hands. 'He disapproves of these most of all. I know they are ugly, but I can't see further than my nose without them.'

They weren't ugly at all. They were achingly erotic. 'I like them. I've already told you I think they give you the air of a schoolmistress. All prim and proper and bossy.'

'I *am* a schoolmistress.'

'Are you really?' The profession suited her.

'Yes, I am. Back at Sister Ursuline's I teach literature and grammar to the girls, with a smattering of history.'

'And are you prim, proper and bossy?'

'When the occasion calls for it.'

Because they were now completely shaded by a patch of trees, Jake couldn't resist gently prising the spectacles out of her hand and placing them back on her face. Because he had to, he arranged that stray silken tendril to sit against the soft skin of her cheek. He wanted to kiss her. He wanted to haul her into his arms and kiss her till both felt their knees buckle—instead, he took a step back and pretended to admire his work. 'I'm intrigued. Professionally speaking, how would you deal with a naughty boy, Miss Blunt? A *very* naughty boy. Would you tell him off?'

'I suppose it depends on what he has done.' She shot him a saucy grin which heated his blood quicker than any kiss ever had. 'For a mild misdemeanour, a few terse words might suffice. For something outrageously bad, it would need to be more severe. Perhaps he would be sent to bed without supper and have all privileges withdrawn.'

'Would you spank him?'

She rolled her eyes, but played along. For all her northern bluntness, she had a mischievous sense of humour. She didn't take herself too seriously and enjoyed a laugh. He liked that about her. 'In my opinion, a good teacher should never have to resort to physical violence. The most effective weapon in my arsenal is my disapproval. A *really* disappointed expression works wonders.' She peered at him over the rims of her spectacles, those green eyes hardened like emeralds.

He shuddered for effect. 'That is a terrifyingly disappointed look. I'm positively quaking in my boots.'

'It's been known to bring even the most unrepentant miscreants to tears. I can be fearsome when I put my mind to it.'

'Not to me. Now that I know I shan't be beaten if I'm naughty it's given me ideas to thoroughly earn your disapproval.' Rash and stupid ideas, which blessedly aligned with his mission. A mission he was coming to hate because he suddenly hated lying to her.

'Really?' She feigned boredom. 'I'm not in the mood for your infantile flirting, Mr Warriner. You'd do well to stop it now because my mood is quite foul and I can be very shrewish when annoyed, and despite the flirting, my anger is not directed at you, so it wouldn't be fair to let you take the brunt of it. Besides, I'm leaving it to ferment for the real culprit.' She stopped walking abruptly so that she could angle her head to look back at her uncle. Her eyes widened and those eyebrows Jake was becoming quite fluent in disappeared under her hair. 'Oh, for goodness sake!'

At her exasperated tone, Jake followed her stare and saw the Earl of Redditch hoisting himself into the small pillion seat on the back of Rowley's phaeton and making himself thoroughly comfortable.

'I should have known!' She groaned loudly and narrowed her eyes.

'Oh, dear. It does look as if you will be having a table for three at Gunther's.'

'He did it on purpose! The wretch prevented me from spending a perfectly pleasant day at my leisure so that he could foist Redditch on me again! He must have planned it last night at the ball. He wanted us to get *better acquainted* indeed. Every word that comes out of his mouth is a falsehood. I should have trusted my instincts and said no from the outset.' She was ranting to herself now and pacing around in a small circle, her expressive gloved hand slashing the air like a rapier. 'When is my uncle going to get it into his thick head that I'm not interested in that awful man and resent the interference?'

Outraged she was magnificent. The emerald eyes were stormy behind the lenses of her spectacles, those lush pink lips were pouting and her generous bosom was heaving with each frustrated, angry breath. 'How dare he! He's gone too far this time. Too far…if he thinks he is going dictate to me where I go or to whom I speak, then he has another think coming… He promised me a surprise! I postponed my own plans at his insistence and this is how he repays me?'

Jake shrugged ineffectually because she made a damn good point. The way her uncle was behaving was outrageous and he felt for her. Nobody deserved to have an aged earl thrust upon them as a potential suitor, especially when she had repeatedly voiced her refusal, but some men thought it was acceptable to bully women. Jake's own father had been such a man and had made his mother's life a misery, so, his mission aside, he was predisposed to loathe Rowley.

However, as one of the King's Elite he also needed to closely watch the events play out as the scoundrel intended. The man's sudden interest in both his niece and one of the main investors in the new Regent's Canal was in no way coincidental. The best and most prudent course of action would be to stand back and allow events to naturally unfold. He would be her shoulder to cry on. A sympathetic ear. Whatever was afoot today, duty dictated he should encourage her to go back to her uncle's phaeton and suffer the unwanted attentions of a man nearly three times her age. At Gunther's, she might well hear information that unlocked the case.

'Is there something I can do to help, Fliss?' Not the words he meant to say.

She slowly angled her face to his and Jake could see the cogs whirring inside her clever mind. 'Perhaps...' She inhaled deeply, her eyes closing, and appeared to centre herself from somewhere deep within. When her eyes opened, he knew she had made some sort of decision about the best course of action, because they slowly turned towards him and a new resolute defiance was shining back out of them. 'What are your plans for the rest of the day, Mr Warriner?'

'I don't have any.'

'Would you like to see the lions with me?'

'I can think of nothing I would like more.' Jake's pulse quickened. They would be all alone. Together. For hours. Finally, he could properly seduce her just as he'd been tasked.

'Then do you think you can smuggle me out of here without my uncle seeing?'

'As a matter of fact, I do. I excel at skulduggery.' He held out his gloved hand and she took it, causing intense awareness to shimmer through his fingers despite the layers of leather between them. Business and pleasure. Too good an opportunity to waste on both counts. He'd deal with the uncomfortable guilt which had settled in his gut later. 'Follow me.'

Chapter Nine

Wandering towards Traitor's Gate at the Tower of London

Escaping proved to be scandalously thrilling. Inexcusably irresponsible and definitely childish, but more fun than Fliss had had in years. It had been a very long time since she had allowed the precocious and wayward part of her character to run free and to do so for an ill-advised and fleeting afternoon was exactly the right medicine to cure her irritation at her uncle's conniving.

After Jake had hidden her behind his horse, the pair of them had crept out of Hyde Park giggling like children. He'd found a ragged, dubious-looking fellow with an angry scar running down one side of his face and paid him a few coins to take his mount back to his bachelor lodgings, then flagged down a hackney to spirit them to the medieval castle.

The Tower had proved every bit as fascinating as Fliss had.hoped and Jake was entertaining company. Together they marvelled at the four ragged lions as they tore apart fresh meat, gawped at the elephant, stared at snakes, petted some monkeys and tried to invent stories as to why Old Martin, the curmudgeonly grizzly bear, was so bad tempered. Jake had then paid a Beefeater to show them the jewels and take them on a tour around the fortress. The fellow had been so knowledgeable that Fliss's feet were now aching and her head was swimming with interesting facts she was looking forward to sharing with her students. Finally they were left alone to wander freely and Jake was reading from the guide book he had purchased.

'It says here that Queen Elizabeth passed through Traitor's Gate after being accused of treason by her mad sister, Queen Mary. The poor girl was only twenty and must have been terrified. Especially after what happened to her mother.' The Beefeater's story had been particularly graphic as he had recounted the execution of Anne Boleyn on the green by the White Tower. 'I'm glad I wasn't born back then. History is so gruesome, don't you think?'

'The gruesomeness is what makes it so interesting. Poor Elizabeth. Was she a prisoner here for very long?'

Jake consulted the guide book again. 'Eight weeks apparently. Not sure I could stand being incarcerated here for eight hours. I can't imagine how she suffered. I bet your uncle and the Earl of Redditch would find the story riveting, though. Look, it says she was brought to the Tower on a barge.' He grinned. 'The pair of them do get excited about barges. I wonder why?'

His question reminded Fliss she would soon have to go back to her uncle's soulless house and answer for pathetically running away. 'I'd rather not talk about my uncle just yet.' Although there was no getting away from it really. While she couldn't bring herself to care about Uncle Crispin's feelings, Daphne and Cressida didn't deserve to worry. She would need to apologise to them for causing them undue stress. 'I suppose I should head back. As furious as I am with him, my aunts will be anxious and it'll be dark soon.' February days were too short, she decided. Far too short.

'I still have no idea what I'm going to say to him about his duplicity. It's bound to be ugly.'

Jake picked up her hand and wound it around his arm. 'Hopefully, once his temper has cooled, he'll listen to your objections properly.' They began to stroll towards the gate they had entered a few hours before. 'Perhaps we can rehearse your argument in the carriage?'

'We could.' It couldn't hurt, although Fliss doubted Uncle Crispin would listen. 'Or perhaps I should simply tell him I think it is time for me to return home to Cumbria? I'm tired of his overbearing and dictatorial manner.'

His step slowed briefly and a part of her hoped he would ask her not to leave yet. The silly female part of her which was easily swayed by biology. The part that adored the fact he had singled her out for his attentions among all the other ladies this Season. That same part deflated with disappointment when he made no mention of her leaving. 'I can't even say he's doing it because he cares, Fliss. I suspect he is throwing you at Redditch for his own gain, yet for the life of me I cannot fathom why. There are plenty of wealthy and titled fish in the sea of Mayfair, most of whom don't smell like feet.'

'As you said, he is obsessed with barges, an area in which the Earl of Redditch is a very big fish. I believe I am merely the bait on the hook.' Something Fliss decided right then she needed to clarify with her uncle. Had he really dragged her all the way down the entire length of the country just to tempt a business associate? 'The man leers and ogles me shamelessly, something my uncle is happy to condone because he is so keen to supply those dull barges.'

'Your uncle is a wealthy man and must have many business interests. Maybe something else will suddenly occupy him and distract him from his current fixation with barges. What else does he invest in?'

A laughable question. 'How should I know? As Uncle Crispin barely speaks to me at the best of times, he's hardly going to wax lyrical about his stocks and shares over tea.'

'But you must have some idea? What business, for example, was he discussing in the park this morning? Who are his other business associates?'

'In case it escaped your notice, I was rudely expelled from the phaeton *because* he wanted to talk business. He didn't introduce me to any of the gentlemen he spoke to. Whatever it is he does, he does it very covertly.' Which was a worry.

They had reached the pavement where a line of hackneys waited to pick up the tourists. Jake took his time inspecting all the interiors until he found the cleanest and, to her body's consternation, lifted her into it. His big hands easily spanned her waist and the heat of them seared through the woollen coat and dress, through her stays and seemed to brand her bare skin beneath. It did odd things to her pulse. Because it took him a minute to apprise the driver of their destination and settle himself in the seat next to her, the rapid knocking of her heart lessened—right up until the moment she felt his hard thigh rest against her softer one. As he appeared unaffected by the contact, stretching out his long legs and crossing both his arms and his booted feet comfortably, Fliss let it pass. There was no point in lecturing him about propriety when this whole outing was vastly improper, yet he had been a perfect gentleman all afternoon. Why, he hadn't bothered flirting once. Something which she bizarrely found rather insulting all of a sudden.

The carriage lurched forward and they watched the Tower shrink through the window in comfortable silence before he turned to her, looking devilishly handsome and more than a little inquisitive. 'What makes you say his business is covert?'

'I don't know. Just a feeling.'

'Most feelings are based on a suspicion of some sort.'

'True.' She angled her body to be able to look at him fully. He was a man effortlessly at ease and the casual, informal way he was lounging suited him even if it did make her skin warm at the sight. 'This morning, for instance. He was being very secretive. And the men he discussed business with didn't seem to be very happy with what my uncle had to say to them.' A common occurrence, apparently. 'Perhaps that is why he chose to apprise them of it all in Hyde Park. Less chance of a scene with so many others looking on.' Another worry. It suggested a deviousness about her uncle which didn't sit right.

'Rotten Row is an odd place to meet to talk about business, I'll grant you, not when most men tend to discuss it at either their club or in the privacy of their own study.'

'Uncle Crispin doesn't tend to work in his study. From what I can make out he prefers to work in his dressing room. At least that is where his secretary and solicitor tend to be directed when they come to call.' Another odd thing when her uncle had a perfectly good study crammed full of expensive objects to impress. Or were most of his business associates so unsavoury he didn't want them in the main part of house? The only one she had seen had sneaked out the back in the dead of night. 'Although he did meet one man in his study recently. I only know this because my bed-chamber is directly situated above it and it's rare to hear anything coming from that quarter—but I was awake.' Thinking about Jake. Fliss made the mistake of glancing into his eyes and almost drowned in the fathomless depths, until the carriage bounced awkwardly, shaking her out of the spell and sending Jake sideways.

'I do believe I've found the worst-sprung hackney in all of London.' To prove his point they rattled over a series of cobbles with such intensity that Fliss had to set her jaw hard to stop her teeth from clattering together. They turned on to a blessedly smoother road and both simultaneous let go of the seat. 'Who was the man?'

'I don't know. A nasty sort.'

'Oh, dear. What about him made you think he was nasty?'

'His manner. He was very…' How best to explain the odd chill she had experienced when she had watched the altercation in the garden? 'Threatening. The pair of them argued.'

'About?'

'Why does it matter?'

'I'm simply curious. I did warn you I was a nosy fellow.'

He said it with such nonchalance, but his pupils constricted. Fliss was sure of it. He was lying. It gave her pause. 'Why don't we change the subject? All this talk about my uncle is spoiling what has been a thoroughly lovely day.' If her instinct was correct, he would try to direct the conversation back to her uncle.

He'd pushed her too far too quickly. Her brows had set in a straight line like a barrier. Fliss was too smart to blindly impart personal family information without questioning why a virtual stranger would feel inclined to ask. He and Lord Fennimore would just have to make do with the interesting snippets she had let slip so far. And they were interesting. How had the mystery man got into Rowley's house late at night when Leatham had all entrances on close watch? At least they knew why Flint had never found anything in the study. They hit more painful cobbles which made him wince. 'Let's talk about *Sister* Ursuline's. That sounds scarily like a convent.'

Her golden brows twitched, a sign she suddenly doubted herself, but she was searching his face a little too intently for comfort. Thank goodness he'd had the wherewithal to stop probing when he had. 'It is a convent of sorts, although Sister Ursuline is the only nun in residence, but it's not attached to any church. It's a boarding school for wayward girls.'

'And how did you come to be a prim and proper schoolmistress in a school for wayward girls?'

'I grew up there.'

'You were a wayward girl?'

'I prefer precocious. I'll admit to being a precocious girl. After my mother died, that is, and I was all alone in the world. Sister Ursuline's is my home so it was a natural evolution to go from being a student to a teacher when I became old enough.'

That all sounded rather sad and lonely to Jake. While his own parents had had little involvement in his rearing, at least he'd always had the strong and loving bond of his three brothers growing up. 'I'm sorry. I didn't realise you were an orphan.' One Crispin Rowley had left all alone until it suited his plans to claim her as kin.

'I wasn't an orphan.' Her face changed. Acceptance. She wasn't bitter or angry, merely matter of fact, then a tiny nerve twitched in her brow line and Jake saw the matter-of-fact acceptance was an act. It bothered her. 'My father outlived my mother by another decade, but he was ill equipped to be a parent and, as I have just admitted, I was a tad precocious, so I was sent away. As it turned out, his decision was for the best as I doubt I'd have grown into the woman I am today without the guiding wisdom of Sister Ursuline. She has been both a mentor and a surrogate mother to me all these years.'

'Your father abandoned you!' The sudden surge of anger at yet another example of shocking fatherhood made his voice louder and more forceful than Jake would have liked—but it was an honest emotion and one she seemed to appreciate. She patted his hand and smiled wistfully, trying to hide the pain in her eyes.

'He did—but practically upon birth. I rarely saw him growing up so his loss in my life was hardly a great deprivation. You should also probably know that I had a very happy life at Sister Ursuline's. I had friends and a nice place to live. She might be a nun, but she is not a conventional one.' The wistful expression changed to one of mischief as she grinned. 'She took Holy Orders at the age of forty-two and only after a scandalously successful career as a courtesan.'

'A courtesan?' Jake hadn't expected that and the bark of laughter surprised him.

'Yes, indeed. She was gently bred, but exceedingly wayward. So wayward her family despaired and eventually threw her out. But Sister Ursuline is indomitable and made the best of her situation. She was mistress to some very powerful men and accumulated a small fortune on the back of it. Money she used to build her school and help other spirited girls avoid making the same mistakes she did. Girls who would also have been abandoned if she hadn't have provided their families with a suitable institution to send them to, to help them curb their wayward ways.'

'While I respect your Sister Ursuline for taking on the burden, a part of me cannot help feeling angry that those families have abdicated their responsibility.' Like hers. And exactly like his parents, although they were at least there in body if not in spirit.

'I couldn't agree more, but that doesn't detract from the awful reality. Sister Ursuline's has provided the love and guidance missing in many a precocious girl's life. Mine included. I suppose I was a difficult girl, but Sister Ursuline helped me to control my impulses without weakening my spirit. She taught me to be self-sufficient, resilient and resourceful. Three skills a woman alone in the world needs more than any others. It was an honour to be able to give something back and I enjoy being a teacher.' She shrugged and he realised she had been in the exact same boat as the girls she now taught. Her own kith and kin had offloaded her elsewhere and then had quickly forgotten about her. Both her father and her uncle had abandoned her. All his brothers despaired of Jake's rakish way of life, but they would never cast him out. He was loved. Always had been. He also had always had a proper home to anchor him, one that drew him more and more with each passing day away. What must it feel like to have no one? Was it any wonder Fliss was fiercely independent? She'd had to be. She'd made the best of the poor hand life had dealt her, just as he and all his brothers had, but she had done it all alone from the tender age of ten. The knowledge humbled him.

'Sister Ursuline sounds like a wonderful person.'

'She is. As you would expect for someone with such a colourful history, her stories are hugely entertaining, and because of her background her advice is relevant. She speaks from practical experience and is sympathetic to human weaknesses. Perhaps sometimes too sympathetic as she is prone to forgive most when they have not proved their worth. Of course, very few know about her past outside the walls of the school, so I would ask you to keep it a secret, but she was a wonderful person to grow up with. I admire her tenacity and her outlook on life. She has a great sense of fun and an annoying habit of seeing the good in all people. I suppose that comes from the depth of her faith, which sadly I do not share. I am neither as trusting nor as forgiving.'

'Not a bad thing in this day and age.' Although a very bad thing for a rake like Jake. Seducing Fliss was proving to be a challenge because of exactly that. 'Beware those wolves in sheep's clothing.' Which was exactly what Jake was; an uncomfortable truth that was leaving an increasingly bad taste in the mouth.

She turned and stared at him. 'Thank you. Sister Ursuline says I am in danger of becoming a cynic, but I think caution is prudent when dealing with new people. I find few who live up to my high expectations.'

'Spoken like a true cynic with the highest of expectations.'

'Unlike Sister Ursuline, I have *realistic* expectations. Some people can't change, or won't, and it's better to accept that about them than hold out futile hope they will improve. If calling a spade a spade makes me a cynic, then I am one and gladly so. It is quite possible to still like a person and be mindful or wary of their character flaws. Let's take you, for example. I dare say a blossoming friendship between a scandalous rake and a schoolmistress from a convent is unconventional, but because I recognise and accept your flaws I can still thoroughly enjoy your company while remaining gloriously immune to your obvious charms.'

A comment which certainly put Jake in his place, although it was probably not meant to. She had called him a philanderer on their first meeting, a label which grated but was deserved. Something this canny, ill-treated northern lass was obviously very mindful of. He should be grateful that she at least liked him despite that glaring character flaw—but he wasn't. 'My obvious charms will grow on you.' Or at least he hoped they would. Regardless of King and country, he still wanted to seduce her for himself. Fliss was becoming an itch which he couldn't scratch. 'I am famously irresistible to all women.'

Chapter Ten

Bouncing in a hackney through the city

'And yet here I am, resisting you.' One wheel hit a pothole and she groped for the strap to steady herself as it bounced out, forcing Jake to watch certain parts of her bounce as well. 'Gracious, this *is* a dreadful carriage!'

He grabbed his own strap as the tired, corroded springs did little to stop the shoddy road surface rattling his bones. 'You'd think in a city as rich as this one they could manage to make a decent road... Ah, look! We're passing St Paul's.' Jake put his hand up to point, then instantly used it to brace himself on the seat as they rumbled along possibly the worst stretch of road in the whole capital.

As she stared out at the massive cathedral in wonder, he took the opportunity to move closer, ostensibly to point things out, but more because the sight of one of England's greatest edifices reminded him that he was supposed to be seducing vital information out of her. 'Did you know it is the fourth St Paul's to sit on the site? The first was built over a thousand years ago, some time after the Romans left.'

'Really?' Her head whipped around to grin at him, then quickly returned to the building. 'You truly are a font of knowledge on the history of London, Jake.' It was the first time she had used his name and he liked the sound of it on her lips.

'Everybody knows this building was designed by Wren, but few know he was still designing it even as it was being built. Especially the dome. He wanted to create the dome without any visible supports inside. You should see it. It's a shame we have run out of time today as I would love to show you around it. We could climb up to the top and whisper at each other across the gallery.'

'I'd love to.' She turned her head and he recognised the instant she became aware of his close proximity, because she unconsciously licked her lips and looked down at her hands. 'I'd have to bring Cressida and Daphne, of course. Today has been highly improper.'

If that was intended as his cue to move back to his side of the seat, Jake skilfully ignored it. 'Hardly improper. I've been a perfect gentleman. Why, I've barely even flirted.' But there were other ways to flirt which required no words and his eyes were currently gazing deeply into hers. 'But we have laughed a lot, haven't we?' Humour was another excellent way of cutting through a lady's defences. Jake had laughed a few into his bed in his time, too. A goodly few.

She smiled at him and began to relax in the seat. 'It has been a perfectly lovely after— *Ooh*!' The hackney lunged to the right and tilted, sending Fliss sliding across the bench towards him. Jake only just caught her before they both slammed into the side, her forehead bashing against his chin and making him cry out.

'I'm so sorry!' As she looked up at him, her spectacles were dangling at an odd angle on her face. The engaging sight did a great deal to alleviate the brief, sharp pain of bone hitting bone. Because she wasn't looking through the lenses, she instinctively leaned nearer to see if he was hurt. 'Are you bleeding?'

'No. No, I'm fine.'

A lie. Being so close to her was playing havoc

with his senses. That perfume—fat summer roses, fresh air and sunshine—so uniquely her and divine. Those stormy-green, short-sighted eyes. The honey-gold hair. Those damned erotic spectacles which haunted his dreams. Everything made his body yearn and his heart pump. Her fingers touched his lip. If ever fate had presented him with the perfect opportunity to kiss her, this was it. Yet he hesitated, feeling suddenly awkward.

'Are you sure? I gave you quite a clonk.' And now she was torturing him. The sensitive skin tingled beneath her gentle touch, her face inches from his as she studied his mouth.

'I have a very hard head.' Gentlemanly good manners dictated he didn't tell her which part of him was currently harder. Jake stifled the groan. His fingers went to the spectacles and righted them, then simply stared at her mouth.

Longingly.

He wanted to kiss her. Desperately wanted to kiss her. Slowly he moved his face closer, watched her lips part. Was she game?

Perhaps.

Her eyes drifted to his mouth again. She didn't move away.

Good grief, why was he lingering? His mission

dictated he should jolly well get on with it… The bad taste and the uncharacteristic guilt churning in his gut made him sit back instead. She deserved better. Honesty at least. A sobering thought for a man who made a living from lying. 'I have a very stiff upper lip.' As well as a stiff bulge in his breeches. 'I'm sorry for my appalling choice of hackney…still at least it's an adventure. Of sorts.'

'It is that.' He watched her blink, her long lashes and fine eyes making his heart stutter. 'I hope we survive it. Being shaken to death in a hackney is not how I had planned on leaving this mortal coil.' She was so very beautiful he found himself looking away because he couldn't think of a single sensible thing to say which did not make him sound gauche. Not a single witticism sprung to mind. No flattering words. Nothing flirtatious. Just nothing. The memorised script of seduction had disappeared out of his mind, or been buried under a whole swathe of new thoughts. Questioning thoughts which had him second-guessing himself. Jake had never felt so strange in his own skin. It was as if it didn't fit. There were at least another twenty minutes till they arrived in Mayfair. Twenty painful, awkward minutes now that he had apparently lost his ability for seduction thanks to the distasteful flavour of his deception.

Perhaps if she hadn't told him about her lonely past and perhaps if he didn't genuinely yearn to have her for himself, Fliss would be just another mission for King and country. Somewhere along the way he had developed both a conscience and she had thoroughly charmed him when he had failed so spectacularly in charming her. When had that happened?

Admitting momentary defeat, Jake shifted his bottom back to his side of the bench. 'Tell me about your work at the convent. What is your favourite subject to teach?'

It was easier to let her talk than to attempt to do what he had been sent to do. All the while she was talking about her love of books, Jake pondered his odd mood and his odder growing attachment to the bespectacled woman sat next to him. While she might not have any messy feelings for him, he had some for her. That was a revelation. Feelings that made his heart both ache as well as soar and which had sneaked up on him when he hadn't been looking. Warm and comforting feelings. A sense of rightness. Of wonder and excitement. Complicated feelings which were unlike anything he'd encountered and not entirely as abhorrent as he had always assumed such attachments would be. It was more than a desire to know her better or to lose himself in her body. Among those familiar feelings lurked others.

A need to protect. The last place Jake wanted to deliver her back to was Rowley's house in Mayfair—yet that was exactly where the British government needed her to be. There was also a worryingly possessive edge to it. He didn't want her being used by her uncle any more than he wanted her to spend her life hidden in a convent making the best of the hand that fate had dealt her. He wanted Fliss to have a wonderful life, filled with laughter and family and the sense of belonging she deserved to have. The woman needed a family of her own. An adoring husband. A dependable, solid man of impeccable morals. Someone who recognised the precious jewel he had married and who spent the rest of his days living just to see her smile—except thinking about that faceless, lucky fellow filled his head with rage and irrational jealousy.

Now there was a thought. Possessiveness, the primal need to protect and irrational male jealousy were all emotions Jake had witnessed his brothers experience for the three women they had chosen to spend eternity with. Those and *romantic* love, of course. Jack, Jamie and Joe were all hopelessly in love with their women, too, the sort of love which transcended sibling love. All-consuming and passionate love, but in their case it had not turned malignant. Was it too risky to allow himself the same luxury? Probably. Because he knew there was a little too much of his father in him for comfort and he did have the reliable habit of disappointing people. Horrifically.

And now he could add maudlin to the awful yearning which had apparently numbed his powers of seduction.

Capital.

With Fliss, it seemed, he was doomed to fail on that score for ever.

If he could temper his odd feelings with the reassuring certainty that he was seducing Fliss with for ever on his mind, secure in the knowledge that he would never let her down with his own inherited selfishness, then he would seduce her now. Guilt free. And he'd put himself immediately out of his self-imposed misery. But Jake could never be guilt-free any more than he could fail to be a disappointment. Reliably unreliable Warriners, of which he was merely one in a very long line, couldn't be trusted with the happiness of others. Especially when they were out to seduce them under false pretences in the first place.

'Oh, no!' They hit another unforgiving road of cobbles and Fliss giggled as she was thrown about the carriage. 'This driver should supply his passengers with anchors, or something.' Being lighter and shorter than him, the poor thing did seem to be bearing the brunt of his shocking choice of carriage.

'Here—let me help.' Jake wound his arm firmly about her shoulders and used some of his weight to hold her down, frantically trying to ignore how utterly wonderful she felt against him and how desperately he wanted to kiss her. 'When we visit St Paul's we'll take a smelly hackney and some nosegays.'

She giggled again. 'You do make me smile, Jake.' That smile rendered all the maudlin regrets temporarily forgotten and he chuckled alongside her. That smile, the warmth of her body next to him, the inexplicable lightness in his chest and the perfect feel of her beneath his arm proved to be his undoing. Lord, she was lovely. Just this innocent touch fired his body and soothed his aching heart. Made him temporarily forget all the reasons why he shouldn't be listening to his heart.

'Berkeley Square!' The driver's shout accompanied the sudden jolt as the carriage began to slow.

Reluctantly he let go of her, internally cursing the swiftness of the journey while simultaneously thankful he had resisted. Because if he hadn't then he knew that a mere kiss would be more than a mere kiss. It would be the start of something he didn't have the strength to stop. A path he was too terrified to go down, yet so very tempted to that denying himself hurt. Deep in his chest. Dangerously in the vicinity of his black heart. Fliss reached for her small reticule and clutched it in both hands as she turned to him. Her smile this time was wistful.

'Thank you for today. For everything. Thank heavens you happened to be in Hyde Park this morning. You do have an uncanny knack of being in exactly the right place at exactly the right time. At times, you almost seem dependable.'

'Perhaps fate is trying to tell us something?' Something certainly seemed to want to tell him something. Jake was feeling decidedly off-kilter and didn't give a damn.

'I don't believe in fate. Coincidence, perhaps.

But even so, today has been the best fun I have had since arriving in London.'

'It's been the most fun I've had in months. Years, probably.' As soon as he said them, he realised the words were true. Somewhere along the line he had become jaded and his profession as a seducer had become dull. Each seduction a memorised routine offering little challenge and culminating in less and less satisfaction. But then Jake usually only offered his body and kept his heart guarded. It had never beat with such purpose before, or stuttered in his chest because of a pair of wonky spectacles or a smile as bright and as therapeutic as warm summer sunshine. 'Don't go back to Cumbria yet.' An odd knot formed in his throat. Jake would be bereft if she left now. Perhaps even heartbroken.

Definitely heartbroken.

Her green eyes gazed deeply into his to see if the words were sincere and he saw the exact moment that she did. 'Oh, Jake...' Perhaps because it was now as necessary as breathing, his head dipped of its own accord this time. Jake had no control over it. He didn't recall a Lord Fennimore, or a Crispin Rowley or his well-used seducer's arsenal or his parents' toxic love. Instead, nature and the overwhelming rightness of Fliss guided his actions. His nose gently brushed hers. He nuzzled her cheek. Then he surrendered to the uncontrollable need to taste her.

By his usual standards it was a clumsy kiss. A little too eager. A little too fast and too loaded with meaning, but all the sweeter for it. The kiss was innocently soft, for both his own sanity and because he was too busy glorying in the perfection of the moment to push for more. Gentle and tender somehow seemed right as this was not a seduction, it was an exploration. An overture from his foolish, wary heart to hers. To see if it might miraculously want more, too, despite both their better judgements, but the moment her lips responded he was ablaze. The simple, chaste kiss became more significant than any other before. Obliterated all previous kisses and conquests completely from his memory until there were no other kisses. Had never been any other conquests. It wasn't the master seducer who was kissing Fliss. It was just Jake.

Heart and soul.

She tasted of ripe summer peaches, but was as intoxicating and as addictive as absinthe. Fliss melted against him, sighing into his mouth and splaying her hands on his chest to steady them as the dusty carriage shuddered to a stop. It shouldn't have been perfect, but it was. It shouldn't have felt right, but it did. His aching heart swelled with the knowledge that this—right here and right now— was suddenly everything.

It took all his strength to pull away, but when he did, he was glad. Those lush, plump lips were parted. Her lovely eyes were wide and had darkened with desire. He knew women too well to confuse it with anything else. She wanted him and he wanted her. It was that simple and that wonderful. Whatever battle they had been waging was lost, yet Jake had no idea quite who the victor was. He traced the soft curve of her cheek with the pad of one finger, drinking in the wholly wonderful sight of her undone.

'That was a mistake.' Her voice was breathy, her chest rising and falling erratically. Those green eyes saying the exact opposite to her canny northern mouth.

'No, it wasn't.' He cupped her cheek with his palm and allowed himself to drown in her gorgeous eyes. 'It was inevitable. Fate.' As if drawn by some magical force they both inched together again. As their lips almost touched, Fliss broke the spell by scrambling across the seat.

'I should go. Aunt Daphne and Cressida will be worried.' Her clumsy fingers wrestled ineffectually with the latch.

'Let me help you.' He placed his hand possessively in the small of her back and she leapt away as if burned.

'No, thank you. I can manage.' The door swung open and she practically fell out on to the street, then tried, and failed, to compose herself. 'Thank you again for...saving me earlier. And for today... and...and... Goodbye, Mr Warriner.'

At the formal use of the word *mister* her eyes flicked to his lips again. He watched her swallow nervously, noting the becoming warm flush which heated her cheeks. She was flustered, but not angry. A little baffled, yet clearly stunned by her equally enthusiastic part in the proceedings. Her eyes finally sought out his in question and she stared for a few seconds incredulous, gloriously lost for words for once and that made him happy because he felt the same. A little baffled. A little giddy. Almost drunk with the power of it all. When her words came, they came in a squeak.

'You're incorrigible.'

'Yes, I am…but you like me anyway.' She didn't deny it. 'I've reserved an alcove at Almack's tomorrow. I shall see you there.' Nor did she answer. But she turned and scurried off, clumsily tripping over her own feet in her hurry to run away, emphasising how rattled she felt.

It mirrored Jake's own feelings. He was beyond rattled, yet strangely happily so and couldn't say why. He sat contentedly and watched her lovely bottom sway in time to her marching and allowed himself a satisfied smile. Fliss was neither prim nor proper, nor was she as immune to his charms as she repeatedly claimed and rather bizarrely, rattled or not, more than a little bit scared by it all, Jake was suddenly looking forward to Almack's for the first time in his life.

Chapter Eleven

Changing for another smelly dinner with the Earl

'Where is my blue gown?' Fliss didn't own many outfits, but the blue watered silk was her best dress and she wanted to wear her own clothes for tonight's ball, rather than any from the new wardrobe she had been gifted. Those bold clothes did not feel like hers. The day dresses were cut too close to hug her figure and the evening gowns, although stunning, were more daring than she felt comfortable with. Comfortable being the operative word, as she hadn't felt anything close in over twenty-four hours and was desperate to restore some equilibrium to her own off-kilter biology. Thanks to Jake, and a very foolhardy kiss, her natural, primal, carnal urges were creating chaos within her body.

Even the new shift she was stood in wasn't helping. The gossamer fabric was practically translucent and did little to cover her modesty, but as it was the only garment the young maid had brought to her after her bath, Fliss had had no choice other than to put it on while her hair was dressed. It did serve to make her supremely conscious of her needy body though. Each time the wispy fabric whispered against the tips of her breasts, a fresh wave of desire coursed through her which inevitably led to her reliving that splendid kiss over and over again. In her own clothes, Fliss would feel more like herself, or at least she hoped she would, rather than this shamelessly wanton stranger who currently occupied her skin.

If only she wasn't so tempted. Sorely tempted. Not that she had any doubts about the unreliability of the man. Gracious, no. Fliss's feet were still firmly on the ground despite the lure of those twinkling stars in his eyes. Jake Warriner was a bad bet if ever there was one. However, she was not looking for for ever. Not in her wildest dreams would she contemplate such nonsense with a man like him but… Surely there was no harm in a mild flirtation? A tiny romantic adventure with a man who her instincts told her was noble and trustworthy despite his shocking reputation. A man who called himself a disappointment, but seemed angry to be one. A man who had the uncanny knack of being in just the right place at just the right time, saving her from her uncle's meddling or her own maudlin thoughts. That peculiar jolt of awareness she experienced whenever he was close by was as comforting as it was alarming. A man she was coming to suspect might be one she could truly depend on. All the time. Or at least her heart hoped he was. She was honest enough with herself to admit that. Perhaps it *was* fate that had decided Jake was destined to be Fliss's knight in shining armour? Her lips tingled in anticipation at the prospect.

Fate! Destiny! Knights! What in heaven's name was the matter with her to be so…so…ripe for the taking? She knew better than to kiss a rake. Or at least she had always believed she did. Until she had succumbed to one and now couldn't get the dratted kiss out of her mind. 'I need to wear my blue gown.' As both a reminder of who she truly was and as armour.

Her maid's eyes dropped guiltily to the floor. 'I believe it has been sent to be laundered, miss.

I have taken the liberty of laying out a gown already for this evening.'

Fliss had just seen it and heartily disapproved. The emerald-green taffeta was scandalously low at the front and significantly lower in the back. She would feel practically naked from the waist up in that thing, especially if Jake Warriner saw her in it. Already that man had taken enough liberties with her person—or at least he had in her fevered dreams where she had happily let him because that one kiss had apparently set her fevered body into a carnal frenzy. 'If I remember correctly, Kitty, you said exactly the same thing the other night despite the fact it didn't need cleaning in the first place. I fail to believe that the laundry takes so long in a household of this size.'

Fliss couldn't leave a room without crashing into a giant footman. One in particular seemed to follow her everywhere. Uncle Crispin had more staff than one bachelor who usually lived alone could possibly need. He had ten maids that Fliss knew of and a veritable army of footmen and even with the addition of her aunts and herself as temporary guests, that was excessive. A cool draught made her newly wanton nipples harden further and she crossed her arms over them in case the maid saw. 'Go and retrieve it, please.' The blue silk would cover up most of her suddenly heavy, over-sensitive bosom.

The maid hesitated and then shook her head. 'I'm sorry, miss, but his lordship has instructed that you must wear one of your new gowns tonight.'

'Has he now?' The very idea was preposterous after yesterday—unless her uncle desperately wanted a tongue lashing. He was certainly due one. 'I'm afraid his lordship has no say in my attire. In fact, now that I consider it, I think I would prefer to wear something warmer tonight.' Something that didn't make her feel bold and attractive and ripe. Something which might encourage her dashing rake to lose interest and the wanton peaks under the scandalous chemise to flatten.

Her dashing rake! Gracious. This was getting dangerously out of hand.

If her blue silk was missing, then Fliss would jolly well turn up for dinner and the subsequent ball in one of her plain day dresses. A very warm one over layer upon layer of sensible underthings. Actions *had* been speaking louder than words for days now, so much so she was beginning to enjoy watching her uncle's mouth set into a disapproving line.

It was the only communication they seemed to share which he listened to, but at least he noticed her, which had to account for something. Yesterday he had been furious when she had returned home, somewhat flushed thanks to her indiscretion, but still buoyed from her rebellion. They had exchanged words. His had been angry, hers had been matter of fact.

'I am my own mistress, Uncle Crispin, and I shall do as I please with or without your permission. If that causes you a problem, I am happy to curtail my visit here.'

When he stormed off, Fliss knew she had won. She had refused to tell him where she had gone and who she had been with. She wouldn't make Jake take the blame when the decision to leave Rotten Row had been hers and hers alone. That, and a tiny part of her, a part wholly ruled by her reckless biology, didn't want to alert her uncle to any potential chance liaisons in deserted alcoves in the future. Or tonight as Jake had suggested...

And she was doing it again! Thinking of Jake when she was supposed to be cleansing him and her momentary lapse in judgement from her mind. It was just a kiss, for pity's sake, and certainly not her first. Hardly something to get so worked up about. She would brush it off just as she had his flirting. Just as she had brushed off countless similar overtures from gentlemen in the past. A meaningless kiss meant nothing, after all. Although if she was brutally honest with herself, which of course she always was, this one felt entirely different. Worryingly different. All-consuming and gloriously different. The exact opposite of meaningless.

Why was that?

'What about the pink gown, miss?' The flustered maid's face matched it in colour as she dragged another wholly inappropriate dress out of the wardrobe. 'I think Madame Devy has excelled herself with this one. I love the ruffles around the neckline.'

So did Fliss. 'If only the ruffles hid more from lecherous, old eyes, then perhaps I might consider it.' Appreciative, twinkling blue ones, for instance, she didn't mind at all. Which was a great part of the problem. Being friends with Jake Warriner and being attracted to the scoundrel was a totally different, and entirely unsatisfactory, kettle of fish. Jake the Rake Warriner was too much like all the men who had waylaid all the wayward girls at the convent. The sort of man Sister Ursuline had been tempted by. The sort of man who had seduced her normally sensible mother and doomed her to a lifetime of marital disappointment. Jake was a charmer and a philanderer, entirely not the sort of man she would ever allow herself to become romantically involved with. She had more sense than all those wayward girls. More sense than her mother and certainly far more than Sister Ursuline had ever had in her youth. She would continue to learn by example, not from personal experience. She had to fight this unwelcome and visceral attraction for the sake of her own sanity, as falling for a rake, even a noble, and entertaining one, could never end well.

Fliss stalked over to the wardrobe and began to rifle through it for a suitable garment to inform Uncle Crispin he had no authority over her appearance any more than he could control her movements.

Not one of her dresses was there.

'Where are my clothes, Kitty? The ones I brought with me from Cumbria.'

'I can't say that I know, miss.' The young girl couldn't meet her eye, a sure sign she did know. 'Perhaps they are all being laundered?'

'My uncle has had them removed, hasn't he?'

His petty revenge for her rebellion yesterday. Another way to assert his dominance over her when all else thus far had failed. How typical he would use the contents of her wardrobe! His annoyance at the simple ensemble she had worn to Rotten Row had been evident in his expression from the outset and he had once again made a huge fuss about her insistence on wearing her spectacles. Spectacles she'd had the foresight to wear to read in the bath this evening, else they would probably have been sent to the *laundry* as well.

'I couldn't say, miss.'

The maid looked close to tears, but they both knew all her clothes had been in there this morning. Neatly organised according to the occasion. Gone were her favourite walking boots, the heavy wool pelisse she wore when climbing the Cumbrian hills, her favourite long-sleeved day dresses and sensible, soft slippers. The plain, navy outfit she had worn to Rotten Row and foolishly kissed Jake in. In their stead were an array of more new gowns stitched by the sought-after Madame Devy—because all the very best ladies in Mayfair wore Devy—but Fliss wouldn't any more on principle.

Uncle Crispin must have paid the modiste handsomely to have sewn an entire new wardrobe in less than ten days, but while the gowns were intended to turn heads Fliss had no desire to be the body stuffed inside them. Not when that body appeared to turn Jake's head as much as his turned hers. And certainly not when they made an old lecher like Redditch drool—her uncle's only reason for insisting she wear them in the first place!

As the anger bubbled, she rummaged beneath the rows of strange new shoes, heeled boots and the rainbow of satin slippers dyed to match the fashionable and revealing gowns and huffed out a sigh of relief when she found the sturdy wooden box. At least that was still there.

Regardless, she still checked the precious contents inside. Her mother's few items of paste jewellery had been spared the cull, worthless to most but priceless to Fliss. As had her embroidered handkerchief, made by her mother's hand as a present for her only daughter in the final months of her life, and the small bundle of letters tied in a pink ribbon were exactly as she had left them. The last things Fliss owned which connected her to her past. But the purse containing her money was gone. It wasn't a great deal of money, enough to buy her passage back to Cumbria and to cover

emergencies, but having none made her financially dependent on her uncle and conveniently
trapped here until he deemed otherwise.

The rage was instantaneous. 'Did he steal my
money as well, Kitty?'

'I don't know, miss.' The girl was already back-
ing away towards the door, her eyes wide and
guilty.

'Kitty!'

The maid bolted and Fliss went to go after her,
but then remembered she was wearing nought but
a see-through shift and there was bound to be a
footman hovering close by. There was *always* a
footman hovering close by. If her uncle seriously
thought she would take this outrage lying down,
he was vastly mistaken and his actions could go to
hell. Tonight, they would be sharing more words.
The final words ever to be uttered on the subject,
or so help her God.

She snatched the green dress off the bed and
hastily stepped into it. Like a woman possessed
she wrestled with the difficult laces down the back
and tugged up the scandalous neckline as far as
she could before stuffing her feet into the matching jewelled slippers, grabbing her spectacles in
her clenched fist and stomping out of the room.

It made no difference that she had dispensed with the need to truss herself into a corset or that she had neglected to put on stockings. The clothes would not be on long enough to matter once she had put dear Uncle Crispin firmly in his place, then she would leave this godforsaken town, with its dictatorial relatives and tempting rascals, and never come back. She had tried to be part of the family. However, as far as her dear, matchmaking and aloof uncle was concerned, Fliss did all the trying. His sole mission was apparently to see her decorated like a mannequin for the lascivious entertainment of an old man.

'Where is he?'

The burly footman stood like a sentry in the hallway was startled by her venomous tone and nervously gestured towards the dining room. She slammed open the door without knocking. At least twenty faces stared back at her curiously. Patently there were more guests than merely Redditch tonight. Another unwelcome surprise in a day full of them.

'There you are, Felicity.' He smiled genially to the rest of the predominately male table. 'Didn't I tell you all that my niece was a beauty?'

At least six of the men ogled her shamelessly.

One of them was the Earl of Redditch. 'She is a beauty, indeed. May I be the first to ask you for a dance at Almack's this evening, Miss Felicity?' His eyes dropped to her unrestrained bosom and feasted. She should have put on the corset. Her bare breasts felt exposed under the thin material of the gown and above the low bodice. She clamped her arms over them and patently ignored the request.

'Might I have a word, Uncle?' Her tone was brittle, but her glare was granite. 'In private.'

'Not at the moment, Felicity. Dinner is about to be served and our guests have waited long enough for you to finish your *toilette*.' He turned to the handsome blond man at his right. A man she had seen a number of times in her uncle's circle, but whose name she hadn't bothered remembering. 'Young ladies and their vanity. Felicity always likes to look her best. A splendid attribute in a woman, I think you'll agree. Who doesn't enjoy a tempting morsel at dinner, Flint?' He winked and a couple of the men laughed.

'I'm afraid I must insist, Uncle.'

His eyes locked with hers with such cold intensity that for a moment she wavered. He suddenly scared her, but her pride wouldn't allow him to see it. He stood, tossed his napkin down and apologised to his guests. 'We shall only be a moment. In the meantime, enjoy the first course.' The well-trained servants snapped to attention, serving the soup as her uncle stalked past her with such speed he caused a small gust of wind as he headed towards his study.

Once Fliss was inside he closed the door. 'You have caused a scene.'

'You have stolen my clothes and my money.'

'I have bought you new clothes. More suitable ones. I will not have the *ton* gossiping about my niece's woeful attire. It reflects badly on me. Most young ladies would be grateful at the generosity.'

'I am grateful.' Hard to say with her teeth grinding. 'You have been *most* generous.' With his money, at least. 'However, that does not give you the right to take my things or dictate how I must dress, any more than it gives you the right to dictate my every movement. Your overbearingness is spoiling my visit. I should like the items back immediately.'

'Impossible, I'm afraid. When I saw the sorry state of those garments, I had them donated to the poor.'

How dare he! Her outrage returned and served

to dim her new fearlessness. 'They were not yours to donate.'

He shrugged unapologetically. 'What is done cannot be undone. Thankfully you have an extensive collection of ridiculously expensive new gowns to make up for the loss, so I feel no guilt. The new clothes are yours to do what you want with. I shall not *dictate* which you wear as all of them are appropriate for a woman of your status.'

'Status! I have no care for status. Where is my money?'

'I know nothing about that.' He was lying. Nothing about his expression hinted at it, but Fliss felt it deep in her soul. Uncle Crispin was a man with a casual relationship with the truth. A consummate and compulsive liar. Another thing she had no evidence of, but felt inside.

'How convenient. You had my bedchamber stripped of every stitch of clothing and every shoe I own in petty revenge for yesterday, yet you have no knowledge of the coins hidden in the same wardrobe?'

His pale grey eyes pinned hers and Fliss wanted to shudder. Cruel. That was the first adjective which came to her and once that thought took root, she wondered why she had not seen it before. He was more than merely cold. Cruel, callous and calculated. If eyes were indeed the windows of the soul, then his soul was tainted. He was not a nice man and neither was he one to mess with. She knew that with the same certainty she now knew accepting his invitation to stay had been a big mistake.

'I have no need of a paltry few coins, Felicity, and I resent the implication. One of the servants must have taken them. Your maid, perhaps? I shall have her dismissed.'

'Kitty didn't take my money. You did. What I want to know is *why* you took it.'

He exhaled as if greatly put upon. 'Have I not provided for your every need, Felicity? Do you doubt that I will continue to indulge you? Tell me what you need and I shall buy it for you.'

'I do not want *your* money. I want *my* money. And as soon as I get it, I am going home.'

'A tad melodramatic for a petty theft, don't you think?'

'Not when the thief is family. I've put up with your dictatorial and stand-offish manner, put up with your flagrant attempts at matchmaking and the way you have used my good nature to dominate my time and force me to follow your agenda, but this time you have gone too far. You have no jurisdiction over me, Uncle Crispin. None. I am not beholden to you, or anyone, for anything. Yet here, I am bullied into dressing how you want, attending the entertainments you deem fitting and degraded again in front of your cronies.'

'Degraded? My, you have you mother's flair for the dramatic, Felicity.'

'Yes! Degraded. In front of Redditch, and those other men just now, you reduced me from person to a piece of...of...' Was meat too extreme? 'Visual entertainment.'

He didn't bother looking affronted, his features remaining impassive and cold. 'I am a man of business, Felicity. I do what is necessary to expand that business successfully. Hence I host dinners, flatter and fawn over my guests and, from time to time, I see no harm in providing them with—what did you call it? *Visual entertainment.* A pretty face, some mild flirting and the tantalising promise of more can help facilitate that. I fail to see why it offends you so.'

Where to start?

'For twenty-five years we have been estranged— and that is of your making, Uncle, not mine. I wrote to you for years and every letter went unanswered. What gives you the right to feel as if you can have any say in my life now?'

'I am trying to make amends, Felicity. The new clothes are surely evidence of my desire to atone for all the years I couldn't provide for you as I had promised your mother I would.'

Once again he was using her mother to justify his actions. 'I don't believe you. This house, all this opulence, these are things you have enjoyed for a goodly few years. Yet in all that time you failed to make any contact at all. Now, suddenly, we are family because it suits your ends and you use my mother's apparent words to bend me to your will. But you don't care about my mother's last wishes. Admit it, you dragged me here for Redditch, didn't you?' His flat stare confirmed she had hit the nail on the head. 'You did! You brought me here to be paraded in front of that old lecher...'

'Is your tantrum done?' He made to walk away and she pulled on his arm.

'My *tantrum*? You are attempting to use me to further *your* business. I am your only niece, yet I am to be bartered for a few *barges*. Have you no heart? No shame? If my mother was alive...'

Uncle Crispin turned to her, his face an ugly

mask of pure malice. 'Your mother was a fool. With her beauty, she could have had any man she chose. She could have married sensibly and hauled our family out of debt in the process. Instead she shamed herself with a penniless scoundrel and wasted her God-given gifts on a wastrel with no thought for me. I couldn't give a damn about what she might think of me now!' Hearing her beloved mother so shockingly maligned stunned Fliss into silence. While she had known the half-siblings were not close, she had never realised her mother's brother had resented her. Hated her even, if his hideous expression was to be believed. 'While I was delighted to learn you were the spitting image of your mother, I had hoped that you might have more sense than her. I had certainly hoped that your years in that convent would have made you less headstrong and difficult. Can you not see the Earl of Redditch is a very wealthy man? As his wife you could have all your heart desires.'

'You are mad if you believe I would ever agree to his proposal. I'm going back to Cumbria in the morning!'

His hands lunged out and he grabbed her firmly by her upper arms, his ghostly pale eyes narrowed. 'You will not jeopardise my relationship with the Earl. Our business negotiations are at a critical stage.'

'They have nothing to do with me.'

'Yes, they have.' He shook her as she tried to free herself from his vice-like grip. 'I promised him a stunning virgin. A woman he could proudly parade around on his arm and salivate over in the bedroom. A malleable, pliable woman, not a rebellious shrew! He wants you, or at least the illusion of you that I have created, and you will stay here until our business is concluded and continue to drive the old fool mad with lust.'

Clearly he'd gone insane. Fliss finally managed to jerk herself free by planting her hands in the centre of his chest and pushing with all her might. 'Over my dead body!'

Her uncle stalked to the door and grasped the handle, but before he opened it he turned back. Those flat grey eyes hardened. 'If you want the money to buy your passage to freedom, then you will earn it by being pleasant to the Earl. The quicker you comply and reel the old fool in, the quicker you can head back to whence you came.' He neatened his coat and his expression became bland again, devoid of any discernible emotion.

It was chilling to watch. 'You are excused dinner, but you *will* waltz with Redditch tonight. The carriage will leave at precisely nine o'clock.'

Her mouth fell open, but Fliss struggled for exactly the right words to convey her utter incredulity and disgust. Before the right words came, Uncle Crispin strode out the door and slammed it behind him.

Chapter Twelve

A cold corner of Hays Mews and Hill Street, behind Berkeley Square

The moment Jake stepped into the dark lane Leatham appeared out of the shadows. 'What brings you here?'

A certain honey-haired temptress and an overwhelming desire to see her sooner. 'I had time to kill before Almack's and thought it might be a good opportunity to catch up.' He eyed the line of waiting carriages. 'What's going on?'

'Rowley's hosting a dinner. There are around ten other men including Redditch. Flint's there, so we'll have to wait for the full list of names to investigate.' The flash of jealousy at Flint spending time with her around the dinner table while Jake loitered outside yearning didn't help his mood and he grunted. 'How was the Tower?' Leatham's bland expression belied the wicked glimmer in his eyes. No doubt he, or one of his Invisibles, had followed Jake's every move and his monosyllabic friend knew exactly what had happened all too briefly in that hackney.

'I'm making progress.'

'Slow progress by your standards, Warriner. I'd have thought you'd have bedded the wench by now.'

Hearing her talked about like that made his blood boil, but Jake covered it with lazy charm. 'That's why I do the seducing and you get to lurk in the stables, my friend. You don't know the first thing about women. Fliss is not the sort of woman you rush.'

A knowing grin split the other man's face. 'Fliss, is it? Suits her. She's got to you, hasn't she?'

Yes.

'Of course not.'

'Then you won't mind that Fennimore's told Flint to try his hand with her, too. Belt and braces...'

'You know damn well two men trying to woo the same woman would muddy the water. What the hell is Fennimore playing at? Flint's got his mission and I've got mine!' And he'd happily flatten the charming Flint if he so much as laid one finger on her. At his furious glare, Seb threw his head back and laughed.

'It was a test, Warriner. One that you failed. Miserably. I saw the soppy grin on your face after you ravished her in that carriage. She's been wearing a matching one most of the day.'

She had? His silly heart soared.

'Have your fun elsewhere, Seb. I was *sent* to ravish the girl as you well know. So what if I enjoy my work? It's better than loitering in the gutters like you.' And Jake was digging himself a deeper hole by seeking to explain it so vigorously. 'Has Flint got into Rowley's dressing room yet?'

'It's his intention to try again tonight if he can distract the guards. There's tighter security inside that house than outside. Rowley has a man on practically every door.' Which was why they were currently chatting at the end of the cluttered mews which served the whole of Berkcley Square and well away from Rowley's small fortress of a stables. 'He's going to try and hang back till after most of the guests and Rowley have left… unless he can inveigle his way into the family carriage.' His friend slanted him a mischievous glance, waiting to see if Jake would bite. When he didn't, he changed the subject. 'The River Police have doubled their patrols, not that it amounts to much. They're spread too thin and their resources are woefully inadequate to cope with an operation of this scale, but they are focusing on the smaller boats coming up from the estuary. There are currently three of Rowley's ships that have been moored at the docks for a week now and show no signs of either unloading or leaving. I've had men watching them and they say the crews seem to know they are being watched, which leads me to believe they want us to watch them. My nose tells me they're decoys or have already been unloaded, there to taunt us while the little *laden* boats sail on by.'

As Leatham's intuition was scarily accurate, Jake was not inclined to argue with his assessment. 'Which explains Rowley's sudden interest in the Regent's Canal. It'll open up a new route all the way up to the Midlands.'

'And why he's throwing his niece at the man.' Something Jake was becoming increasingly annoyed by. If it drove Fliss to return to Cumbria… The back of his neck prickled with awareness seconds before his friend frowned. 'Hold on…' He strained his head to get a better look. 'Unless my eyes deceive me, that's her?' Seb pointed to the lone figure hurriedly crossing the next road along, her head darting left and right before she made a mad dash out of sight. 'What's she doing out all alone?'

Everything about the situation raised Jake's hackles, from the furtive nature of her movements to the fact she was out in the chilly February night without so much as a shawl to protect her from the elements. Jake immediately broke into a run, his long legs eating up the distance between them until he could see her properly in the darkness. Her skirts were gathered in her hands as she ran in what looked terrifyingly like panic.

'Fliss!'

She hesitated at the sound of her name, then sped up, blindly heading towards Park Lane, seeming oblivious to the dangers of the many carriages which were trundling along the thoroughfare. She wasn't wearing her spectacles, which meant she couldn't see properly. In the darkness, a horse might not see her until it was too late. It spurred Jake's legs to pump faster before he called out again.

'Fliss, it's me! Jake!'

She skidded to a halt as her head whipped around. Most of her hair was in disarray, but her eyes were as wide as dinner plates. 'Jake?' Her hands went to her mouth and, as he finally caught her and dragged her into his arms, she crumpled. 'Oh, Jake…'

Her skin was like ice. The delicate silk of her dress was already damp with the frigid evening mist. Jake shrugged out of his coat and wrapped it around her, then guided her towards an alleyway and out of sight. If she was running, then there was probably a damn good reason why. Nothing fazed his canny northern lass normally, therefore he would err on the side of caution in case she was in some danger. 'What's happened?'

It took her a few moments to choke out any words. When they came, her voice was shaking. 'He stole my money…all of it.'

'Who?' Jake scanned the street for any signs of the villain. 'Where were you?'

'All my clothes are gone. My money. Everything is.' She clutched at his lapels and he saw the tears streaming down her cheeks. She swiped them away impatiently. 'The footmen are watching me.'

'Your uncle stole your money?' Or at least that was the gist he was getting from her breathless staccato phrases. She nodded.

'Petty revenge to get his own way. To keep me here. He wants me to be nice to Redditch.' She stared anxiously down the street she had just run down. 'I had to get away, Jake. He scares me… I c-c-can't go back there.'

'You don't have to go back there.' His mind was whirring as he enveloped her in his arms, the desire to take care of her warring with the urgent need to give Rowley a sound thrashing. 'I'll help you.'

She reached up to touch his face and he saw relief and total trust in her eyes. 'You always are in the right place, aren't you? I *can* trust you.'

Guilt strangled any answer because he couldn't bring himself to lie to her, so he hugged her fiercely instead. 'I have lodgings at the Albany, less than ten minutes from here. Why don't we get you out of the cold and then we can plan what to do next?'

'I know what to do next. I need to go back to Cumbria. Back to Sister Ursuline's where I belong. I'll walk there if I have to! All three hundred miles of it in these silly shoes!' The old Fliss was rapidly returning. The feisty, no-nonsense, indomitable Fliss. The one he knew he had to leave regardless of how much it hurt to watch her go.

As long as she was away from Rowley, he could bear it.

'I'll take you back home. In a carriage. It'll save those silly shoes.' She offered him a tremulous smile, happily absorbing his strength and the heat of his body. When she rose on tiptoes and placed a grateful, soft kiss on his lips, a surge of wholly inappropriate lust hit him with such force Jake closed his eyes to guard against it. Beneath his hands he could feel the softness of her body under the damp silk—unfettered by stays—and knew that only that one layer of silk and one gauzy layer of linen from his shirt and the inconvenient buttons on his waistcoat separated their naked skin. Knowledge which he didn't need while he was trying to be selflessly noble. Her knight in shining armour. 'We'll leave tonight if you want to?'

'You'll take me all the way back to Cumbria?'

'Yes.' And then he would say goodbye. Why did that thought already make his heart ache?

'Not a good idea.' At the sound of Leatham's gravelly voice behind, Fliss stiffened, her fingers gripping Jake's back. 'We need to take her to Fennimore.'

'No. We *don't*.'

'*Yes*, we *do*, Jake.'

At the familiar use of his first name, Fliss's eyes swivelled from Seb's to his warily, that clever mind of hers already doubting him. 'Who is he? Jake?' Her pretty eyes widened. 'I recognise him...the scar...this is the man who took your horse that morning. You *know* him?' She took a decisive step back, severing all physical contact between them, wrapping her own arms around her body protectively rather than stand any longer in his embrace. Her voice was all at once both mistrusting and brittle. 'What's going on?'

Jake felt sick to his stomach. Guilty, ashamed and furious simultaneously at both Seb, his own duplicity and this impossible dilemma he wished with all his heart he wasn't facing. 'This is my friend Seb Leatham. He is...' His voice trailed off. How to explain the truth without having her hate him?

'We work for his Majesty's government, Miss Blunt. You are quite safe with us, but I hope you understand we will need to question you before we arrange for your safe passage back to Cumbria.'

'Question me about what?'

'Your uncle. We have been investigating some of his business dealings.'

* * *

Jake couldn't meet her eyes. He didn't need to deny it because his body radiated guilt. His dark head was bent. Broad shoulders slumped. For a man always supremely confident in his own body, he suddenly didn't appear to know what to do with his hands. Shocked, Fliss complied and allowed the other man in ragged labourer's clothes to escort her down the back alleys of Mayfair as she tried to digest it all. She didn't recognise the mews they entered, or the stables they went through, but she recognised the bitter taste of betrayal and the heavy weight of humiliation as she accompanied the two men. Both strangers to her now.

Jake was blessedly silent and walked several paces behind. It was just as well. If he had offered her any empty platitudes, she would have happily slapped his duplicitous and handsome face raw for his part in this. They were investigating her uncle! It had all been a lie.

What a foolish, trusting dolt she had been. Jacob Warriner had a canny knack of being in the right place at exactly the right time because he was apparently paid by the King himself to be there. He wasn't dependable, he was doing his job. He had wormed his way into her affections only to extract information for the crown. Every charming word out of his tempting mouth was a lie. Every stupid thing she had imagined between them was a mirage, too. The odd sense of kinship. The mutual attraction. The seductive allure of temptation. The hope that his feelings for her were as deep as hers had become for him. The perfection of that kiss... Fate! It would be laughable if she didn't feel like crying.

His empty words would be galling if she wasn't bleeding inside. He'd played every trick in the successful rakes' book and she had fallen for them. Just as she supposed a great many other women had in the past.

And it hurt.

Fliss so wanted to turn around to look at him to see if he was hurting, too, as if the sight of his remorse would make her feel better about his treachery. Fortunately, her pride kept her eyes front and centre and her shoulders fortified with steel. As soon as they crossed the garden and entered the French doors of the smart Mayfair town house, she shrugged off Jake's offending coat, not wanting any part of him left touching her skin. She heard him bend to retrieve it, but refused to look back as he did. Let him feel the frigid cold of her indifference. He was nought but an untrust-worthy philanderer just as she had first thought. A consummate and cruel liar. A chameleon who adapted seamlessly according to his environment and the situation; a wastrel like her father and one who had misused her as grievously as her horrid uncle.

An older man with a serious face greeted her in what looked to be his study. 'Miss Blunt. I wish I could have made your acquaintance under bet-ter circumstances and I hope you will forgive us our cloak-and-dagger methods, but until very re-cently we had no idea that you weren't in any way involved in your uncle's skulduggery. I am Lord Fennimore and I head up an organisation called the King's Elite. Warriner and Leatham work for me. As does another operative embedded within your uncle's social circle. I assume you have met Lord Peter Flint?'

Now she knew who the handsome blond crony was. He had always smiled kindly at her, as if he felt a little bit sorry for her—now she knew why. He knew what Jake saw in her. Fliss nodded once, curtly, and sat primly in the chair Lord Fennimore placed in front of the fire. As she sipped the hot tea she had been given, she felt the soft wool of a blanket be placed about her shoulders and felt the painful tingle of awareness which told her which of the King's minions had put it there. She didn't bother thanking him for that single genuine kindness.

'I suppose you have a great many questions, Miss Blunt, and now that Warriner has assured me we can trust you, I shall do my best to answer them, but for now I shall cut to the heart of the matter...'

A cut to the heart. How apt. Hers felt shredded.

'The King's Elite is a secret branch of the Home Office. We are tasked with unmasking and bringing to justice all those who seek to undermine the British economy through large-scale smuggling. For two years, we have been desperately trying to bring down a very dangerous group who have flooded the market with brandy. While smuggled liquor is nothing new, what concerns us most about this particular bunch are their links to the loyal supporters of Napoleon. The same men who helped him escape from Elba are once again plotting to return him to power—only this time they are using British coin to purchase weapons and amass an army, coin raised from the thousands of gallons of French brandy smuggled onto our shores every single month. Brandy they provide. Until recently, we had no plausible leads to follow. You see, this gang are as brutal and secretive as they are powerful and every smuggled cargo we've seized has led us to yet another dead end. The smugglers either did not know who they worked for or were prepared to go to the gallows rather than betray their masters. However, six months ago, one of those smugglers gave us a name. The man who he claims is the sole distributor for the goods in London and the Home Counties. I'm sorry to tell you that name was Crispin Rowley.'

Jake's shabby accomplice lowered himself into the seat opposite her. 'We believe the brandy is coming through London via the Thames and suspect your uncle is responsible for finding buyers and distributing it from there. He is a significant link in a very long chain, but he covers his tracks well. All we can find are his legitimate business dealings, shares in merchant ships, banks and the like. However, his choice of investments lends itself as the perfect cover for the real source of his impressive new fortune. We believe those same shipping companies are somehow bringing in the cargoes, but we do not know either where or how they are able to hide the contraband from the Excise Men. We are coming to believe he moves the goods entirely on the water and in very large amounts. Thanks to you we now know he is seeking to invest in the new Regent's Canal, which goes some way to confirming those suspicions.' Jake had charmed and prised that information out of her, claiming the dull conversation would cure his insomnia. One of his many lies. They tripped off his tongue with such ease, no wonder he was so good at his job. She could feel his eyes boring into her back, willing her to turn around, but his dishonesty sickened her far more than her disgust at her own stupidity did. If he had been a decent man to begin with, he would have told her the truth from the outset and she would have happily still told him everything. Honestly. Upfront. He wouldn't have needed to try to seduce it out of her!

But lies and deception were a rake's stock in trade and she had pathetically fallen for them as well as him, so instead Fliss clutched the blanket tighter, and ignored him, focusing back on his friend. All these years she had stalwartly guarded her heart, waiting for someone worthy, only to discover she had unwittingly given it to the unworthiest man possible. He wasn't simply a selfish hedonist taking his pleasure where he could. He was paid to seduce. Somehow that felt worse. Humiliating. Even more of a betrayal.

'So you see, any information you can add to what we already know will be a godsend, Miss Blunt. Your testimony could help us infiltrate that gang, or it could help clear your uncle's name of any wrongdoing.' The scarred man hesitated, obviously conscious of the fact that his every word condemned his friend further in her eyes. 'Jake said you overhead a meeting between your uncle and another man which bothered you.'

She shook her head and laughed bitterly. Had their every conversation been reported in great detail? Very probably. Snippets of the nocturnal argument she had overheard in the garden filtered back and suddenly made sense. 'Dead men can't spend.'

'I'm sorry?'

So was Fliss. 'I should have trusted my instincts.' All of them.

Mr Leatham and Lord Fennimore sat forward in their seats with interest. 'Go on.'

'That's what the man said. Dead men can't spend. I did overhear a conversation between my uncle and another man in the garden a few nights ago. My bedchamber is directly above his study and faces out on to the garden. It was past midnight and I couldn't sleep. I'd left my window ajar.' And now she hated Jake, too. It had been his fault she had been hot and restless, and all the while he had been tricking her into confiding in him. The Biblical snake in the Garden of Eden, luring her to sin and damn near succeeding. 'My uncle was in a state. Desperate. He offered to pay double, then triple his usual for a shipment of some sort. The other man refused. Said it would make no difference because *dead men* couldn't spend. He said the boss wouldn't like it if his cargo got seized. That he'd lost enough already this month because there were many new eyes along the water. Or words to that effect.'

'You're sure he used the words the Boss?'

'It is my judgement that has been impaired, Lord Fennimore, not my memory. Because the conversation was in the middle of night and out of the ordinary, it sticks in the mind.'

'What else did they say?'

'I got the distinct impression the other man was the one in charge of the situation. My uncle seemed scared of him. He was pleading with him, complaining he was out of pocket every time a shipment was late and saying that people were relying on him. Now that I come to think about it, yesterday morning in Hyde Park, my uncle discussed a great deal of business with some other gentlemen, none of whom looked particularly happy by what he had to say.'

'Their names are in the list I gave you,' Mr Leatham said matter of factly, letting Fliss know he had also been following her around the park, and probably to the Tower. All three men were probably well aware she had been silly enough to welcome Jake's kiss. Had lost herself temporarily in it.

'Were both of you tasked to watch me, Mr Leatham? Was one charming nursemaid not enough?'

He had the decency to appear embarrassed. 'My mission was to follow your uncle's movements, Miss Blunt, not you. Jake was assigned...' His voice trailed off as he looked at his boots.

'I am well aware Mr Warriner was tasked with seducing me, Mr Leatham. I am a fool, not an imbecile. I suppose that is the usual manner in which you operate?' Fliss forced a brightness in her voice she didn't feel, because she refused to allow him to see how much he had hurt her. 'Assign a *dedi-*

cated and highly *skilled* man to everyone. Already I have worked out that your particular skill, Mr Leatham, is to blend into the background—am I right?' The other man nodded. The tips of his ears blushed incongruously with the rest of his harsh exterior. 'Then it is hardly surprising that Mr Warriner would be assigned to question the ladies. How *clever* of the British government to utilise his talent for philandering so *thoroughly*.'

'The man your uncle met with—what can you tell us about him?' Lord Fennimore clicked his fingers and gestured towards his desk to hastily change the subject and save his man, and it was Jake who quickly fetched paper and a pen and pressed them into his hand. He took himself to stand behind the other two, directly in her eye line. She resolutely ignored him. 'We will need a thorough description, Miss Blunt. All you remember.'

'He wasn't a gentleman, my lord, by the accepted definition of the word *gentleman*.' Neither was Jake the Rake, henceforth to be known as Jake the Snake for ever. She shot a few daggers at him in case he was in any doubt she loathed him for his deceit but wasn't broken by it. She'd been let down before by men. Continually let down by them. Expected nothing less. 'He was a Londoner. His accent coarse like a working man's. His clothes were scruffy. He was big. He loomed over my uncle.'

'And his features?' Lord Fennimore looked up from his notes.

'It was dark and I wasn't wearing my spectacles. At best his face was a smudge.'

'Was he fair? Dark?'

'He was wearing a hat. I never saw. It was an odd and short exchange, my lord. Once it was over the man disappeared behind the shrubbery. I haven't seen him since.'

'What of your uncle's dealings with the Earl of Redditch? Is there a chance he is involved somehow?'

Fliss considered it, then dismissed it out of hand. 'If he was, then there would be no reason for my uncle to thrust me in front of the man's nose. Tonight he made it clear that his negotiations with the Earl are at a crucial stage and that he expects to use me as a bargaining chip. I am to be *nice* to the man, apparently. Allow myself to be fawned and drooled over while the negotiations are concluded. Drive him mad with lust to scramble his wits.' Just thinking about it made Fliss shudder and she unconsciously rubbed her arms where her uncle had gripped her. 'He intended to keep me a virtual prisoner until the contracts were signed.'

Chapter Thirteen

Suffering an Arctic chill in Lord Fennimore's study

Fliss rubbed her arms and the blanket fell. It was only then that Jake's eyes were drawn to the dark finger-shaped bruises marring her upper arms. The urge to kill Rowley was primal and visceral. 'He hurt you!'

Her eyes flicked to his, hardened, then turned back to Lord Fennimore. 'We argued after I discovered he had destroyed all the clothes I had brought with me from Cumbria and had taken the money I had intended to use to pay my passage back. Clearly he assumed that would make me more compliant, when instead it only spurred my desire to escape.'

'How did you get away? My men have the front and back entrances under strict surveillance.'

She eyed Seb with marginally less disgust than she had Jake. 'The whole house and all its occupants are under surveillance, Mr Leatham. My uncle's henchmen are disguised as footmen, I now realise. There is one posted on every door. They watched me like hawks, I believe I have been *assigned* one in particular who is irritatingly diligent, but like most men he underestimated the resourcefulness and tenacity of women. When I realised I was being watched, I pretended to be distraught and dashed up the stairs and slammed my bedchamber door. When he went to talk to the man guarding the front door, I crept back down and returned to my uncle's study because I knew it would be easier to hide in the darkness of the garden than it would be anywhere on Berkeley Square. I climbed out of the window and followed the route I saw the Londoner take as he left that night. Low and behold, behind the shrubbery is a convenient ladder which he must have used to scale the ten-foot wall between my uncle's house and the neighbour's. I went over it and followed the path alongside it and away from the house. At the back of that garden is another pathway—a servants' alleyway of some sort. It runs between the gardens of the houses on Berkeley Square and whatever street is behind. Eventually, I could hear the carriages rattling past, so knew that it must be one of the main roads rather than the mews, so I managed to scale the wall and jump to the pavement. Then I ran.' Her eyes turned to Jake again fleetingly. They were as hostile as it was humanly possible for a pair of eyes to be. No less than he deserved, he supposed, but they made him feel utterly wretched none the less.

To avoid her gaze and his own guilt, he turned towards his comrades, only to watch a telling look pass between Fennimore and Leatham. 'Does your uncle *know* that you have escaped, Miss Blunt?'

'As I was excused dinner to compose myself, maybe not yet, but I was told in no uncertain terms the carriage would be leaving at nine and he expected me to bc on it, I'm assuming he's in for a bit of a surprise.'

'Then perhaps—'

'No!' Jake interrupted before Lord Fennimore could vocalise what he and Leatham were clearly thinking. 'She's not going back there!'

'We cannot let this opportunity pass.'

'I won't have her put in more danger.'

'It's not your decision to make Jake. It's hers.'

Seb's tone was intended to calm him, instead it fired Jake's temper further.

'She's told you all she knows and we promised her safe passage back to Cumbria.'

'Think logically, man! Think about the bigger picture. She has unprecedented access.' Lord Fennimore reached forward and took her hands in his. 'I know this is a great deal to ask of you, Miss Blunt, but these are dire times and we desperately need your help. If your uncle assumes you will back down and comply to his edicts, I propose we allow him to think he has won...it is a matter of national security...'

King and country could go to hell. 'I said no, damn it! I won't let her go back to that man and see her forced to suffer more of his brutality.' Those bruises on her arms were injury enough and Rowley would pay for them. Jake turned to her then, purposefully ignoring the others. 'I'll take you back to Cumbria in the morning, Fliss. Just as I promised. You don't have to do this. I won't let you do this.'

Instead of appearing grateful, her face contorted in a sneer. 'I'd rather face a month enduring Redditch's drooling than spend another second in your lying company, thank you very much.' To spite him she turned her head towards Lord Fennimore. 'What would you have me do? My uncle doesn't confide in me. To be frank, we barely converse at all. I'm not entirely sure how much use I could be.'

'You can be our eyes and ears inside the building. Monitor the comings and goings, memorise the names of your uncle's associates, pump the Earl of Redditch for more information about the potential partnership with your uncle. You said the man was taken with you.'

'He is. His eyes are on stalks whenever he's within ten feet of me.'

'Then let us use that to our advantage. Your uncle will be thrilled with your newly compliant attitude and the Earl will be beside himself to have such a lovely young woman hanging on his every word.'

Now things were getting out of hand. 'What you are suggesting is as deplorable as what Rowley was doing! I won't stand by while you put her in grave danger and at the mercy of an old lecher! She'll be all alone in there.'

Lord Fennimore appeared affronted at the suggestion. 'Hardly. Leatham will be a stone's throw away outside and Flint will be inside as much as he can be. The house and any movements within it are already under close watch. Miss Blunt will be under our full protection going forward. She'll be perfectly safe.'

'You cannot guarantee that. Nobody can. These smugglers are ruthless and she's a blasted school-mistress, for pity's sake. She's hardly equipped with the skills necessary to spy on the lot of them. She'll slip up somewhere and then she will be entirely at their mercy.' Thinking of Fliss in peril, her life at risk, made his insides clench painfully. He should never have listened to Seb. Never have brought her to Lord Fennimore's house. Jake had put her in this danger when he should have listened to his heart and helped her to escape. 'She's better off back home where she belongs.' As far away from her cruel uncle and his bloodthirsty associates as it was possible to be. 'We'll find another way to infiltrate Rowley's web.'

'Not like this we won't.' Seb placed a reassuring hand on Jake's shoulder and then sighed when he furiously jerked away. 'Think about it, Jake. We've been trying for months to get on the inside. Flint is occasionally there, but the best we've really managed is to cling on the periphery. We've learnt more about his business dealings through Miss Blunt in one week than we have by throwing all our resources at it for six months. Even if she just sits by her bedchamber window night after night we'll find out more about this Londoner. He has to be the link between Rowley and the Boss. He will lead us to where they hide the cargos and eventually to the mastermind himself. Within weeks we could have all the keys to unlocking this case and bring the empire to its knees.'

'She's spent her entire life sheltered in a damned convent, Seb! She's not up to this!'

'She had the wherewithal to escape unseen from Rowley's fortress.'

Fennimore nodded. 'She is also incredibly intelligent and astute.'

'She's not doing it!'

'*She* has a mind of her own and the ability to use it!' Fliss sprang to her feet, her hands clenched into tight fists she looked intent to use at any moment. 'Stop talking about me as if I am not here!'

Seb and Fennimore instantly apologised, but Jake was too furious and too concerned to back down. 'She's not cut out for any of this and I strongly recommend we put her on the first available coach north.'

Later, Jake would recall that those words lit the fuse which caused the full force of her temper

to explode directly in his face. 'I *strongly recommend* you take your *strong* recommendations
and place them elsewhere.' Her finger jabbed him
hard in the chest. 'How dare you speak for me! If
there are any decisions to be made and any risk
to be taken, then they are mine to own and mine
to take, *Mr* Warriner! How dare you say I'm not
up to the task! If *you* can be a spy, then I doubt
it is that hard to do. What are the main attributes
of one? To lie? To sneak around? To flirt? To say
one thing when I mean another? To shamelessly
use my attractiveness to the opposite sex to seduce
information out of them? Hardly skills which re-
quire a great deal of intelligence and, if your example is anything to go by, one doesn't need to
have a great deal of finesse either!'

She was hurting. He'd hurt her and in doing
so had mortally wounded himself in the bargain.
'Fliss, I'm—'

She didn't give him a chance to say sorry. 'I'll
do as you ask, Lord Fennimore.'

After that the decision was taken firmly out of
Jake's hands. While he silently seethed and flailed
himself for his incompetence at handling the situation, Leatham and Fennimore briefed her on
everything they suspected, what to listen out for

and how messages could be quickly and covertly passed between them. As the chiming clock signalled their brief time was nearly up, it was agreed that Seb would escort her back to the street they had found her on. If the coast was clear, she would re-enter the garden in the same way she'd left it. They had a story all worked out so she could explain her appearance and where she had been should they have missed her. All Jake could do was stand by and impotently watch it all unfold.

'Godspeed, Miss Blunt.' Lord Fennimore walked her back to the stables and personally helped her into the shabby carriage they kept for such occasions. 'We are in your debt.'

As Leatham was already in the driver's seat, Jake went to climb in beside her, only to find his arm stayed by his superior. 'Best to leave this to the pair of them, Warriner. Too many bodies will only serve to arouse suspicion if you're seen.'

'I won't be seen.' Before he could put his boot back on the step, the irritated, stubborn minx in the carriage slammed the door closed. She did it with such force even Lord Fennimore was taken aback.

'Come on, man. Leave the girl be. While your concern does you credit, the bad feeling between you is not good for this mission. Leatham and Flint will look after her now. She's in good hands.'

They weren't Jake's hands. 'I'll work with Leatham and the Invisibles.'

'Do you think that is wise? She could do with some distance to get her head around things and focus on what she needs to. I suspect the last thing she'll want to see is you for at least the next few days and we all need her to be calm and rational. Her safety depends upon it.' More words Jake didn't want to hear. 'For now, your part in this is over. I know you feel bad about the way things have turned out, but the mission has to come first. You know that. Take that well-earned leave I cancelled. Have a rest. In no time at all she'll be out of there. You can explain it all then. Rationally. When you are both calm and the danger is past.'

'If you don't mind, sir, I'd like to explain a few things now.' And Jake would do his level best to talk her out of this madness before it was too late. 'You owe me that.'

His superior consulted his pocket watch, then rolled his eyes. 'Two minutes, Warriner. But it is a mistake.'

Jake swiftly opened the door and quickly inserted himself into the small carriage in case she had a mind to stop him, then promptly closed it behind him. Fliss was still incandescent with rage, although it was quietly white hot now rather than raging red, and regarded him from the opposite seat with cold contempt. He steeled himself for the onslaught and prepared to do some serious grovelling. 'I wanted to apologise for lying to you.'

Silence.

'And I wanted to explain that…' What? Not everything had been a lie when the foundations were rotten? The friendship had been real, even if it had been contrived. So had the kiss. Very real. Although he had been tasked to kiss her and had been frantically planning exactly how to go about it just a few minutes before. If only they had met under different circumstances. 'I know this looks bad, Fliss, and I know you probably hate me right now, but…' As he struggled to find the right words to fully convey his own disgust at using her while assuring her he had some seriously complicated feelings he didn't fully understand himself, she slowly turned her head away to look out of the other window. That cold, dead stare out to nothingness his mother had always done so well. The utter disgust at who he really was. His stomach lurched at the comparison.

'I understand. It was your job.'

'Yes, but not entirely... The thing is...' She turned back to look at him, or rather look through him, and her expression cut him to the quick. It wasn't hurt. It wasn't angry. It was resigned. As if she had been expecting to be grievously let down all along and had fully expected nothing less. The trust was dead. Its corpse a foul stench that hung between them in the air. 'It wasn't all a lie, Fliss. I promise you.'

'I know that.' His silly heart soared. 'Among all those lies, all those convenient chance meetings and all hose tempting glances and poisonous kisses, there was one irrefutable grain of truth which I should have listened to. You *are* a disappointment, Jake. Perhaps the biggest I have ever met.'

Well, that was a well-aimed dart and one he couldn't argue with. 'You don't have to do this, Fliss. There is still time to back out. Go home to Cumbria. Be safe. This is not your fight, it's ours.'

She sighed, her face for once inscrutable, then reached over his lap to open the door. This time she didn't fumble clumsily. The lock gave quickly. 'Your part in this is done. As are we. Take your leave, Jake. I dare say you've earned it.'

Chapter Fourteen

Somewhere in Piccadilly, one week later

Fliss forced herself to smile at the Earl of Red-ditch, even though the smell of the man in the confined space of her uncle's carriage threatened to make her retch. Her uncle still persisted in play-ing silly games, as if his decision to secretly swap carriages with the Earl so he could go home early had really been sudden. It had all the subtlety and finesse of a blacksmith's hammer, but for King and country she would make the best of it. 'That is fascinating, my lord. One hundred tons of cargo in one year alone! No wonder you need to increase your fleet of barges.'

The silly old fool preened at the compliment.

'Indeed, Felicity, and I expect my *own* fortune to be doubled as a result.' Since she had resigned herself to her uncle's threat, Redditch kept dropping in little hints about his wealth in the hope it would make him more appealing. It didn't—Fliss had maintained a healthy disinterest. She doubted her scheming uncle would be convinced by an abrupt about-turn and decided a mildly belligerent stance would ultimately be more convincing. At best, she tolerated Redditch and reluctantly allowed him one dance, although much to her uncle's chagrin it was never the waltz, and her tongue still dripped the same acid, but with a sugary smile on her face.

While her behaviour added a layer of authenticity to the proceedings, the charitable part of her also wanted the Earl to get exactly the same message. She couldn't bring herself to give the poor man too much false hope, yet he still persisted in trying to impress her with his money, which served to do two things. Firstly, it made her pity the Earl. To feel that one's worth was inextricably linked to money was a very sad state of affairs, and, despite the fact Redditch was still an ogling, repulsive and shallow man with little respect for her beyond the sight of her now shamelessly displayed bosoms, Fliss couldn't help feeling sorry for him. He was also a sad, ageing, childless man who was clearly happy to settle for a woman who *only* wanted him for his money. That smacked of desperation and the more she was forced to get to know him, the more she wanted to take him to one side and tell him he was going about finding a wife all wrong. *Bathe more often, lift your greedy eyes and look at the woman in the face for once rather than the chest, listen to her rather than constantly bragging and then perhaps you will find the personal happiness you seem to crave.*

The urge to be honest with him for his own good was a double-edged sword, because the other thing it made Fliss ponder was how truly miserable Jake's deception had made her. She doubted his shocking lies had left him feeling a quarter as guilty and dishonest as hers now did; rakes who did their raking for King and country had to have hard hearts and no conscience. After a week of attempting to find evidence of her uncle's criminality, Fliss now appreciated how dangerous and precarious such work could be. Half the time she was on tenterhooks, the other half simply terrified and both states were exhausting. She had never been so conscious of every word she said, every nuance, every movement and, aside from now knowing the ins and outs of the river-haulage business, she had gleaned precious little for all her hard work. Spies clearly needed vast wells of patience as well as nerves of steel.

However, knowing she had been nought but a job to be done, when she was still grieving the loss of *him*, made her feel ridiculously foolish, naïve and—if she was being entirely honest— more than a little bit heartbroken. While he had been busy working, Fliss had been nurturing a friendship which had quickly spiralled out of her control. Somewhere during their brief but eventful liaison her guarded heart had let its guard down, then had usurped her sensible, pragmatic head. Jake the Snake had become so much more than a friend. He'd been her Knight in Shining Armour. A man she had confided in and allowed to kiss her. That kiss had changed everything. In that one heady and unexpected moment she had begun to hope he was more. A few hours later, those dreams had been crushed just as brutally as all her childish dreams had before.

One day, she would be able to look back on the whole sorry affair and sagely warn her students of the sort of techniques the most dangerous and predatory philanderers used to woo the unsuspecting. Or at least Fliss hoped she would get to that point, because right now, she sincerely doubted she could even confide her misery to Sister Ursuline without weeping like a pathetic victim and flagellating herself for her own stupidity.

'My future wife will enjoy all of life's comforts.' The Earl had smiled and settled himself back against the seat and his eyes drifted back below her chin again. Fliss ignored the compulsion to drag her thin evening shawl around her. Like the calculating Jake, she now also had a job to do and one which was easier if her lecherous companion was occupied. His tongue was looser when it was hungrily hanging out of his mouth. Something which did nothing to make her feel any better.

'Tell me, my lord, while I appreciate business is business and that you make coin by hauling the cargos of others, do you have some mechanism to rigorously vet what is carried.'

'Why would I do that?'

'I have heard stories about smuggling. Apparently, it is still as rife as it ever was, yet more secretive. What if the smugglers were using your boats to transport their goods? Are you not concerned for the consequences?'

His eyes flicked back to her face for a second before he shrugged and returned to staring at her décolleté as it gently moved with the motion of Uncle Crispin's well-sprung carriage.

'Why should I be? As a gentleman, I do not concern myself with the day-to-day machinations of *business*.' He pulled a face as if such a thing was below him. 'I merely provide the capital. The barges are leased by the wherrymen who benefit from the numerous opportunities my good name provides them. I offer hold space for hire. The price is fixed according to the distance regardless of the contents carried. I get half of that fee and the wherrymen get the other. If anything, being able to categorically state I had no clue as to what is being transported means the Excise Men cannot blame me, any more than they can attribute blame to any of the other gentlemen of business who invest in the same trade.'

'But these are illicit, ill-gotten gains, my lord. Aren't you worried it will end badly for you if the Excise Men board one of them and seize the cargo?'

'If the crews are silly enough to take the risk of transporting something illegal, then that is down to them as they will ultimately pay the price. New crews are ten a penny. Especially when a business is as lucrative as mine.'

Fliss began to feel less sympathy for the man. 'Surely you wouldn't want boats sailing under your name to carry illegal cargo and rob the crown of its rightful taxes?'

'Better the coin falls into my purse than the Treasury's. They get more than enough from me as it is, so I shall not complain if I inadvertently get a little something back?'

'Even if it brings down the British economy?'

He laughed, flinging himself back into the seat in a musty waft and smiling at her in that patronising way sanctimonious men did when they thought they knew better. 'Oh, bless your good heart, Felicity! Your strong morals are one of the many things I adore about you, but you have a scant understanding of the workings of the British economy. Smuggling is inherently part of it. The free traders have operated within it for centuries and will continue to operate for centuries more.' He pointed to the intricately patterned lace laid over the burgundy silk of her tight-fitting bodice. 'Where do you think that exquisite trim came from? Chantilly lace is a small fortune and few pay the extortionate prices from the merchants who are silly enough to pay the duties. And after the wars, we prefer not to *openly* trade with the enemy. While the *ton* loves its fripperies, smuggling will continue to flourish. Everyone knows the best lace comes from France.'

'So does the best soap.' Next to him, Aunt Daphne was blatantly wielding a perfumed vinaigrette in front of her nostrils and wearing an expression of complete distaste. 'You might consider using some!'

The Earl laughed, assuming Daphne's words were a joke just as the carriage slowed as it turned into the narrow lane which housed the mews servicing Berkeley Square, and like a fool Fliss allowed her gaze to drift out of the window. Although she had promised herself faithfully she would *not* look again tonight, her silly eyes had a mind of their own and of course they briefly locked with *his* before she resolutely turned away, heartily disgusted with her wayward urges.

In scruffy workmen's clothes, Jacob Warriner was no less attractive than he was in his evening finery and her silly heart gave a little sigh before she hardened it against him. Those beautiful blue eyes were liar's eyes and she would not be relieved or reassured by the sight of him. Not when she had Mr Leatham and Mr Flint close by to help her should she need it. Jake the Snake was the last person Fliss wanted standing guard. Or within one hundred miles of her for that matter. He was history. The past. Done and dusted. Why couldn't the man have taken the leave he'd been offered? Why did she have to see his dratted face day after day, night after night, popping up wherever she went. Watching.

Why, she had already had to suffer the knowledge he had been in the alcove of the very ballroom she had just left! Did the man race his horse across Mayfair night after night and change his clothes en route? The very last image she wanted in her confused and exhausted mind was the thought of him shrugging out of his splendid evening clothes in some darkened alleyway and then pulling on the roughened ensemble he wore to blend into the mews, only the moonlight illuminating his broad shoulders and the muscles on his strong arms. Coarse clothes which should not make him appealing, but which suited him just as well. Oh, how she loathed him for his magnetic attractiveness and diligent persistence to see the job finished!

Nor did she want to think he was there because he cared. About her rather than his mission. Except his heated and poignant looks led her to believe he might, which made her waver in her resolve to loathe him for all eternity, constantly flitting between disappointment and raw hatred and a disturbing and foolish desire to put herself in his big, fibbing and fetching boots, hoping to find a way to forgive him for the unforgivable. He would be so much easier to despise if she wasn't confronted with those troubled eyes every single day.

Watching.

Protecting.

While she doubted he cared about her in quite the same way as she had been coming to care about him, Fliss was prepared to concede he did seem to have a genuine interest in her safety, else why would he be everywhere when he could be at home.

Instead, he had become her shadow and whenever she was out she could feel the intense weight of his stare as he followed her every movement. At balls, he seemed to become particularly stern whenever Fliss danced with another man, something she had taken to doing a great deal now that hiding in alcoves was out of the question. She justified her sudden transformation from reluctant debutante to eager social butterfly by telling herself that it reassured Uncle Crispin that she was partially abiding by his rules in her own rebellious way and in so doing was attempting to drive the Earl of Redditch mad with lust. However, it didn't hurt that the sight of her laughing and flirting with a succession of handsome new gentlemen made Jake's sapphire eyes harden and narrow while he watched her like the hawk she had once accused him of being.

Fliss had spent the entire interval of the opera yesterday giggling with Lord Peter Flint and had barely cast the traitorous Mr Warriner a glance. As the lights had dimmed for the second act and she had pulled her opera glasses up to cover her face, she'd needed to bite very hard on the inside of her cheek to avoid smiling at the splendid vision of Jake's hands clenched into tight fists on his lap. The wayward part of her hoped he was burning with jealousy. The sensible part wished she didn't care either way.

Lord Flint, of course, had some pity for his friend and used every opportunity to quietly reassure her that Jake was worried about her and that he was sorry for having to keep his true identity at secret. Neither comment made Fliss more inclined to feel any leniency towards him because he hadn't apologised for not telling her the truth sooner. A true friend would have.

It wasn't all a lie, Fliss. I promise you…

Ha! Roughly translated, that meant a great deal of the silky poison which oozed out of his mouth to loosen hers had been and she would not be the sort of dolt who sought clarification. It made no difference to her which bits had been true.

It didn't!

It wouldn't.

The tiny hairs on the back of her neck prickled, alerting her to the fact that the dratted man was still staring at her and willing her to glance back. 'Oh, for goodness sake! Why have we stopped?' The driver had brought them around the back because the lines of carriages going into the square had been horrendous. 'This was supposed to be the quicker route home!'

The Earl of Redditch reached over and patted her knee. 'The whole of Berkeley Square are doubtless all coming home at the same time. We are in the thick of the Season and Saturdays are always the busiest nights. I suspect there is quite the queue. On the bright side, we get to converse a little longer…'

Fliss offered him a tight smile and then glared at

the offending palm which was still resting posses-sively on her leg. Fortunately, Aunt Cressida had spotted it, too, and thwacked him smartly over the knuckles with her folded ivory fan. He retracted the offending appendage immediately only to face the outraged wrath of Aunt Daphne as well. 'Keep all of your digits to yourself in future, my lord, else I'll have you banned from my niece's com-pany!' While they all knew Uncle Crispin would do no such thing, the Earl certainly didn't and the threat was enough to make him apologise.

'Dearest Felicity, I meant no offence. The close confines of this carriage make it very difficult to move without encroaching on another's person.'

Daphne pinned him with a withering look. 'Idle hands are the devil's workshop, my lord, and yours seem quite possessed. I suggest you sit on them in case they are tempted to wander again. Do you remember Nuneaton, Sister?'

Cressida glared imperiously. 'Indeed *I do* and we'll have *none* of that here today, my lord.'

Fliss gave both old ladies a thankful, enigmatic smile even though she didn't have the first clue what they were talking about as was so often the case. They had become the two guards she found she was grateful to have. In the week since the awful night when she had discovered the true hideous measure of both her only living relative and the only friend she had made in London, Fliss had come to rely on the comforting presence of these two eccentric, formerly scandalous and often useless chaperons. They meant well, seemed to have the same low regard for Uncle Crispin as she did and had appeared to understand her predicament—or at least some of it—without her having to tell them any of it. They assumed she had been bullied by their nephew into suffering the Earl while he concluded his business and Fliss didn't have the heart to apprise them of the terrifying reality. Her uncle dallied with murderers, stole from the crown and was not averse to practically imprisoning and blackmailing his only niece for his own profit. It was bad enough that Fliss knew some of the tangled web of danger they were all in—alerting them to the real truth was asking for trouble.

The Earl of Redditch wore a sad puppy-dog expression which she assumed he thought was charming and guaranteed to earn him her forgiveness, so purposefully looked away so that the obnoxious fellow knew he had overstepped the mark on this short carriage ride he shouldn't have been on. When she found her eyes drifting back towards the handsome scoundrel still stood on the corner of Hays Mews, the one who had very definitely overstepped the mark during *their* carriage ride with her blessing, she stubbornly pulled them back. For five long minutes she sat but a stone's throw away and ignored him. Fliss didn't realise how much of her strength that took until the carriage eventually edged forward and she finally allowed her tense muscles to relax.

In the seclusion of the Rowley stables, Fliss made sure she clambered out of the carriage before the creaking Earl, thwarting any attempt at his lifting her down, and stood to the side waiting as her aunts alighted, too. They were soon met by the butler, a man who rarely ventured out of the house, who bowed politely to the Earl. 'My lord, his lordship sends his deepest apologies, but begs you understand he cannot continue to entertain you this evening. He has been afflicted with a sudden chill and has gone to bed. Your own equipage has been readied to take you home immediately.'

The temporary relief at being spared more time in the Earl's company was overshadowed by her unease. Her uncle never went to bed until the small hours and in the few weeks Fliss had been a guest in his house, she had never known him to pass up on an opportunity to impress the man he desperately wanted to do business with. As her uncle had also been as fit as a fiddle less than an hour ago, she smelled something rotten and, for once, it wasn't Redditch.

With her mind racing, she suffered through the polite goodbyes and made her own excuses to head to bed. A crack of light bled out from under her uncle's rarely used study door, but with several footmen guarding the hallway and his door, she dared not attempt to get any closer and rouse their suspicions. In her bedchamber, her maid insisted on helping her into her nightgown and plaiting her hair, and Fliss made a great show of going to bed. Twenty painful minutes ticked by before she heard her bedchamber door quietly open. Only when Kitty heard the slow, deep breathing of a woman lost in slumber did she leave. Fliss heard her mumble something to the footman on the landing and a few minutes later she heard his heavy tread move away from her door. Now that she knew the ritual of her gaolers, she knew he would take himself to the strategically placed chair at the end of the hallway and, if he was satisfied his charge was sleeping, he might nod off.

On silent feet, Fliss went to the window, slid her hand behind the heavy curtain and released the window latch. She never dared open it more than half an inch in case it could be seen below, then she threw water on the fire burning in the grate and snuffed out the single candle Kitty always left burning in the corner. Only when her bedchamber was shrouded in blackness did she risk cracking open the curtains and peering out into the garden.

It was empty, but the soft lighting in her uncle's study illuminated the ground directly below, suggesting that he still had a guest. Fliss fetched the glass from her nightstand and stealthily rolled up a corner of the Persian rug covering the wooden floor. On her hands and knees, she pressed her ear to the glass and struggle to listen.

The sounds were too faint and muffled to discern more than male voices speaking. After five minutes of straining, Fliss gave up and sat back on her heels. She had to get closer somehow. Even if her bodyguard was asleep, taking the main staircase was pointless. Not only was his chair directly next to them, there were more footmen posted downstairs, none of whom could risk the luxury of a sneaky forty winks. She supposed she could pretend to go fetch a book or a drink, but then one of them would undoubtedly assist her and then escort her back. However, the kitchen did lead out to the garden.

Deciding to take a chance, Fliss carefully opened her door. The burly footman's head was leaning heavily against the wall, his eyes closed. In the last week, because she had been compliant, she had lulled him into a false sense of security and she thanked her lucky stars she'd had the wherewithal to do that one small thing. Keeping to the wall, she edged out of the room, mindful of gently closing the door behind her. Instead of heading towards the main staircase, she crept in the opposite direction, hoping the servants' staircase might lead her where she needed to be.

The narrow stairs were as black as pitch on the upper floors, so she used cautious feet and hands to feel her way down them. At the bottom was a dingy corridor with doors leading out to different parts of the house. Her appalling sense of direction made her dither. If she went out of the wrong door, then the game would be up. In desperation, she closed her eyes and tried to picture the house in relation to the route she had just taken. If the servants' stairs were behind her, then the garden had to be to the left. The kitchen had to be nearby.

Fliss stopped at the second door to the end and put her ear against it. Only when she was certain there was no sound coming from behind did she dare open it. The room beyond was blessedly empty, but well shy of the kitchens. The silhouette of the enormous gilt harp and the expensive Italian pianoforte told her that she had stupidly managed to get herself to the room furthest from the kitchen. The Music Room was the least used and most ostentatious of Uncle Crispin's showy entertainment spaces. The only other door led directly out towards the main staircase and the biggest concentration of guards. She was about to retrace her steps when the moonlight disappeared behind a cloud, plunging her into complete darkness again. Her eyes drifted to the windows. At least they overlooked the garden, although wholly in the wrong place… This new knowledge made her dizzy as Fliss heard her own heartbeat bang loudly in her head. Before she could talk herself out of it, she had pushed open the sash, hoisted up her billowing and flimsy nightgown, then clumsily lowered her body out.

The February cold made her skin prickle with goosebumps, although the rush of excitement and the forbidden made her hot all over. Taking a convoluted route behind the screen of shrubbery and flowerbeds, it took a few minutes to get to the wall directly outside her uncle's study and she pressed her back against the icy brickwork, willing herself to look like a brick in a feeble attempt to blend in.

Barely breathing, Fliss shuffled a little closer to the window, then closer again until the back of her head came level with the frame. With her heart in her mouth, her pulse drowning out all other sounds, she had to give herself a stern talking to. Several deep cleansing breaths later, she was finally able to hear something. A London accent. Broad and flat. Common. More menacing now that she knew who he worked for. She concentrated hard on the sounds, trying to discern the non-existent consonants from the vowels. Eventually Fliss was able pick out one or two words, hearing them clearer because they kept being repeated.

Tomorrow and *fobbing*—whatever that meant?

The scrape of a chair and the sounds of movement had her leaping away, hugging the wall until she risked darting behind the skeleton of a rose-bush and crouching low in the prickly branches to avoid the pristine white linen of her nightgown being discovered by the transient moon. As an afterthought, Fliss dragged off her spectacles, too, in case their lenses reflected the light, and squinted as the door to the garden opened and the Londoner appeared out of it.

Thanks to her poor vision and the hat pulled low, casting shadows over his face, she still could not make out his features and within seconds he had disappeared into the trees. She considered following him and decided against it. Just this had been terrifying enough and she was in no hurry to die. She had two words more now than she had had before and the King and Lord Fennimore would have to make do with that for now. In the meantime, she had to get back into the house unseen and then count the hours until she could surreptitiously pass the information to someone from the King's Elite on her morning walk.

Chapter Fifteen

Hidden in the mist on Fobbing Marshes

Jake methodically tried to close all the gaps in his greatcoat for the hundredth time, then pulled his thick woollen scarf up to the rims of his eyeballs. After close to six hours exposed, he was prepared to do anything which might make his frozen body less cold. Beside him, Seb seemed cheerfully unaffected by the temperature and his legendary patience was driving Jake insane. 'What time is it?'

'Probably ten minutes on from when I last checked.'

'Can you look at your damned pocket watch?'

'I find time moves much more slowly when you watch it tick past.'

'It'll be light soon.' Which meant that Jake would have wasted an entire night for nothing, worrying about Fliss the whole time and wishing he was there in Berkeley Square, in case she needed him, rather than here hoping to end her torment once and for all.

Seb rolled his eyes, then promptly closed one to stare through his telescope. 'We've got at least another two hours before the dawn breaks. A lot can happen in two hours.'

'Because so much has happened in six! And what have you got to be so blasted cheerful about? There must be something wrong with you that you are incapable of feeling the cold.'

'I feel it, but like the time I choose to ignore it. What can I say? Some of us are cut out for field work and some of us aren't.'

'I've spent years working in the field.'

'Yes—but your fields have feather eiderdowns and perfumed sheets.'

Jake didn't want to be reminded about those again, not after Fliss had made him more ashamed of what he did than anyone ever had before. His friend must have seen the flash of pain cross his face and assumed it was because of their situation. 'You did insist on coming here tonight, so you only have yourself to blame for your current predicament. You could be tucked up in a nice warm bed somewhere and have left this to the Excise Men.'

'Just as you could have. But like me you knew they're likely to make a ham-fisted hash of it.' The eager bunch who had been assigned to chase Fliss's sketchy intelligence were currently dotted around the marshes, hiding just as Jake and Seb were, waiting for their signal to move a muscle. 'We need the blighters alive, not peppered with musket balls.' So that Jake could shake the truth out of them and then snatch Fliss out of that monster's house.

If only they had more to go on. While Fobbing was a small village sat conveniently on one of the many marshy tributaries of the Thames, it was large enough to mean they could be in entirely the wrong place to see the smugglers if they turned up. Just because the Norman-built tall tower of St Michael's Church behind them had once been a beacon guiding the boats into these treacherous waters didn't mean it still did. The Excise Men firmly believed they had eradicated free trading from this stretch of Essex nearly twenty years before. The increasing sea defences built since had blocked off many of the small inlets which the boats used and much of the marshland had been drained to make way for grazing land. But they were currently camped near a shallow creek, one of the few barely navigable ones left. One which had been getting progressively deeper over the last couple of hours as the tide came in and tides only came from the sea.

'Tell me what if feels like to be you right now? I mean, it must be quite alien for you to desperately want the love of a woman and to be confronted with the cold shoulder of abject disappointment and total disgust.'

It wasn't. Something which caused his chest to constrict painfully every time Fliss looked through him. The disappointment in her eyes eerily mirrored that of his mother's, except this time it wasn't caused because he merely happened to look like someone. Fliss's disappointment was real and well —earned. With hindsight, Jake wished he had broken ranks and told her the whole truth early on. The deception now created a chasm between them which he didn't know how to breach because she wasn't the usual sort of woman he dealt with. She was frustratingly resistant to his charms. She saw right through it and Jake only had the truth left in his arsenal. Truth which she had no interest in hearing because she had already worked out most of it for herself.

'I want her forgiveness, not her love, Seb.' Although the latter should frighten him, his heart craved it none the less.

His friend grinned, clearly enjoying his misery. 'I doubt she'll ever forgive you for pretending to want her and then pursuing her relentlessly till you wore her down. I'm no expert on women, but I should imagine a woman like her, one who prides herself in her own common sense around men, would be furious at falling for a man who was only kissing her because he had been told to do so.'

'That wasn't...' He clamped his mouth shut, but it was too late. Seb was staring at him incredulous.

'Good grief... I never thought I'd see the day... You have *genuine* feelings for the girl. Proper romantic ones. You *do* want her to love you back!' He chuckled softly and shook his head. 'Now your belligerent mood makes perfect sense. Jacob Warriner is in love! And with a woman who now loathes him! Oh, how the mighty have fallen.'

'I haven't fallen.' Although he was beginning to suspect he had. This last week had been pure torture. Jake had followed her everywhere, hoping he would see a chink in her frosty, indifferent armour and when he hadn't it had hurt. Real pain. A constant knot in his chest. A head which ached because of his constantly furrowed brow. A tightness in his throat. Hell, last night when she had glared at him as if he were as abhorrent as something foul she had stepped in, he had experienced the overwhelming urge to hide himself in some dark corner and weep. He was even displaying all the irrational behaviours he had watched his normally sensible brothers go through when their hearts had been lost to the women who were now their wives. Jake couldn't sleep, eat or think straight because the only thing on his mind was her.

Her. Her. *Her.*

Blunt by Name and Nature.

The woman he very probably loved.

Good grief, he was doomed.

The knowledge came with a wave of nausea so acute that for a moment Jake thought he was about to lose his long-ago consumed dinner. How had he let that happen? And, more importantly, what was he going to do about it? She hated him. Rightly so. He'd lied to her from the outset. It didn't matter that he had always lied to women, justifiably for the good of the nation, but Fliss wasn't most women. The second bout of nausea was accompanied by the depressing knowledge she would likely never forgive him for using her. Like every man she had knowledge of he had been wholly undependable in the end. The knot in his chest throbbed painfully and the urge to weep into his frozen hands sprung afresh. He'd made a ham-fisted hash of things…

The pathetic sound of one of the Excise Men attempting to mimic a herring gull, the call they had insisted would not arouse suspicion, made a welcome diversion from his maudlin introspection. Someone must have seen something. Seb scanned the waterway with his telescope until it fixed on one spot. 'There,' he whispered, pointing. 'I see a lantern.'

Jake soon saw it for himself, although barely. Smugglers were very good at blacking out all but the essential light and this one was no bigger than a shilling, flickering as it passed through the long marsh reeds. It made slow progress as it navigated the shallow creek, the long flat-bottomed hull of the barge sitting low in the shallow water. After an interminable age it finally moored at the bottom of the very hill the church stood on.

In the gloomy silence, one man jumped off the boat and raised the miserly lantern in the air. Only when he was satisfied they were all alone did he signal his mate. For the next ten minutes Jake watched the two men offload barrel after barrel from the vessel. When Seb nudged him, Jake readied his pistols and nodded, focusing on the scene in front while his friend moved towards them under the cover of the grass. It was quite a haul, but as yet nobody else had arrived to collect it. They couldn't make a move until they did.

'Put your hands in the air! In the name of his Majesty!' At the shout behind him, Jake wanted to scream in frustration. The Excise Men had jumped the gun and jeopardised the whole mission. The smuggler stood on the deck of the barge immediately dived over the side into the water and disappeared out of sight. The man on the shore partially raised his hands, but appeared ready to bolt at any moment.

'Hold your fire!' Jake stood up and raised one fist in the air to stay the idiots behind, pointing one of his own pistols directly at the smuggler's head. 'Stand still or I will kill you!'

The man paused, his gaze furtively darting from left to right as the Excise Men lit all their own lanterns and exposed him to their eyes. He took a step backwards towards the water's edge, then yelped as Jake's warning shot sent the turf next to his feet spraying in the air.

'I said stand still! Don't do anything silly...'

In his peripheral vision he saw Seb less than twenty feet away from the man, ready to strike, and calmly raised the second pistol in the air, making sure the smuggler saw the slow cock of the hammer and the deadly aim of the barrel. They couldn't afford to lose this man, too, now their only link to Rowley and the Londoner, and by default Fliss's safety.

Seb inched closer, his head finally emerging from the reeds. A genuine herring gull call spooked the smuggler and he took another clumsy step back, his hands groping at his belt. Jake heard the blast of a shot behind a split second before it exploded in the smuggler's chest, flinging him back into the water. He held his breath while Seb plunged in to retrieve the body and felt the boiling fury course through his veins when his friend shook his head. Their only link was now dead.

'Which one of you fools fired?' Jake grabbed

the closest Excise Man by the lapels and shook him. 'We needed him alive, damn it!' This was about more than a few paltry barrels of brandy. The woman he was head over heels in love with was in danger! Grave danger and this was Jake's one chance to get her out swiftly.

Their captain stepped forward, unrepentant. 'He was reaching for his weapon. My man did the right thing. At least the cargo has been seized.' He gave a signal to his men and they all came towards the now-crewless barge, only to be stayed by Leatham.

'You can board it once we've looked it over and not before.'

For the next half an hour the pair of them searched in vain for clues before reluctantly handing the vessel over to the others. All they could find were tankers filled with brandy. As the dawn began to break they made their way wearily back to the horses they had left almost half a mile away, exhaustion, the cold and Jake's ridiculously heavy heart making each step an effort. He'd failed her again. Now he would need some divine intervention if he was to—

Jake paused and pulled Seb's coat. 'Why were

they here? Specifically here?' He stopped and turned full circle and took in the desolate marshland. There was the odd cottage, but the only building of any significance was the church. 'One of us would have seen something if a welcoming party had arrived.'

'Not if they'd heard the gunfire beforehand. Those idiots probably scared them off.'

'But what if there wasn't a welcoming party?' An idea was germinating in Jake's mind. 'We're assuming they came here because the creek runs off the Thames—but what if they came here because that church also used to hide contraband in its cellars?'

As one, they started up the hill. The heavy oak-arched doors were open, as church doors were often prone to be offering sanctuary to all comers, but at this early hour the church was deserted. They wandered past the silent pews to the vestry, locating the entrance to the cellar under a large, threadbare rug.

Jake squeezed his body into the small opening first and allowed his eyes to adjust to the pale lamplight as his friend followed. Ahead a long, narrow tunnel disappeared into the darkness. Together they moved along it, crouched at first as it twisted and turned, but then it evened out and widened. Eventually they came to a crossroads of sorts as the tunnel veered both left and right. Knowing they'd have to follow both, they turned left and followed it to the end. The wooden door in the ceiling came out on the edge of desolate marsh land. Not a sign of human habitation marred the landscape. There was water, though. Plenty of it and a solitary wooden quay built of strong new timber. In the distance, Jake could make out the sails of the ships traversing the busy Thames beyond and the miniature signs of civilisation that dotted the banks as the river wended its way directly into London.

The second tunnel took them to another cellar, although thanks to a heavy barrel placed over the trap door, they couldn't see more than a small glimpse of the room beyond without dislodging the barrel and potentially alerting its owners to their presence. It was obviously a storeroom. A smuggler's storeroom. Barrels and boxes were piled several deep along the edges. Above that were the sounds of people. Lots of people. Metal plates and mugs clattered as they were plonked down on tables, the smell of ale and beer hung heavy in the air. All they needed to do now was work out the name of the inn.

It was a little past ten when all hell broke loose at Uncle Crispin's. One minute Fliss had been quietly reading in the drawing room, waiting for her aunts to surface, and the next the silence was filled with the angry growl of her uncle's shouting and what sounded like furniture being thrown. She immediately went to investigate and was held at bay outside his bedchamber door by a shocked footman who politely suggested she make herself scarce until he had calmed down.

The cacophony persisted for almost ten minutes and was so loud it succeeded in rousing both Cressida and Daphne from their sherry-induced deep slumber. After that, while the ladies quietly discussed the possible cause of his fury, Uncle Crispin locked himself away for the rest of the day upstairs and Fliss watched a succession of harried-looking footmen disappear in and out of the house ferrying messages.

Close to seven, and in the middle of dressing, Fliss was informed that they would no longer be expecting guests for dinner and that neither would they be attending Almack's as had been intended. With no way of colliding with either Mr Flint or dropping a paper message for Mr Leatham to find, Fliss could do little other than worry and speculate, convinced that, somehow, she must have been the cause.

Her uncle didn't appear at the quiet, tense dinner table or in the hours after, and by the time Fliss pleaded a sudden headache and excused herself for bed in order to stress about it all alone, he was firmly ensconced in his study. The place he only holed up in when he was expecting his menacing nocturnal visitor.

Kitty, much like the rest of the staff, was nervously preoccupied. A full hour after putting her charge to bed, she had still not materialised to check Fliss was asleep and Fliss couldn't stand to waste one more minute. Something was up and as each hour ticked by, it seemed less and less likely she had come under any suspicion. If anything, it was the staff who were marched into his office, if the steady stream of them leaving with pale, drawn faces at the end of the inquisition was anything to go by. When she could stand the waiting no more she raided her wardrobe and, using another nightgown, pillows and a filigree shawl which she hoped might pass for hair in the darkness, made a body-shaped lump in the bed. After extinguishing both the fire and the candle, she cracked open her bedchamber door and, seeing the coast was miraculously clear for once, crept out.

The rain fell in a miserable, erratic drizzle which quickly seeped through her shawl and thin nightgown. Fliss ignored it while she found a place behind some bushes to watch her uncle's study. He was alone. Pacing furiously and wringing his hands. Far from being angry, he looked scared, his angular features pinched with worry. Several times he stopped and went to the window, his pale eyes nervously searching the garden.

His nervousness increased her own, heightening all her senses. She felt the air change before she heard the ominous sounds of boots crunching on the gravel in the distance and pushed her body further into the bush instinctively as she heard him scale the wall and drop with a thud as he landed on the ground.

He strode less than three feet in front of her, his big body vibrating with anger, and for the first time Fliss saw his features in profile. Dark hair, fuzzy whiskers covering both his cheeks and curling into a thick moustache under his nose. That nose was bent as if it had once been very badly broken, the large nostrils flared as his breath came in heavy bursts, but it was his hooded eyes which petrified her. They positively burned with hate.

Her uncle recoiled as the Londoner ripped open the French door and stalked inside; it slammed behind him with such force the pane quivered. Fliss watched, horrified, as her uncle was grabbed around the throat and smashed against the wall. The Londoner spat something in Uncle Crispin's choking face, then let him go. Both men began to speak in a rapid tattoo which she could neither hear nor follow from her spot a few yards away. The Londoner did lots of finger pointing, her uncle mostly cowered, and everything about the exchange smacked of something very important. Something urgent.

With her heart in her throat Fliss darted towards the wall and, exactly as she had two nights previously, she edged her body closer and closer until she could hear what was being said. Thankfully this time, because of their respective anger, neither was whispering.

'A month's hard work is gone because of your incompetence!'

'I've told you—I never told a soul outside of the usual few where the boat was headed!'

'You have a leak, Rowley! A big one! Someone tipped off the Excise Men and it sure as hell wasn't me or any of my men! The place is crawling with them now. The tunnels, the inn! We've lost everything. All the stock, our supply route... and all because someone in this house couldn't keep their trap shut!'

'My staff wouldn't dare talk. They know better. I pay them to know better...'

'What about Redditch eh? You've been cosying up to him a lot of late! Maybe you let something slip?'

'I promise you I didn't. I wouldn't. You know full well why I tolerate the old fool. It was you who put me on to him in the first place! Why would I jeopardise all the effort I've put into wooing the man? The leak has to have come from somewhere else.'

'Mayhap you've employed someone else. Fresh eyes who see too much?'

'There's nobody new. I run a tight ship. Everyone in this house is exactly the same as they were last month, and the month before and the year before that...*unless...*' Fliss covered her mouth in case the cry escaped. Her uncle was no fool.

'Unless what?'

'Forget it. I was going to say my niece might have said something, but I have her under close watch. She doesn't go anywhere or speak to anyone now without me knowing about it.'

'*Now?* What the hell does that mean?'

Fliss felt tears sting her eyes as her uncle regaled him with how she had escaped, how she had rebelliously refused to comply with his demands. It didn't take long for the finger of suspicion to point firmly in her direction. 'I'll expect you to deal with it, Rowley.'

'You can't be suggesting...?'

'I am. You knew what you'd signed up for. You take the Boss's shilling. You carry out his justice. Plug the leak. I want her silenced for good. And tie up the loose ends. All of them. The two old ladies, too, in case she's talked to them as well as the authorities!'

'I can't kill family! What if we're wrong? What if—?'

'We can't risk what if! Put the three of them in a carriage tomorrow. I'll deal with the rest.'

'But...'

The sound of a body hitting the wall again and her uncle's involuntary squeal suggested the Londoner had resorted to violence again. 'No buts. No excuses. No loose ends! Or do you want me to tell the Boss you are prepared to put his entire operation at risk for the sake of a bunch of women we both know you couldn't care less about...?'

Fliss didn't bother waiting to hear the rest of the conversation. She ran as fast as her legs would take her back to the window of the Music Room, all the time praying she could find a way to save Daphne, Cressida and herself before it was too late.

Chapter Sixteen

Aunt Daphne's bedchamber

Soaked to the skin, terrified and with her words tumbling over each other, Fliss managed to explain the whole story to her aunts in less than five minutes. Their initial disbelief was soon replaced by the same urgent fear which pushed her on. 'We have to escape! Now! Tonight!'

'But all my clothes are in my bedchamber.' Cressida gestured to her nightgown and her hair wrapped tightly in rags. 'I can't leave the house like this!'

'We don't have time to change! It was hard enough sneaking back into the house and rousing you both without the servants seeing, we daren't risk letting them see us prepare for an excursion!' Although the house had been ominously quiet as most of the footmen were now gathered in her uncle's study. They had one opportunity to escape. It was now.

'To be honest, if the servants see us in our nightclothes, we can pretend to be in need of a nighttime beverage.' At least Daphne saw sense. 'How do you propose we leave, Felicity?'

'Through the gardens. We have to climb over the wall into the neighbours, then there is an alleyway and...'

Daphne held up her hand and shook her head. 'Out of the question. It is one thing for a lady to be outside in her nightrail, we've all *done that* a time or two, but quite another to be scaling walls. We shall leave by the front door as is proper.'

Cressida nodded enthusiastically. 'Yes, indeed. With my rheumatism I can't be climbing walls.' Before Fliss could argue, Daphne held up her bony hand again.

'Think, Felicity. The front door leads us on to Berkeley Square. My nephew can hardly murder the three of us in full view of the *ton*.' A valid point. 'And if your Mr Leatham has men watching the front then there will be someone around to save us.'

'But how do you suppose we get past the footmen?'

Daphne grinned. 'Do you remember Lord Wivenhoe's house party, Sister?'

A mischievous smile appeared on Cressida's face. 'I do believe I do, Daphne.'

And so it came to pass that Fliss found herself blindly following the lead of two incorrigible old ladies in their hasty bid for freedom. Daphne collected an array of assorted items from around her bedchamber, including a tiny lady's pistol, and concealed them about her person. Fliss was stripped of her soggy nightgown and swathed in the one her scandalous aunt claimed she kept for special occasions. If Fliss had thought her new underthings daring, this billowing, sheer confection made her reconsider. Without the matching silk peignoir, it left little to the imagination, but it was nightwear and therefore apparently essential to the old ladies' plan so she didn't argue. If it came to it, she would run out of this house stark naked.

Daphne handed the poker to her. 'Hide it in the folds, dear, and do not use it until I give you the signal.' She executed an exaggerated wink, the agreed signal for mayhem to be unleashed.

Cressida retrieved a bottle of rum from her sister's trunk, popped the cork and took a healthy swig. 'I'm ready.'

With more calm than Fliss could muster she

sauntered to the door and began to sing loudly as she swayed into the hallway waving the bottle.

'*The Dey of Algiers, when afraid of his ears, A messenger sent to the Court, sir. As he knew in our state the women had weight, He chose one well-hung for the sport, sir.*'

She giggled as Fliss and Daphne chased after her.

'Aunt Cressida. You are ill. Let us put you back to bed.'

'Sister, dear, come. Sleep it off.'

As they had hoped the noise drew the attention of the footmen on duty in the hall below and they rushed towards the staircase to help.

Cressida pointed at one and wiggled her finger at him suggestively. '*He searched the divan till he found out a man—* Whoops!' She tripped for effect at the bottom step and drunkenly pushed the footman towards the front door. '*And he lately came o'er from the Barbary shore, as the great Plen... As the great Plen...* Oh, dear I always get stuck on that last word.'

She leaned heavily on the footman and grinned up at him while the second footman supported her elbow, and Daphne and Fliss gathered around to help. They were less than six feet from the door.

Daphne winked and Cressida threw out her arms, smacking the footman in the face with her bottle as she sang at the top of her lungs, '*As the great Plenipotentiary*!'

Fliss cracked the second footmen over the head with her poker as Daphne whacked the first smartly with a full bottle of rum that hadn't been opened. Both men staggered woozily from the blows, leaving the three of them free to make a dash for the door.

They had the late hour and the element of surprise on their side, but not for long. There were so many bolts to slide, that it took all three of them to get the thing open before they tumbled out into Berkeley Square.

'Help! Help!'

Fliss scanned the darkness for the watchmen Lord Fennimore had promised her, all the while dragging her aunts with her into the night. When nobody appeared, they ran to the corner where a solitary hackney stood waiting, while back at the house there was already the sound of panicked shouts calling for help. Fliss managed to stuff both old ladies in as one of the footmen ran haphazardly from her uncle's house. His forehead was bleeding and he clutched at his head. Behind him, three more men hurried out and sprinted towards them, far too close for comfort. From the shadows, some shabby men appeared, but no Mr Leatham. They dashed towards her uncle's men, grabbing them and slowing their pursuit and giving Fliss just enough time to throw herself into the hackney. She screamed at the coachman, 'Just drive!'

Panicked, he cracked his whip repeatedly and the coach lurched forward the moment her feet left the pavement and thankfully didn't stop as one of the footmen came perilously close to grabbing the door handle. The horses picked up speed and the carriage clattered out of the square. Blessedly they were soon flying along the deserted streets away from the danger. Thanks to Mr Leatham's men, nobody appeared to have followed them. Eventually, when they were a significant distance away, he slowed enough to ask directions and Fliss barked the address of the only place she could think of. The only place her heart wanted to be.

'The Albany! Take us to the Albany!'

The city was wide awake as Jake finally wove his way to St James's practically dead on his feet, the sun valiantly poking its head through the miserable blanket of clouds for the first time in weeks. Typically, the fine weather decided to appear now, rather than overnight or the whole day before when he might have benefitted from it. After the discovery of the underground tunnel system, they had sent to London for Lord Fennimore and reinforcements, believing the smuggling gang might be spooked by the loss of their cargo and suspecting they would move swiftly to relocate their reserves. That suspicion had proved correct. The moment the darkness fell, the innkeeper and his staff set to work shifting the barrels towards the deserted quay he and Seb had found in the marshes, clearly waiting for some boats to come and retrieve it all. Jake and Seb spent another freezing, wet, sleepless night watching and waiting in the reeds with Lord Fennimore. At dawn, like the jumpy innkeeper, they realised those boats were never going to come. The Boss would rather relinquish that supply chain and those profits rather than jeopardise his entire operation.

They'd rounded up the terrified publican and his accomplices for questioning, seized everything in the cellar and left the Excise Men crawling through the tunnel like a colony of ants. While it wasn't the satisfying conclusion they had hoped for, Jake was philosophical. At least they had enough circumstantial evidence to arrest Rowley on suspicion of aiding and abetting free traders and, despite Jake's soggy clothes, aching body and heavy heart filled with worry, Lord Fennimore now finally agreed Fliss's work was done. As soon as Jake was washed, shaved and presentable, he fully intended to head to Berkeley Square and find some way to get her out of there.

When the doorman told him he had visitors, his first instinct was to pat the pistol on his belt as his hackles rose. Upon learning those visitors were female, three of them and all in nightgowns, he practically sprinted up the stairs in a blind panic. Something must have happened in his absence and he prayed it wasn't bad. But if three of them were there…

He burst through the door to see his valet pouring brandy into two outstretched teacups.

'Don't be stingy, there's a good fellow. We *have* been through an ordeal.' Daphne Sawyer's head turned and she smiled at the sight of Jake, her grey hair still wound in curling rags. 'Ah, finally! We've been waiting for you for hours, young man.

Hours and hours. I suppose you've been out gallivanting.' The smile quickly turned into a frosty frown of disapproval. 'You could have timed your urges better. We were almost murdered in our beds and would have been had Felicity not had the wherewithal to get us out! My nephew has gone quite mad, hasn't he, Sister?'

'Yes, indeed. We had to overpower the footmen and flee in a hackney.' Cressida swigged the entire potent contents of her cup and held it out for more. 'My nerves are shot to pieces.'

'Where's Fliss?' Because her absence in his tiny bachelor parlour petrified him. 'Has she been harmed?' If she had, someone was going to die.

'She is as well as can be expected under the circumstances and quite determined to go home today.'

'She is unharmed?' Jake barked out the question.

Watching his worried face, the old lady smiled. 'You *do* care! That *is* encouraging.' Both ladies shared a knowing smile. 'Since we arrived here, she's been in a foul mood and was getting more agitated by the minute. I thought she was going to wear a groove in the floor with her pacing.'

'But where is she now?' Their amusement irritated him.

'Gone to find some suitable travelling clothes in your bedchamber, sir.' His valet gestured backwards with an incline of his head. 'I've already sent a message to Lord Fennimore appraising him of her whereabouts.'

He didn't wait to ask more questions. The only thing he cared about was seeing her. Jake crashed through the door and stopped dead in his tracks as the sight of one very feminine, very bare back caught him completely by surprise. Fliss squealed and clutched the front of the nightgown quickly to her chin before she turned around, oblivious to the fact the weak February sun streaming through the window made the gossamer nightgown translucent. Every mouth-watering curve was shown in stark silhouette and the dusty peaks of her breasts were easy to find.

'Don't you believe in knocking!'

'I was worried about you.'

'Oh, please! I doubt you've given me a single thought in the hours you've been out philandering!' The snippy, jealous tone buoyed him. 'Why—your shirt is undone and you're not even wearing a cravat. It's obvious you have just fallen out of some hussy's bed!'

'I haven't been out philandering and I haven't been in anything resembling a bed in days.' He quietly closed the door behind him and leaned against it, enjoying the way the daylight picked out the rich caramel tones in her hair as it tumbled over her naked shoulders. 'There have also been no hussies. Nor have there been since the night I met you at Almack's.' After his epiphany on the marshes, he had promised himself he would tell her nothing but the whole truth going forward—if he was ever given the chance to. Now that she was here, there was no time like the present. 'I fear you have ruined me for all other women, Fliss. I've missed you.' At her disbelieving eye roll he smiled. 'If you must know, I've been in Fobbing.'

'Fobbing is a place?'

'A very cold and damp place. Filled with smuggled brandy ferried down the Thames on barges.' As he spoke she wiggled her arms back into the nightgown and tightly tied the ribbons at her neck. Jake decided not to tell her it made precious little difference. Thanks to the blessed return of the sun his view was still spectacular and the wiggling, combined with her presence, was doing wonders in taking his mind off his exhaustion. As were the erotic spectacles she had primly placed back on her delectable nose. 'Thanks to you we intercepted a fresh delivery and then discovered where the rest of the contraband was hidden.'

'Ah… My useless information proved not to be useless at all, then. I did wonder if I was responsible for my uncle's irrational behaviour yesterday.' She sank down to sit on the bed. His bed. The home of those fevered dreams and yearning. The irony was not lost on him. 'Hardly a surprise, then, that suspicion fell on me.'

Jake should have anticipated that and the guilt was instant. 'I put you in danger and then wasn't there for you.' Instead, he had insisted on accompanying Leatham when he should have remained watching over her.

For the first time since she had discovered his mission, Fliss smiled kindly. 'I seem to recall I put myself in danger. You were dead set against it. Mind you, I might not have been so gracious had I known my uncle and his associates would happily kill me and those two dear old ladies out there to save his own sorry hide. Still, we escaped. I didn't know where else to go.'

'I'm glad you came to me. Fliss, I know now is

not a good time, but I need to explain.' Her eyes lifted to his—they were so troubled and sad he had to go to her, but as he sat down on the mattress beside her, wrapping one arm around her shoulders to draw her into his embrace, she folded her arms across her chest and angled her body ever so slightly away from his. The message was clear. She didn't want his comfort. Coming here had been a last resort. The knowledge cut like a knife into his poor, confused and ill-prepared heart.

'There is nothing to explain.' She stood and, still hugging her body, calmly put several feet between them. 'They are dangerous men and the world will be a better place with them off the streets. You did what you had to do. What you are trained to do. We don't need to discuss it.'

'But, Fliss...'

'Please, Jake, don't.' Her golden eyebrows pleaded with him to stop and her eyes glistened with pain, then both faded only to be replaced with that flat, emotionless stare which destroyed him.

'We do.' He rose and edged towards her, his palms flat, imploring. He owed her the truth. What she did with it was up to her, but if there was any hope for them it had to start with honesty. 'To begin with, my pursuit of you was a mission, but from the outset I struggled with it. Before I knew who you were I was drawn to you, and then...' He sighed, not quite knowing how to put it all into words. The feelings he had for Fliss were so new and so different from any he had wrestled with before. They had broadsided him. 'I wish I'd been honest with you sooner.' Although would he have been? Knowing there were messy and complicated feelings involved, he knew himself too well to believe he'd have done anything differently if he'd have had any whiff of what was happening to his heart. If anything, Jake would have panicked and doubled his efforts to seduce her quickly so that he could get away. He'd spent a lifetime avoiding the painful emotion which came when a man and a woman became too attached. 'And I wish I had been able to tell you the truth myself. The way you found out...the timing...well, it was not as I would have wanted.'

'If wishes were horses, beggars would ride. I wish I had never wandered into that alcove in Almack's.'

'You don't mean that.'

She shrugged and walked to the window, denying him the chance to watch her face to know for sure. 'I saw him. The Londoner, I mean. He was dark. Swarthy. His hair was black, I think, and he had bushy whiskers and a moustache. His nose was quite Roman. If I were to hazard a guess I would say it had been badly broken many times. He wasn't as tall as you, maybe an inch or so off six feet, but much stockier. Very big hands. Very frightening.'

Slowly, Jake had come to stand behind her. He resisted the urge to touch her, sensing it wouldn't be welcome. 'Information you can tell Lord Fennimore when he arrives. I want to talk about us.'

'There is no us, Jake.'

'I want there to be.' When she didn't respond, he risked putting one hand on her hip before allowing it to coil possessively around her waist. 'I know I am the very last sort of man you want. I have a past. One I'm not particularly proud of now. But the truth is, my heart…' His throat choked with emotion. Every messy and complicated feeling was suddenly clawing its way up his neck and demanding to be let out. It was both terrifying and humbling, but at least it was honest. She shifted round and was staring into his eyes so intently he felt vulnerable and exposed, and he couldn't bear to see her expression in case she rejected him. Instead he closed his eyes. 'The truth is my heart is yours now. I… I love you, Fliss.' He exhaled, then instantly sucked in a breath to hold as he waited for her response.

She turned away and her head fell back to rest on his shoulder while her eyes stared out of the window. For several long moments, they simply stood there. Jake waiting. Fliss thinking. When she stiffened he knew he'd lost.

'I don't trust you, Jake.'

She gently prised his arm away and turned to face him again. He could see the doubt warring with some other powerful emotion. He hoped it was affection or temptation for him. Her lovely face was etched with pain. Seeing his wise northern owl with a broken wing of his making was eating him from the inside like a cancer. 'Do you think you might be able to? One day?' Again, she didn't respond straight away which gave him some hope. The tiny flame warmed his battered heart. A decisive flat no would have taken no thought.

'I don't know, Jake.'

That had to be enough until he worked out a solution and there and then he decided he *had* to find a solution. He had to find a way to make the badness good. A way to earn her forgiveness and her trust again. Even if it took him a lifetime.

A lifetime!

Good grief, he was doomed. Or blessed. Or just plain mad to be contemplating for ever with any woman, let alone the one who saw straight through him. Yet in her time of need, she had come to him first. That had to count for something.

'I'll make this right, Fliss. I swear it.'

Her lovely eyes searched his for the truth and he held her stare this time, willing her to see it. Jake wanted to hold her and reassure her it would be all right. He took a step forward to do exactly that, but the soft knock on the door was followed by his valet's voice.

'Lord Fennimore is here and so are the others. There has been a complication, sir.'

Chapter Seventeen

On the Great North Road, bound for Nottinghamshire

Fliss stretched out her aching neck and opened the carriage curtains. The sharp shard of sunlight made her wince and drop it back in place. This was the second sunrise she had witnessed in this carriage and the second night she had attempted to snatch a few hours of sleep on the uncomfortable bench as it sped north, barely stopping long enough to change the horses and fill their bellies with food.

As uncomfortable as the three ladies were, every mile away from London couldn't come soon enough. The more miles the better. Each one helped to relieve the enormous knot of fear which had formed in her chest when she had first learned she was a loose end to be tied and had doubled when she had learned that the Londoner had murdered her uncle for the very same reason and probably within hours of Fliss's epic escape.

Since then, the whole world had been turned upside down. At least that's what it felt like. She was no longer a naïve schoolmistress from Cumbria or an unlikely spy for his Majesty's government. Now she was a target. The only person still alive who could identify her uncle's murderer and his links to the dangerous underworld he had become involved in.

When the astounding news came that Uncle Crispin had been found hanging in his study within hours of her watching him, nobody believed it was suicide. Not when there were meaty hand-shaped bruises apparent beneath the silken bell-pull wrapped around his neck. Uncharitably Fliss knew he would have happily seen Daphne, Cressida and herself garrotted by convenient footpads to save his own skin. When push came to shove, he might have even done the deed himself, he was that cold and self-serving. So she couldn't find it in her heart to grieve for him and fully blamed him for the danger she now found herself in. There was no room in her mind for grief; having a price on one's head was petrifying.

Thank the Lord she had escaped and fled to Jake's, because he had been reassuringly adamant about her continued safety since Lord Fennimore, Mr Leatham and Lord Flint had arrived that morning at the Albany. At his insistence, they had left the capital that morning. The carriage they were travelling in bore the colours of the Post, so the sight of it speeding up the Great North Road would not arouse suspicion. Knowing he and Mr Leatham were driving it, that they were both heavily armed and that a huge escort travelled both ahead and behind them also made her feel better, although only marginally. Until she was safely locked within the fortress he had assured her he had grown up in, and many, many weeks had passed, she doubted the crippling and all-consuming fear would begin to subside. Lord Fennimore was hopeful Fliss's final destination was obscure enough to be safe but, with what was highly likely to be an enormous bounty for her whereabouts, there was still the chance somebody might tell them she had gone first to the Albany and then from there perhaps they would link her to Jake.

Another group was being led by Flint and headed further north to Sister Ursuline's, to evacuate the school and lay in wait should the Londoner attempt to search for her there. Local battalions of Excise Men were also being drafted in to stand guard in Cumbria. Both Jake and Mr Leatham were of the belief the shadowy criminal behind it all, the elusive Boss, had men or informants from within their ranks and so involving the Excise Men while neglecting to apprise them of her true location would lure the men to the convent and ultimately to their arrest.

As the carriage began to slow, Cressida stirred beside her and gazed bleary-eyed around the dim carriage. 'Where are we?'

'I have no idea, but it's morning.' Fliss lifted the curtain again and forced her tired eyes to adjust to the brightness. They were no longer on a main road. The narrow lane was flanked on either side by dense trees. Eventually, a twenty-foot wall loomed in the distance. When they passed through it there was an orchard, orderly lines of trees echoing with the sounds of children's laughter. The carriage came to a halt and Jake jumped down. For the first time since they had begun this arduous journey, neither he nor Mr Leatham had warned them to keep the curtains closed as they had at the busy inns they had stopped at.

Fliss took the opportunity to lower the window and poke her head out. Their scruffy-looking entourage rattled past the giant, sturdy gates which stood wide open. As the last cart of Mr Leatham's Invisibles trundled through, Jake, Leatham and several men began to close them. It reassuringly took a great deal of strength.

'I think you might be lost…this is private land.' A man the spitting image of Jake, only slightly older, limping and draped with little dark-haired girls, approached the carriage. His deep blue eyes flicked to hers first, then towards the gate. 'Jake? Is that you?' The sight of his brother sporting several days' worth of beard and dressed in the red uniform of the Post men clearly amused him. 'Our big brother will be pleased that you've finally got yourself a job.' His face fell when he saw the gates shut and he instantly wrapped his arms around his daughters. 'What's wrong?'

Jake strode towards his brother and hugged him. 'Too complicated to explain here. Where are Jack and Joe?'

'Both at home as far as I know as it's early, but you know Joe.'

'Round them up, Jamie. I'll see them inside.'

With that he climbed back in the driver's seat and the carriage lurched forward again.

Within minutes they had reached an impressive Tudor manor house and were met by servants at the door. Another dark haired and blue-eyed man came to greet Jake with a beautiful woman still in her dressing gown. A riot of blonde corkscrew curls hung loose over her shoulders. As the men talked she came towards them smiling. 'I'm Letty Warriner—Jake's sister-in-law. I can see you are exhausted. Come. Let us get you inside. Chivers, our butler, will fetch tea.'

After that, Fliss and the Sawyer sisters were made a huge fuss of. Hot tea and breakfast came in quick succession, which Fliss fell upon gratefully, and then sighed with relief when she was shown into a beautiful bedchamber. A steaming bath had been drawn and wafted a deliciously floral scent about the room. A selection of clean clothes and a beautiful embroidered nightrail had also been laid out.

'Jake said you haven't slept properly for days, so if you want to sleep then please go ahead and do so. We are very informal here.' Letty laid a soft hand on her shoulder and it appeared to have the power to trigger the waterworks. Tears streamed down Fliss's cheeks and, to her acute embarrassment, she couldn't appear to stop them.

'I'm so sorry.'

'Oh, don't be. You've been through an ordeal. I was kidnapped once, so I completely sympathise. I've often thought female tears are more a release of pent-up anger and frustration rather than a sign of weakness and from what I can gather you have been quite brave enough so far.'

Another woman burst through the door at that exact moment, copper hair tied back in a single ribbon and her freckled face smiling. 'Apparently we are in the midst of a crisis, or so my curmudgeonly husband tells me, so I brought cake. I know it's early but everything is better with cake, don't you think? I'm Cassie Warriner and I made this myself.' The sight of the charmingly wonky concoction only made Fliss's tears worse and she began to hiccup and snort as she wept into the pretty handkerchief her hostess had just pressed into her hand. 'Clearly I've arrived just in time. I've sent Chivers for more tea. You can't have cake without tea.' Unfazed by her overtly emotional state, Cassie wrapped an arm about her shoulders and squeezed. 'Get it all out. Bottling stuff up inside is never good. Bella will be here soon. She's finding mornings a bit trying at the moment.'

The butler scratched at the door and didn't blink an eyelid at Fliss's grizzling as he deposited the second tea tray on the bedside table. He was closely followed by a dark-haired woman who looked worryingly green around the gills. 'Sorry I'm late to the party. I am counting the days till this morning sickness fades. Joe is adamant that it's not unusual for it to continue past three months and it's at least four months now and the slightest thing sets me off. Is that cake?' She eyed it suspiciously. 'Move it out of the way, Cassie, or I will disgrace myself in front of our guest.' A guest who would welcome some company in the disgracing. 'My goodness, you look pale...'

A large black medical bag appeared out of nowhere and the third Warriner wife rifled in it. She produced three bottles. The first two she measured out on a teaspoon and dropped in Fliss's tea. 'A few drops of these should help with your mood. Gorse relieves despair and willow apparently eases the tendency towards self-pity. I mixed them with plenty of sugar so even if their therapeutic abilities are dubious they will make your tea taste nice. But this…' Bella grinned and wiggled the third bottle '…is heaven in the bath.' She pulled out the cork and, after depositing the whole bottle into the steaming tub, the scent of lavender tickled Fliss's nostrils. 'A nice cup of tea in the bath is just what you need.'

'I happen to think my cake in the bath will be more beneficial than your grass in her tea, Bella.' Cassie Warriner was already sawing off a slice which she placed on the side table she had dragged next to the bathtub, next to Fliss's tea. 'And then when you are fully refreshed we shall all gather again and get to know each other.'

'Yes,' said Letty as the three walked towards the door. 'We are all intrigued to learn about your dealings with our dear brother Jake. None of us has ever seen him quite so…ferocious before.'

Joe was the last to arrive and took his place at the scarred kitchen table where they had always held important discussions. In the hours since Jake had come home, they hadn't pressed him for information, merely aided him in making the grounds secure without questioning why. That solid, loyal reinforcement was exactly the reason he had brought Fliss here. When you messed with one Warriner, you messed with them all and to-gether they had always been a force to be reck-oned with, although he was dreading telling them all he'd been lying about for five long years.

Jack's quirked eyebrow signalled they had waited long enough. 'Why have we battened down the hatches and why is there a small army en-camped on my lawn?'

'I've not been being entirely honest with you all.'

'You don't say?' His elder brother folded his arms across his chest, a sure sign his patience was wearing thin. 'There are a lot of guns out there for a mail coach. What the hell are you involved in?'

There was no easy way of saying. 'I suppose the best way of explaining it is to tell you that I've been working for the government. I have been since Cambridge. I belong to a secret branch called the King's Elite. We work with the Home Office, the Foreign Office and alongside the Ex-cise Men tracking large-scale smuggling opera-tions.'

Two pairs of blue eyes stared back at him agog. Only Jamie didn't appear the least bit surprised. But then only Jamie had alluded to knowing the truth before.

'And you've done this for five years?'

'Yes, Jack. I was recruited almost as soon as I left university.'

'Why?'

Now came the part he was dreading. 'They recognised that some of my skills might be useful in procuring difficult information.' A painfully convoluted and shoddy description which he hoped might be enough. Typically, Jamie understood straight away because he'd done similar in the Peninsula, although he had nobly kept his clothes on.

'So you are a spy?'

'You're a spy!' Joe was flabbergasted.

'That's the long and short of it, yes.'

There was a painful beat of silence while they all digested this, and then, of course, came the narrowed eyes. 'What skills?' Because Jack knew he possessed few and frequently lamented his lack of attempting to acquire more.

'My way with the…ah…ladies.' Saying it out loud made him feel like a doxy for hire, only it was the crown, not a client, who left the money on his nightstand.

'You lucky devil!' Joe threw his head back and laughed. 'Only you would land a job which allowed you to be horizontal most of the time.' He slapped him on the back jovially. 'All these years we've nagged you about being a rake isn't a career and all the while it was! That's priceless. You've always had the luck of the devil.'

'I wouldn't call myself lucky. I hardly had a choice as to whom I…' Oh, good grief, this was painful. For years he had told himself he was pleased with being a rake. He got to enjoy women without any of the messy complications, but now he felt sordid—a shameful philanderer, just as Fliss had first said.

'The young lady upstairs, I take it she is one of your *assigned* conquests?' Jack didn't appear the slightest bit amused at his confession.

'Yes. No!' Jake ran an angry hand through his hair. 'It's complicated. I *was* sent to seduce her. Her uncle was involved in a major smuggling ring which we believe is funding Napoleon's supporters. We had been trying for months to get deep into his inner circle and I was drafted in when they dragged Fliss into the mess.'

'Fliss?' Another cocked eyebrow. 'How very cosy. Does she know you bedded her on the King's shilling or are we expected to help you perpetuate the charade?' As the devoted father of four girls,

Jamie's stormy expression conveyed his outrage at such a situation perfectly.

'I haven't bedded her and, if you must know, at this point in the proceedings I am highly unlikely to.' Getting her to actually talk to him would be something. He and Fliss hadn't exchanged anything other than essential words in days. It was as if she had erected an invisible yet impenetrable wall around herself, one which let most people in except Jake. This morning she had barely looked at him and the widening chasm between them was killing him. 'She currently loathes me because she learned about the King's blasted shilling. I wish I knew what to do to fix that!' Three pairs of dark eyebrows rose at his frustrated tone and Jake wished he couldn't speak fluent eyebrow, or that the world would suddenly be completely eyebrow free and thus spare him from reading the meaning of one ever again. Embarrassed, he went on the defensive. 'Anyway, whether or not I bedded her is by the by. She's in danger. Grave danger and it's all my fault!'

They listened intently as he told them all about Rowley, the murderous Londoner and the mysterious and ever-elusive Boss. Jake left nothing out of the whole sordid story, knowing that each of them deserved to know the full truth because he was bringing that danger to their door. Their families. His family. To their credit, none of his brothers passed comment when he told them how he had sought Fliss out, how he had teased information out of her or how he had allowed her to walk alone into the lion's den after he had promised her he would help her. Three awful truths where he wished with all his heart he had behaved more honourably—as the three of them would have undoubtedly done in his shoes. By the end of the tale, he hoped he had adequately and dispassionately conveyed the seriousness of the situation. 'If you want me to move her, I completely understand. Just let us rest here for a few hours because I am dead on my feet and I can't protect her properly if I am not on my game.'

Everyone looked to Jack to make the decision, just as they had always looked to Jack their whole lives, and he made them wait while he considered all the ramifications. 'This affects you all. Jamie's and Joe's houses lie within the walls of Markham Manor.' Both men nodded slowly. '*If* we do this—and it's a *big* if at this stage—then I think it's safest you all move back into the main house until the danger is past. It might also be prudent to attempt to convince the ladies to move away temporarily. For their safety.' The second nod was less decisive as all three knew there was little chance of dislodging their devoted and determined spouses. Especially if they banded together, as they were prone to do, and dug their heels in. More silent seconds ticked by until his eldest brother pinned Jake with his stare. 'Give me one good reason why we should invite trouble to our door for a stranger.'

'Fliss is…she is…' Emotion clogged Jake's throat.

'You love her.' It was a statement, not a question.

'With all my heart.'

All three sighed in that matter-of-fact way he also loved about them and regarded him with pity. Joe and Jamie simultaneously wrapped strong arms about his shoulders while Jack huffed out a deep breath. 'Then I suppose we need to start the preparations for a potential siege. Jamie, dust off your arsenal, I fear we might need it, and then we'll tackle the ladies. I suspect your smugglers might be easier to defeat.'

Chapter Eighteen

*Around the dinner table at Markham Manor,
eating Letty's traditional Foul à la Braise*

'Could you pass the salt?' Too late Fliss realised it sat next to his hand. Jake smiled and passed it to her, but in her clumsy hurry to grab it as quickly as possible, their fingers brushed and she ended up yanking it away as if she'd been burned. Which she had. The instant warmth zinged up her fingers and bounced around all her nerve endings before blooming into an embarrassing blush on her cheeks. A blush she willed away by concentrating hard on sprinkling a few grains of the dratted salt over her potatoes. Good gracious, she had never felt so awkward, but then again she had never before sat down to a dinner with three strange women who had recently seen her blubbing like a baby and a scoundrel who had kissed her and made her fingers zing without trying and his entire family. It was beyond unnerving, yet apparently only to her. Nobody else appeared particularly fazed.

According to her generous hostess, whenever there was a significant occasion, good or bad, the Warriners gathered together and ate chicken. It was a tradition and one which gave them strength, apparently, so Fliss found herself very much the centre of attention around their giant dining table. All the adults, aside from her vexing rescuer, were unsubtly watching the peculiar atmosphere between her and Jake.

She had done her best to reassure the ladies after her bath that she and Jake were merely acquainted through circumstances and that she was nothing more than a mission to him. She was grateful for his rescuing her, of course she was, but that was the full extent of their brief and odd relationship. But then, when she had related everything which had happened to her in the last few weeks, her uncle's treachery and the threat to her life by the Londoner, Fliss had conveniently left out how she had welcomed, then come to depend on, Jake's friendship. In her story, they happened to collide. They never danced, or ran away and spent the day laughing at the Tower, and they certainly never shared an earth-shattering and inappropriate kiss in a hackney.

In glossing over the truth she had hoped to maintain her dignity—the last thing she wanted was them knowing that most of those noisy tears had been shed because she was heartbroken. The constant knot in her chest she had carried since she had discovered he had been lying could be nothing else. And if she was brutally honest with herself, which of course she always was, she couldn't be heartbroken unless she had given her heart in the first place and somewhere in a ballroom, or in Hyde Park or in the worst hackney in the world, Fliss had given Jake hers and he had stepped on it repeatedly—just as she had his feet during their one and only waltz. If only he wasn't a professional liar and if only she had not been stupid enough to ask for salt! Her silly cheeks were still glowing crimson.

Joe, the nearest brother in age to Jake, seemed to find the spectacle highly amusing and was making no attempt to disguise the fact he was studying their behaviour, much like an ornithologist would scrutinise rare nesting birds in the wild. Jack and Jamie were making a better show of uninterest, but even they had smiled at the salt incident. The wives put on a good show, but then they'd had a hand in placing her purposefully just opposite their untrustworthy brother-in-law and then distributed themselves specifically to get the best view, so that hardly counted. They all had their suspicions and she sincerely hoped Jake the Snake had been discreet in his own explanations. Surely he owed her that much?

The other end of the table was worse, so Fliss tried her best to avoid glancing left. Daphne and Cressida, already pickled in several glasses of wine, were openly grinning at her gauche and guilty reactions and Jake's feeble attempts to appear normal as he picked at his food. Periodically, though, his eyes would lock with hers and all manner of inappropriate emotions were visible in those intense swirling-blue depths. Each one of them doing strange things to her heart, which she was determined to harden against him and was failing to do with alarming frequency. Past him, several sets of identical bright-blue eyes were openly staring at her. All of them under the age of seven.

It didn't help that the nieces and nephews had insisted on sitting close to Jake, because he was a charmingly doting uncle with a wonderfully patient way with children. The sight of him so obviously affectionate and paternal was making her womb ache and her mind wonder. Damn him for being a natural father! Jake didn't need any more points in his favour. That one was now noted alongside fiercely protective, quick witted, intuitive, devilishly handsome, always there when she needed him and a splendid kisser. Her heart wanted to add beautifully contrite and tortured in his remorse, but if she relented and added those then she would have to allow her sensible head to believe his sweet and heartfelt declaration of love was real when he had resolutely refused to meet her eyes when he said it, which meant she was doomed to surrender and he would have won. Although doomed didn't seem half as bad now as it had a few days ago and a growing part of her was coming to hope he might give up his womanising ways if the right woman came along. Was she the right woman?

Clearly, Fliss was now suffering from the blind naivety that had afflicted many of the wayward girls, Sister Ursuline and her own beloved mother, if she believed that nonsense, and she knew full well how all those liaisons had turned out.

Badly.

She had to be strong. Rise above her biological urges and uncharacteristic romantic tendencies. Ignore the persistent knot in her chest and the urgent call of her womb. Call of her womb! Biology was quickly becoming her least favourite science. He had not looked her in the eye and, deep down, she knew that meant he was probably lying. 'How long do you think it will be before I can return home to Cumbria?'

Jake's head snapped up because they were the first words she had directed towards him since they had sat down half an hour ago. 'I suppose that depends on how swiftly the Londoner decides to tie up the last remaining loose end.' And there it was again, that fierce, protective gleam in his eyes. 'When he is standing on the scaffold—unless he meets his maker before.'

'What happens if you can't find him?'

'We'll find him.' Certainty. Roiling hatred on her behalf. 'Until then, you are safe here. You don't have to live in fear, Fliss.'

'Can I call you Auntie Fliss?' The eldest son of Letty and Jack asked this with the innocent face of an angel.

'You may call me Fliss, as that is my name and we are friends now.'

'But when you marry Uncle Jake you will be my aunt, won't you?' There was an audible hiss as the entire table collectively breathed in.

Fliss didn't dare look up. 'I'm not marrying your uncle, poppet.'

'Mama says you will. If Uncle Jake apologises properly.'

Her eyes flicked to Letty, who had the good grace to look sheepish at the end of the table before she glowered at her son. 'I *did not* say that, Jonathan!'

'Well, if you didn't Papa certainly did. I heard him discussing it with Uncle Jamie. He said it was about time the notches on his bedpost had finally caught up with him.'

The eldest two Warriners' eyes widened as they struggled to find the words to apologise. However, young Jonathan was far from finished turning the screw.

He tugged on the now-furious Jake's sleeve. 'Why do you have notches on your bedpost, Uncle Jake?'

Letty shot to her feet. 'Right, I think it's past your bedtimes, children. Come along!' She sent a mortified glance at Fliss while everyone else stared at their plates, except for Joe, who watched Cressida frantically chase a lone pea around her plate with her fork.

Fliss did the same, but found tears prickling her eyes. Tears she would never allow him to see. 'I think I shall retire, too. It's been a trying couple of days… Goodnight, everyone.'

She scraped her chair back too loudly and the sound reverberated around the dreadful silence like a hammer on an anvil at the crack of dawn. In her hurry, her skirts got tangled and she almost stumbled as she tried, and failed, to glide like a swan out of the room with the last vestiges of her dignity holding her ramrod straight. So straight she feared her shoulder blades might snap.

They all knew what had happened.

With her innate skills at reading people, she could see it written plainly on every face. The straightened brows, the chewed bottom lips, the downcast eyes, their irises brim full of pity. Because they knew. He'd told them. How she'd almost become another one of those silly notches. Every hideously shameful detail had been shared with his family, because he was lucky enough to have the luxury of one.

Suddenly all those intuitive and identical Warriner eyes bored into her soul and stripped it bare and she had to get away. She didn't look at any of them as she swept out of the dining room. Alone, Fliss could curl up into a ball and cry. She heard more wood grinding against floor and purposeful footsteps behind her, and picked up her pace as she reached the staircase. The dratted tears fell regardless, silently and miserably, spurring her onwards.

'Fliss, wait!'

'Leave me alone, Jake.' At the top of the stairs she forgot about pride or propriety and simply ran towards her bedchamber. With his longer legs he was right behind her as she reached the door.

'We need to talk. Please.'

'You told them, didn't you? I'm so humiliated! Do they all know you were paid to kiss me?'

'Fliss—it wasn't like that—'

She cut him off by slamming the door in his face and resting her back heavily against it.

'Don't make me talk to the door.'

'Go away. I honestly have nothing to say to you. Just g-go away.' Fliss hated that her voice cracked. 'I wish I'd never met you, Jake Warriner! I hate you!'

That comment was met with silence, but when she craned her ears she could still hear his soft breathing outside. To her horror more tears fell, when she had never been one for crying. Silent, devastated tears of self-pity. For everything. Her situation, the danger, Jake's lies and the humiliation of knowing the last vestiges of her dignity now lay in tattered and public ruins at her feet.

'If it's any consolation, I hate myself, too.' His voice was a muffled whisper, as if his face was also laid against the door. 'I can't eat. I can't sleep. My mind keeps rolling, searching over everything and suggesting a hundred different ways I could have done this or that. I loathe myself for hurting you and for lying and for letting you go back to your uncle. I wasn't there when you had to escape and I hate myself because you had to deal with that all alone. The danger you are in now is gnawing at me, too. I keep running through every scenario and imagining you hurt, and I blame myself for that, too. If you hadn't escaped, you would have been murdered that night just like your uncle. I can't get that image out of my mind. If I'd said no to Leatham and taken you straight back to Cumbria like I promised then you'd still be safe and none of this would have happened.'

His voice sounded choked and her heart went out to him.

'That is my uncle's fault, Jake, not yours.'

'I could have stopped it.'

'Could you?' Without thinking, she traced her fingers over the wood his voice hid behind. 'Who's to say my uncle wouldn't have tripped up somewhere and those men still would have headed north to tie up loose ends? I would have been all alone, unsuspecting and unguarded. Maybe fate intended this to happen all along.'

'You don't believe in fate.'

'But you do.' Or at least he had claimed to when he had been tasked with seducing her. Her hand dropped back to her side and she felt betrayed all over again. 'When it suits you. It's impossible to separate the pretty lies from the facts.'

She heard him exhale slowly. 'You seem to always have my measure, Fliss, and that terrifies me because I'm stripped bare before you. You've always seen through the charm and the bravado, but actually I do believe in fate. That is a fact. I believe that sometimes we have no control over things even when we try with all our might to direct them. The honest truth is I'm painfully aware of my own failings. I always have been. My brothers are right. I've spent my entire life avoiding emotional entanglements and responsibility.

'Growing up, I watched it destroy my parents. They both loathed and loved each other to the exclusion of all else. My father couldn't handle responsibility either and sought his solace at the bottom of a bottle for all the mistakes he made. My mother lived in the past and resented the life he had dragged her into. They were always arguing, often violently, and that constant battleground slowly killed both of them.

'My mother committed suicide. Or at least that's what the world believes. In reality, she was always threatening to harm herself in order to get my father's attention and it always worked. She would cry and he'd come running, then the pair of them would fight and then lose themselves in passion, then the toxic vicious circle would begin all over again.

'As a child I found it exhausting and terrifying, and I have no doubt those early impressions have stuck with me as I've grown. On that day, as she had on so many others before, my mother told me she was going to throw herself in the river and sent me to fetch him, but because I wasn't keen on facing my father's wrath I dawdled,and because of that she died.

'I'm not asking for your pity. I know I don't deserve it. My brothers tell me it was her choice to do what she did. That she was a selfish woman who never cared for any of us, me least of all because I was so much like my father. Another pretty liar with little else of substance behind him. But even so, that event has left deep scars. That dreadful day, their relationship, it left its mark on me and shaped the man I became.

'I never wanted to live with all that angst and drama ever again. It's too painful. Too destructive. I like life to be simple and uncomplicated. I'm not good with guilt or anger or introspection and I certainly never wanted to become my father, although I also know, deep down, that I do not possess any of his worst traits. I would never be intentionally cruel and I'm not violent or unable to discern right from wrong. But I am selfish. I've selfishly protected my heart. I've lived my life ensuring that none of that messy emotional nonsense ever touched me. Aside from my brothers, I've kept everyone else at arm's length. Purposefully so. But then I met you and all those necessary defences dissolved and that terrifies me.

'I didn't want to get involved, yet I did regardless. I didn't want to show you my true colours, but you saw them anyway and the very last thing I ever wanted to do was fall in love, because I knew I couldn't bear the heartbreak if it went wrong and I was right. I'm dying inside, Fliss, because I love you so much and you quite rightly hate me. But know that, despite you loathing me, I will fight till my dying breath to keep you safe. If you cannot bring yourself to trust me with anything else, please trust me to do that, Fliss. I can't face living in a world that you are not in.'

Fliss wanted to believe him. Desperately. But with a solid oak door between them she couldn't see if he was telling the truth. She pulled open the door and sought his eyes. They were blue. So blue they were almost black. His tell-tale pupils were large and awash with tears as she stared into them. One solitary drop fell off his lashes and slowly ran down his cheek. She saw his pain because it mirrored hers exactly. His misery was real and visceral. But alongside that raw, undisguised emotion swirling in his irises Fliss also saw something else. Something as irrefutable as it was unexpected. Something her heart yearned for and which her sensible head couldn't overrule.

Something she'd wanted all her life. Waited for. Would never settle for anything less than. This man—this loyal, incorrigible, flawed man—absolutely adored her. Those beautiful blue eyes of his couldn't lie to her.

It was her feet that closed the short distance between them. Her hands that reached out to cup his face. Her lips which brushed his first. But it was both of them who lost themselves in the honest beauty of the moment before burning, biological need took over.

The second her mouth had touched his, Jake was on fire. His wary heart was bursting with joy that she wanted him and might well have forgiven him; his battered body yearned to join with her. That first kiss had ignited it all—love, desire, longing—and that first kiss was yet to end. What had started gently had simmered as they didn't break apart. Together they had stumbled back into her bedchamber, failing to pause when Jake had kicked the door closed, and tumbled breathless on to the bed. He had shrugged out of his jacket, then set about pulling all the pins from her hair while she clumsily undid the buttons on his waistcoat, before tugging the tail of his shirt roughly from his breeches.

Now, with all her hair gloriously loose he rolled her on top of him so he could fumble with the laces at the back of her dress. As the fabric loosened he smoothed it off her shoulders with his palms, revelling in the warm, silky texture of the skin of her bare arms. He wanted to look at what he was touching, but that meant prising his hungry lips from hers and like a starving man at a banquet he couldn't. So he let his hands see instead, running them greedily down her ribcage, then back up again to cup her breasts while Fliss reached behind and attempted to undo the ribbons of her corset.

She giggled into his mouth and collapsed against him, her breasts squashed wonderfully in his hands. 'It's knotted. Take it off.' An invitation he didn't need to hear twice.

Jake shuffled into a sitting position and tackled the mess, but she was right, the ribbons were hopelessly tangled and his hands lacked the finesse or the patience to solve the puzzle. In desperation he groped for the knife in his boot and in one swift motion sliced through the ribbons to the delight of them both and tossed the offending garment to the floor.

Knelt on the bed in just her chemise, golden hair tousled and smiling, she was a picture. Her gaze never left his fingers as he reached out one hand and slowly tugged the bow on the low bodice. He teased them both by gently tugging the fabric lower, enjoying the way it resisted and strained across her nipples. He let his thumb slip beneath the lace to graze one and had the satisfaction of hearing her sigh at the brief touch. Another tug and the flimsy fabric pooled at her waist and he drank in the sight of her bared before him. Every inch of her was perfect, as he had known she would be. Flawless peachy skin, saucily jutting breasts tipped with dusky pink tips, undulating curves which nipped in at the waist and flared out at the hips. All better than his wildest imaginings or his fevered dreams.

Reverently he bent his head to kiss her again, gentler this time because she deserved better than the rushed and hasty loving he had so far subjected her to. He trailed soft kisses down her throat and over the swells of her breasts, pausing long enough to worship each nipple. The throaty, staccato moans told him she thoroughly enjoyed that, so he lingered longer until those lovely breasts were rising and falling rapidly in time to her erratic breathing. As he nibbled the underside of one he let his fingers wander lower until they rested in the golden curls at the apex of her thighs. She stilled as they wandered lower, but she allowed him to nudge her legs open and gave a lovely whimper of pleasure as he caressed her, but when Jake sat back to look she clamped them shut again and hastily covered them with her chemise. 'What are you doing?'

The prim, missish reaction amused him after her obvious enjoyment thus far. 'I'm fundamentally a nosy fellow, as you know, and I need to see you, Fliss. All of you.'

'Why do you get to see all of me before I get to see all of you?'

'Because you are so beautiful I fear I won't be able to control myself if we are both naked just yet and I want to see to your pleasure first. Try to trust me, my love. It'll be worth it. I promise.'

He sensed her trepidation as she forced herself to relax, a rosy blush of embarrassment pinkening her cheeks and her neck as she allowed him to slide away the last bit of clothing, but the trust in her eyes humbled him and exulted him at the same time. This time when he caressed her, she was tense, but he soon eased that away and she let her legs fall wantonly open as her breathing became more laboured and her hands gripped the sheet beneath her.

Jake knew exactly how to ease her frustration. He also knew enough about the female body to know that the more he built the anticipation, the sweeter her release would be. When he sensed she was close, he lazily smoothed his hand back up her body and went right back to kissing her. As he'd hoped, it was not enough. Her hips bucked and she arched beneath him, but he wouldn't be swayed. His talented mouth and hands remained resolutely above her waist until she was writhing beneath him.

It was Fliss who lost patience first, shamelessly sliding her hands under his shirt and raking her nails over his chest and back, making earthy noises which almost sent him over the edge. 'I want you naked, Jake.' Her green eyes were stormy with desire and her mouth was swollen from his kisses. Jake had never seen anything so erotic in his life. Impatiently he sat up and tugged off his shirt and he had to watch her lounging gloriously naked while his suddenly urgent and clumsy fingers dispensed with his boots and the buttons on his falls, but at her insistence he let her remove his breeches and she tortured him by duplicating the slow, sensuous disrobing he had subjected her to. Except this time, the fabric resisted and strained over his insistent, needy bulge. A bulge she was thoroughly exploring over the blasted fabric with the flat palm of her hand.

She grinned when Jake growled, drawing out the moment before slipping her hand inside and touching him properly. The inquisitive first explorations soon turned bold as she watched how she affected him. It was ecstasy. It was agony. But he endured it stoically by biting down on his lip and clenching his fists as she exposed him inch by inch.

'Is this your revenge?'

'I think you deserve a little punishment.'

'Haven't I suffered enough?'

Fliss pushed the fabric to the floor, her eyes fixed on the impressive sight of him in all his glory, and flicked him a wicked, passion-charged gaze. 'Oh, I think you need to suffer some more.' She had no real idea what she was doing and let her instincts guide her. Jake's magnificent body was an enigma which she burned to explore. Fortunately, that exploration was proving to be scandalously exciting for both of them. Brazenly she let her hands wander where they wanted—the broad expanse of his shoulders, the taut stomach, strong back, the delightfully compact and rounded bottom. Then her mouth, teeth and tongue followed and she learned that his hard, muscled body was as sensitive as her soft one. He shivered when her tongue traced his nipple and followed the dark dusting of hair as it arrowed down his abdomen. In fascination she traced the length and girth of his hardness, smiling as his jaw tightened or when he occasionally hissed out a strangled breath.

Every moan and sigh was accompanied by his heated gaze; deep blue eyes bright with mischief and love. To begin with Jake lay there passive, but soon he paid her back in kind. Every touch of hers which tormented him was parried with a more thrilling intimacy from him, shocking yet unbearably pleasurable intrusions that made her grateful he had been a rake, yet none giving her the elusive fulfilment her newly awakened body seemed to crave.

Only when she was positively vibrating with need and he was breathing heavily did he position himself on top of her, staring straight into her eyes. His hardness cradled against her body. Her body wanting it inside her. That want, the significance of what they were about to do, made her suddenly nervous. She was the novice. He knew what he was doing. What if she didn't compare with the women before or meet his expectations?

'You're my first lover, Jake. Be patient with me.'

He brushed his nose against hers tenderly. 'And you'll be my last lover. That is just as significant. In fact, I fear it's you who needs to be patient with me.' Her mocking smile was met with pure seriousness. Jake laced his fingers with hers and brought her hand to rest snugly between them on his chest, holding it firmly in place. 'Do you feel that?' Beneath her palm his heart drummed steadily.

'I can feel your heart…'

'No, love, it's not my heart any more. It's yours. It always will be. Please be gentle with it because it bruises easily. And be patient with me, Fliss. Falling in love is the most terrifying thing I've ever done. I'm ill prepared for the adventure. So ill prepared I'm bound to make mistakes. I don't want tonight to be one of them. I've shared my body more often than I should have. I can't change that, but I've never *made love* to a woman before, nor wanted to. Making love involves the heart and the body, and up until recently my poor heart was happily encased in cotton wool and robustly barricaded from the world. But as much as it scares me, as much as I fear all those messy and complicated emotions and responsibilities which walk alongside love, I know everything will be all right as long as you are beside me, too. This will be my first time and I don't want to make a hash of it.'

He kissed her softly and that part of him nudged at her entrance, while he nuzzled her neck. 'This is a huge responsibility. I need to show you how much I love you. How much I will always love you.' He gently eased inside, pausing to allow her to adjust to the intrusion. 'I need to make tonight truly special for you. I need to make sure you never look at another man some time in the future and wonder what if?' His expression became fierce and Fliss could feel the tension in his whole body as he held himself in check. There was a look of intense concentration on his handsome face as he came up against the barrier of her maidenhead. 'I don't want to hurt you, but know that I must to make you mine.' She sucked in a breath as he pushed passed it quickly and stilled as he kissed away the pain—only then did he fill her completely. 'I need you to believe that you are the one. My one and only. For always and for ever.'

As he began to move, the alien feeling of this new intimacy began to fade, replaced instead by a sense of complete rightness. Biology and fate. Two unpredictable factors which had made their love inevitable. She loved him so much, wanted him so much, it consumed her. Fliss happily succumbed to the building desire only Jake kindled. Each stroke reverberated down her nerve endings, heating them, heating her and her wary heart. Every kiss fanned the flames. Every touch set her ablaze. With building need, she matched him thrust for thrust, revelling in the solid weight of him around her, shamelessly touching every part of him she could reach with her hands and clenching her internal muscles around the wonderful part of him she couldn't. All the while their eyes were locked. Now words were unnecessary because there were no words to convey how immersed in each other they were. Two bodies in perfect unison; two hearts beating in time with the other.

As the passion built, Fliss surrendered herself to every new sensation whole-heartedly, glorying in the effect their lovemaking was having on him, too. His eyes were so dark. His body so ardent. She had never felt so beautiful or alive. Special. So utterly adored and cherished. She remembered murmuring his name. Telling him she loved him, then the universe exploded in shimmering blue light as bright as his eyes and they dived into the sublime abyss together.

Chapter Nineteen

In the garden at Markham Manor

It had been a peculiar week. Idyllic, yet trying. A time of latent fear and of pure joy, noisy family camaraderie, quiet introspection and passionate intimacy. Jake was a creative and resourceful lover who had initiated her completely into the pleasures of the flesh. During the day, just as he had less than an hour ago, he found ways for them to steal a few minutes of privacy and utilised those scant minutes so fully and thoroughly her body tingled from the experience.

One minute she had been walking purposefully towards the Great Hall the Warriners used as a drawing room and the next she had been outrageously braced against the door inside the linen closet, her skirts around her waist, but her spectacles resolutely on her nose, because that was where Jake liked them when the mood struck, while he had his wicked way with her. Not that Fliss minded one bit. All those naughty wayward tendencies which she had always struggled to suppress happily came to the fore with him and she always rejoiced in the frantic, breathless waylaying.

Late at night, when the house slept, the dynamic between them shifted. He would creep to her room and make slow, tender love to her and then she would drift off to sleep, feeling safe in his arms. In between times, they spent a great deal of time in one another's company, often with the others, but the Warriners and her incorrigible aunts were at great pains to leave them alone together frequently. It seemed everyone was equally keen to see them paired off, actively encouraging their deepening romance, and neither Jake nor Fliss made any attempt to slow things down. There was an inevitability to it all. Serendipity. As if they were destined to be together, so why bother fighting the mysterious forces which pulled them together?

Here, in his home, Fliss felt she was coming to truly know the real Jake. Of course he was charming, that characteristic was etched into his bones, and he shamelessly flirted with each of his brothers' wives and all of the female servants in his good-natured way, but she saw it for what it was and was not the least bit perturbed by it. She owned his heart. Lock, stock and barrel. His eyes told her so every single second they spent together.

But she also saw the other facets of his character which he hid behind his silver tongue. The enviable and unbreakable bond he had with his three brothers and their respective wives. The thoughtful man who took care to spend equal time with all his nieces and nephews in case he appeared to have a favourite. He really was a man who listened and paid attention, and not just to Fliss. He followed every thread of conversation around the dinner table, remembered the tiny idiosyncrasies and details about people, whether that be Letty's latest embroidery project or the current state of little Jonathan's butterfly collection, and while he remembered all this, as well as the names of all of the servants' children as he frequently asked about them, he still tirelessly patrolled the grounds with Leatham and the Invisibles and kept a close eye on her security at all times. That attention to detail was beyond reassuring at a time when her nerves were often strung as taut as a bow.

It helped that Markham Manor was indeed a fortress as he had promised. Three-quarters of the sprawling parkland was surrounded by an enormous stone wall which appeared strong enough to withstand the force of a battering ram. Beyond it, several dense miles of Sherwood Forest cloaked the perimeter. Only one long lane led to the tall, forbidding locked gates. The remaining quarter used nature for protection. The River Idle provided the house with a wide barrier between them and the outside world, and in the dead of winter after all the rain the underlying current was apparently ferocious. The small but deadly battalion of the King's Elite closely monitored the vulnerable areas along the river bank, as well as the wall. While the sight of men wielding pistols constantly gave Fliss the shivers, she was supremely grateful they were there. Their presence allowed her to function relatively normally, or as normally as a displaced schoolmistress from a convent could be in the crammed house of her lover, waiting for evil to strike.

Jake was adamant she would remain here until he was satisfied the danger had passed. Danger he was convinced still might be lurking despite the express they had received two days ago from Flint and Lord Fennimore, informing them that Sister Ursuline's had been attacked by a gang of men and, instead of them finding Fliss as they had anticipated, they walked into a deadly ambush of Excise Men. Of the twenty-six assassins sent to kill her, all but two were now quite thoroughly dead. Lord Fennimore was confident the danger was now passed and they had got their man in the skirmish. Any one of those men could have been the Londoner, but as only Fliss had ever seen him and there was nearly two hundred miles between her and those dead faces, Jake was not taking any chances. His efforts now concentrated on the two. Just in case, although how long his Majesty's government would continue to support her protection was still a mystery. As each new day passed uneventfully, it appeared less and less likely anyone was going to come for her—which in turn meant they were wasting valuable resources which were desperately needed elsewhere. Jake suspected that when Flint and Lord Fennimore arrived back from the north to meet them, then the rest of the King's Elite would leave with them.

She was trying not to think about that.

'Serena cheated!'

'I did not. You're just a sore loser!'

Fliss looked up from the book she wasn't reading at the sound of the two oldest Warriner children bickering again. The enforced proximity and near constant rainfall of the last couple of days had meant the poor dears had been cooped up in Markham Manor and were bored stiff. In desperation, Cassie and Letty had organised a lawn bowls tournament to be played on the carpet. Letty's three boys formed one team, the eldest three of Cassie's girls the other. At the time it had seemed like a brilliant idea; within ten minutes it had descended into more arguing.

'Your cousin didn't cheat, Jonathan. She knocked your ball away fair and square. Play nice.' Fliss recognised the exasperated tone of her hostess and felt guilty for being the cause of it. Every Warriner's life had been disrupted because of her, but they were all being so nice and stoic about it as they fussed over her. It didn't sit right. 'It's your brother's turn.'

'We're still losing.' Jonathan said this to his youngest sibling with all the seriousness of an unimpressed seven-year-old and he clearly blamed him as the cause. 'Please try harder.'

Little James's tongue poked out in concentration, but his childish attempt rolled well shy of the jack, causing more eye rolls from his big brother. When Cassie's four-year-old stepped forward to take her turn, Aunt Daphne came behind her to help. 'Now remember what I told you, young lady, a nice smooth arm motion with a bit of oomph.'

The child eyed the jack with determination and threw it with all her might. It whizzed through the air and crashed into Jonathan's remaining bowl, sending it careening towards the wall as hers gently rolled to kiss the jack.

'I call foul!' Poor Jonathan was outraged. 'She was meant to roll the bowl, not throw it! Throwing is cheating. Isn't it? *Isn't it!*' Six angry children's voices jostled to be heard, while the two eldest cousins squared up to one another. Before outright war broke out, Fliss jumped up to intervene.

'Jonathan. Serena. Why don't we take a walk in the garden seeing as the rain has stopped?' As the two main protagonists, their swift removal and distraction would help to calm the situation. 'You can show me around as I have not seen barely any of it yet.'

Both children nodded, but their mothers both

frowned. 'I'm not sure you should go outside, Fliss.'

'Every inch of the estate is guarded, Letty. What harm can it do? And these poor dears could do with some time outside to expel some of their pent-up energy.'

'Can I bring my ball, Auntie Fliss?' Little Jonathan, like the rest of the Warriner children, had already adopted her as one of the family. 'We could play catch.'

'I love catch,' Serena added with a wistful look. 'And can we show Auntie Fliss the stables? Would you like to meet Orange Blossom and Satan?' Pleading fingers tugged at Fliss's skirts.

'I suppose it wouldn't hurt to take them some carrots.' The frazzled Cassie had relented. 'The little ones do need a nap.'

Bella made the final decision. 'The men are all out there with Jake. I shall instruct Chivers to let them know we are taking some air. I for one could definitely use some.' She stood up and grinned, patting the tiny, growing bump lovingly. 'So could this little Warriner.'

In less than five minutes, they were all in heavy, warm winter coats and walking across the lawn. Daphne and Cressida had also jumped at the chance to leave the confines of the house along with Bella. All three happily watched the two children toss the leather ball back and forth, laughing and giggling now that the ill feeling between them was now forgotten.

The crisp February air felt marvellous, as did the freedom. They set a brisk pace towards the stables, loitered a while to pet the horses, then took a circuitous route around the parkland, allowing Jonathan and Serena to guide them around places of interest. Typically, this meant visiting the very best part of the estate to play in: the wide-open meadow flanked by clumps of weeping willows. Bizarrely, watching those dark-haired cherubs running amok and climbing over everything reminded Fliss that life was much better when it was not shrouded in fear.

Every few minutes they passed one of Leatham's Invisibles, who emerged from their hiding places to offer them a reassuring smile and a wave as they continued on their way, reassuring her that this place *was* safe. It was a fortress filled with loyal brave knights and she was the princess they protected. It went a long way to lightening her mood until the laughing children made her forget the danger entirely and Fliss felt properly light again for the first time in weeks as she forced herself to believe the danger really might be past. Each day of peace surely proved it?

'I need to sit,' said Daphne without preamble as she placed her bottom on a log. 'All this walking is making me thirsty.'

'Now that you come to mention it, I am a bit parched.' Cressida sat beside her and produced a hip flask from her pocket. 'Fortunately, I filled this with some lemonade earlier.'

Lemonade which had doubtless been doctored with something from one of their host's crystal decanters. Fliss glanced at Bella and they shared a smile. The two old dears were incorrigible, but in a delightful way, and the way they embraced life and took everything thrown at them so completely in their stride was an inspiration. To look at them, nobody would know they had recently fled Mayfair for their lives or that the dark cloud of death still loomed on the horizon.

'Who wants to play catch?'

'Auntie Fliss, you can be in my team and Aunt Bella can be on Serena's.' Jonathan marched them to a spot of flat grass close to the trees and organised them to stand in a small square. 'Each time the ball is dropped equals a point for the opposing team.' When nobody dropped in several rounds, he declared the square too small and ordered everyone to take several paces back. Soon that became the game. As the ball hit the grass, the winning team crowed and everyone took another step backwards until poor Serena with her tiny arms could barely bridge the distance. Being plucky and stubborn, she used all her might to hurl it at Fliss, but misjudged it and sent it several feet to the left. The little leather ball bounced hard on the ground, then began to roll downhill towards the clump of trees behind them.

'Oh, Serena.' Jonathan shook his head and began to chase the ball, only to be swiftly halted by Bella.

'No further than the trees, young man. You know you are not allowed near the river in winter.'

Fliss hadn't realised they were that close. She certainly couldn't hear it, but visions of Letty's son tripping over and floundering in the cold water suddenly made her nervous, or perhaps her constant state of nervousness made her imagination more vivid with nasty possibilities? Either way, Fliss was the only adult present neither aged nor pregnant entrusted with keeping him out of harm—Fliss and the two burly men posted at either end of their stretch of river—so retrieving the lost ball and restoring family harmony was her responsibility.

She spied it instantly, a little brown sphere poking out of some long grass near the waterfall of branches, and bent to retrieve it. As she stood, she saw it.

At first it appeared to be a log protruding from the overhanging branches of the largest willow less than five yards away, but as she turned the shadows changed. That log seemed to be wearing boots. Curious, she edged closer, then stopped dead in her tracks. One boot became two; they were attached to a man lying face down. Stood proud between his shoulder blades was the hilt of a knife.

Blind panic had her calling out a warning to the others, screaming at the top of her lungs to Bella and the children to run before she started up the steep incline herself.

'Oh, no, you don't.'

The voice behind Fliss chilled her blood a split second before an arm wrapped itself around her throat like a vice and dragged her choking back towards the trees. She fought and clawed, but the Londoner had strength, surprise and gravity on his side. The heels of her borrowed walking boots slipped on the wet grass, denying her any traction as he pulled her through the branches of the willow. The pressure on her windpipe was starving her of air, making her light-headed.

One meaty hand wove its way into her hair and shoved her down to her knees. 'Well, isn't this fortuitous? Miss Blunt, I presume? How lovely to finally make your acquaintance. You've caused me a bit of bother.'

Chapter Twenty

Under the ancient weeping willow

Denied the sight of his face as he growled close to her ear, Fliss's eyes darted around, searching for an escape route. They were shielded from the world by the ancient willow's cascade of branches. The sounds of the river were amplified in this cocoon, cold mist settling on her face suggesting it was close by. Another corpse lay on the soft mud within, his throat cut. She recognised him as one of the Invisibles and whimpered. He was dead because of her. Probably the other man, too. So many innocent people were now in extreme danger. Jake. His brothers. Their young families.

He forced her head back cruelly, making her look into his manic eyes. 'Were you the one spying on me?'

'I wasn't s-spying.'

'Liar.' The back of his hand slammed hard across her face. 'You took a hackney to the Albany while I was in your uncle's house. I know Jacob Warriner works for the Excise Men. I know they brought you here to hide and I know they set a trap for my men!' His hand whipped across her cheek again, so hard her head snapped back and spun. He violently shook her out of the blackness. 'Was *he* with you that night? Has he seen my face?'

'No!' At least he referred to Jake in the present tense. Fliss forced herself to take some comfort in that.

'Who else has seen me?'

'N-nobody. Just me.' If she couldn't save herself, perhaps she could spare the others the fate of those poor men. 'I heard you telling my uncle you wanted my aunts murdered, too, so I dragged them with me. They know nothing. Only me. I'm the only one who has seen you.' Pride made her look him in the eye. Pure hatred made her brave. 'I'm your loose end.'

'Then come with me, my lovely, and you can tell that to the Boss. Let's hope he believes you, for both our sakes. He don't like loose ends.'

He was so strong, easily dragging her like a dead weight to the water's edge.

'You can get in the boat willingly or I'll drown you and deliver your body to the Boss. Your choice.' She hesitated and he smiled callously. 'I've got what I've come for. The quicker you move, the less chance there is of me killing someone else. Those wee ones or your fancy man, perhaps...'

Thinking fast, Fliss staggered to her feet and stepped into the small tethered rowing boat. Drowning right this minute served no purpose because Jake was coming. She knew that with the same certainty that she knew this monster before her was pure evil. At some point he would have to leave the sanctuary of this willow and sail in open water where he would be vulnerable. Every man in the King's Elite had a pistol. Any one of them could take a decisive shot.

Before he pushed the boat off the muddy bank, the Londoner bound her hands roughly in her lap, the coarse rope so tight it made her fingers throb. Then he used the oars to dislodge the boat, his brawny arms holding one steady in the water to act as a rudder in the current. As they emerged from the branches, that underwater current proved to be too strong, sending the bouncing rowing boat drifting back towards the open meadow rather than in the direction her captor wanted it to go. His arms frantically dragged the oars, but the two opposing forces merely twisted them on the same spot. He'd misjudged things and was panicking. Fliss could see it in the wild darting of his eyes and the hard, determined set of his jaw.

As subtly as she could, she leaned towards the direction of the current to make his job harder and searched the horizon for help. While she was relieved to see no sign of Bella, the children or her aunts, the lack of anyone coming to her rescue was worrying. But the longer they sat here, completely exposed and floundering, the better. Jake would come and with him would come more men and guns. That certainty was like a soothing balm to her soul and gave her the calm she needed to think pragmatically.

The hard thud of a boot on her leg brought her sharply back to the moment. 'Sit up straight!'

Fliss complied roughly, purposely causing the boat to rock and freezing water to slosh in, soaking her feet. The more delays she created, the more chances she afforded Jake and his men. The Londoner's response was to kick her again, which only made the violent rocking worse, and the boat listed and twisted, forcing him to use both oars and all his strength to calm it.

'They are going to kill you. You know that, don't you?' Her voice was sure and prim. Her Miss Blunt schoolmistress tone. Defiant. His eyes briefly narrowed.

'Not before I kill you first.'

Jake and Leatham had crept along the cover of the willows. The rest of the men were either on their way or already in position under cover. They weren't called the Invisibles for nothing. Somewhere, too, were his brothers, because Warriners always stuck together. Knowing that gave him some comfort, but did little to ease the clawing panic which consumed him. The sight of two good men murdered hadn't helped.

'*Not before I kill you first.*'

Both of them stilled at the gravelly sound of the Londoner and Seb silently gestured beyond the branches to pinpoint exactly where the voice had come from. Then he mouthed the word *Fobbing.* Jake understood instantly. He would confront the scoundrel, keep him occupied while his friend crept around and took the shot.

Taking a deep breath, Jake emerged from the curtain of the willow fronds, his pistol aimed. When he saw her, spinning in the river, bound and pale, his heart stopped and his arm wavered. The irony of the situation was not lost on him. Nor was the symbolism. Why did it have to be here? The exact same place…

He wouldn't fail this time.

'Put your hands in the air!'

Fliss turned then and her frightened eyes locked with his in the same moment her captor placed the point of his pistol against her neck. 'Go ahead, Mr Warriner. Shoot me. I'll blow her pretty brains out before your bullet leaves the chamber.'

Jake didn't dare risk flicking a gaze left or right. Fliss's life depended on him trusting Leatham to do the job. 'And then you will also die. You're surrounded. All my men are armed. If you surrender yourself we will provide you protection from the Boss.' The man wouldn't live to step on the shore if Jake had anything to do with it, but now, the official lines might buy them some time if the bastard thought he could save his own sorry skin. 'Testify against him and I guarantee you won't hang.'

The chilling laughter echoed in the silence. 'I'd

rather hang then spend the rest of my short life looking over my shoulder. I'm already a dead man walking. The Boss doesn't take well to failure.' He jabbed the pistol harder under Fliss's jaw. 'But you don't want *her* dead, do you, Warriner? So you'd best let us go.' His other hand groped for the oar and with Fliss clamped against him as a human shield, attempted to row away.

The tiny boat pitched again, and spun, then seemed to wedge itself against some underwater debris. The position was a bad one, denying Jake or Leatham a clean shot that wouldn't hit her as well.

Checkmate.

Jake stood rooted to the spot, his pistol raised in readiness none the less. 'Let. Her. Go.' The second he had a clear line of sight that monster would die.

'Urgh!'

The shout from the willow branches as Leatham launched himself out, pistol waving like an ancient warrior, made the Londoner start. The smuggler's gun hand shifted.

Aimed.

Fired.

The bullet ripped through Jake's friend's body, throwing him backwards in a hideous spray of blood. Jake watched in horror as the Londoner briefly let go of Fliss to reach for another weapon. Like a dream, he saw her lurch to her feet in the boat. Watched her eyes widen and lock with his before they softened. Watched them harden to emeralds as she threw herself over the side and was instantly swept away in the current.

His guttural cry and the explosion from his pistol sliced through the air. Jake didn't care whether he'd hit his target. All he cared about was the woman in the water. Oblivious to everything else he charged in after her, first running, then swimming towards the tangled green skirts which floated on the surface like river weed.

As he got closer, he saw her bound hands had grabbed the willow fronds, but the current was winning. It was greedily flowing around her, each new surge ebbing higher and higher as she struggled to stay afloat. For one heart-stopping moment, her face disappeared under the surface, only to emerge again a few seconds later spluttering as she fought to stay afloat.

Jake battled to swim alongside, wrapping one arm tightly around her as he, too, grabbed the ancient willow, but her woollen winter skirts were like an anchor, sucking her down until he could barely hold her face free of the river. She gasped for air and swallowed a mouthful of river instead, her eyes staring helplessly up at him from beneath the icy tomb. Terrified. She didn't want to die.

Yet he was losing her. He wasn't strong enough. She had trusted him to save her and he was failing, just as he always failed when people stupidly depended on him. He stared back at where his fingers gripped the branch. The irony wasn't lost on him. Fate's last cruel joke at his expense. He should just let go and let the angry river take them both. Selfishly he didn't want to live without her. Knew he wasn't strong enough to carry that burden. Knew his heart only beat for her.

'We've got you!' His eldest brother Jack's voice boomed through the despair. He was waist deep in the water, his other hand locked tightly in Joe's. Behind him was Jamie. Strong as an ox and braced round the same gnarled branch Jake had scrambled along all those years ago.

His brother grabbed his collar and pulled, freeing Jake to finally let go of the willow. He wrapped both his arms tightly around Fliss and kicked for all he was worth, until his feet scraped along the river bank and his lungs burned from the exertion. Together they dragged her to safety.

Except she wasn't safe.

She lay on the ground like a wet rag. Pale. Frozen. Deathly still. Jake stood back to allow Joe to do what he was trained to do, knowing in his unworthy heart it was futile.

'She's not breathing, is she?'

'There's water in her lungs.' His brother's face was grave. Joe turned Fliss's head and river water spewed out of her slack mouth. Then he turned her head upright again and pushed on her chest. When the trickling stopped he bent and began to blow deeply into her mouth while Jake stood powerless and broken, the pain in his own chest so severe he wished he had let go of the branch so that he didn't have to face the future without her. Knowing he'd failed her when she had needed him the most.

His eldest brother's arms went around his shoulder. He didn't offer platitudes or false hope, simply his strength, and as he had all those years before Jake leaned on him and wondered how the hell he was supposed to cope with this. His heart was bleeding. His life now meaningless. Tight bands of pain corded around his body and he wished they'd strangle the life out of him and get it over with.

'This is all my fault.'

'No, it isn't. You did all you could.'

Which was never enough. It was all so hideously familiar. Damn fate and its twisted games! Damn it all to—

Her violent coughing and spluttering was the most beautiful sound Jake had ever heard and he dropped to his knees and wept. He didn't care who saw it or what they thought, he just scrambled towards her and gathered her close while she caught her breath, smoothing her wet hair from her chilled face and telling her how much he loved her.

Close by, Bella and Jamie were bent over Leatham, then Joe joined them, too. All Jake could do was pray for his friend because he couldn't let Fliss go. From somewhere, a dry greatcoat was placed around his shoulders and he used it swaddle her in. After several long minutes, her arms wrapped around his neck. 'Oh, Jake…' Her voice was so weak, hoarse from her ordeal, but hearing it healed his broken heart instantly. They still had today and tomorrow and for ever.

'I thought I'd lost you.' She was going to be the death of him and the light of his life. A life he now couldn't wait to get started on. A new life with a wife and a home. Children perhaps. Love. Laughter. Light. 'What were you thinking, woman? Throwing yourself overboard...'

Her finger pressed against his lips softly, silencing him and she smiled. 'You do have an uncanny knack of being in exactly the right place at exactly the right time, Jacob Warriner. I trusted you implicitly to save me.' One frozen finger brushed a tear from his cheek. 'I knew you wouldn't disappoint me.'

Epilogue

Markham Manor—February 1830

'Jake. It's time.'

Although he'd been on tenterhooks waiting for those words for three long weeks, they still caught him by surprise. He quickly rolled to sit, but fell out of the bed instead.

'Right! Right! Don't panic!'

'I'm not panicking, darling. You are.' She was shaking her head and smiling at him as he stuffed his legs into his boots. Then laughed as he stalked to the door. 'Clothes, Jacob?'

He looked down at his body. Nude except for the Hessians he had jammed on the wrong feet, he smiled, too. 'You'd think I'd be more prepared fourth time around, wouldn't you?'

He tried to be calm as he dressed, tried to ignore the way her pretty face contorted with each contraction and kissed her softly as he went to raise the troops. Each of their three children had been born in Markham Manor. It had become a tradition and they had travelled up from Mayfair a month ago to be with his family for the birth.

Flint was holding the fort in his stead at the King's Elite. Lord Fennimore had made Jake his successor when he had finally retired last year. In Jake's opinion, it should have been Leatham's job. His brave, selfless friend had always been the better spy. But Seb had been lured away by the Prime Minster himself and was helping to create an entire police force for London, so Jake now found himself with the responsibility of the ever-expanding secret service they had created together. To his greater surprise, he rather enjoyed it.

He paused briefly outside his brother's door, wondering if he should wake them at this ungodly hour, then realised Jack would have his guts for garters if he didn't. Jack had quite exacting standards and took his responsibilities very seriously. Those same morals now made him a well-respected magistrate. A man who judged men solely by their deeds rather than their reputations and understood what it meant to be poor.

He tapped lightly. 'Jack, Letty. It's time.'

A few seconds later his brother's dark head appeared, grey now just at the temples but still fiercely handsome. 'Have you sent for the others?'

'Footmen are winging their way to their houses as we speak.' Houses which all stood within the walls of the estate. 'They won't be long.' They never were.

Several hours later and three of them were pacing the floor of the Great Hall, while Joe was irritatingly calm and watching them with amusement as he polished his spectacles. Spectacles his scholarly eyes now needed all the time.

'I thought you said that this labour would be quick!' Snapping at him made Jake feel less helpless. He'd been banished from the birthing room by a very stern Bella some time around dawn, instructed in no uncertain terms to *leave this to the ladies* because he was getting in the way and all his pacing and hand wringing was stressing his poor wife. When the wives all ganged up together, there was no arguing with them.

'It's only been three hours.'

'It feels like three weeks! Why don't you go and write a paper or something!' While his practice was still loyally based in Retford, Joe was now one of the leading lights in the Royal College of Physicians and his words of wisdom were relentlessly hung on by medical students the length and breadth of the land. His calm brother merely grinned in response.

The distant newborn cry had Jake breaking into a run, but he was met at the door by Cassie and Letty. The two sentries took their guard duty very seriously. Their folded arms and firmly planted bodies wouldn't let him pass. 'You can't come in until Bella says so.'

'The hell I can't!'

'Oh, let the poor thing in.' Fliss's voice, strong and healthy, filled him with relief. The door opened and Jake practically floated in, mesmerised by the sight of the fuzzy dark-haired bundle in his exhausted wife's arms. She held out the baby and he took it. Cradling it close. Behind him he felt his brothers, all peering over his shoulder to see the latest addition to the growing Warriner brood. The baby's eyes opened and stared blurrily at him. Deep blue, not the usual blue of a newborn—Warriner blue.

'I told you so.' Joe grinned and held out his

hand and Jack huffed before smacking a pound note into it.

'One of these days, one of us *has* to produce a child with their mother's colouring!' But alas, now all seventeen of their combined children were Wild Warriners through and through, thankfully the only thing they had inherited from their troublesome ancestors.

'Never mind the colouring. What is it?' Jamie limped forward, leaning on the incongruous floral cane his talented third daughter Thea had painted for him. Like Jack, he was greying slightly too, and just like Jack it only improved his appearance. He and Cassie still created magical children's books and remained perfectly content to spend every minute of every day in each other's company.

'A girl.'

'Two from two, then. Pay up.' Joe held out his hand again for Jamie to slap another pound in it, then flapped his winnings in the air. 'Never argue with science, boys. A girl was inevitable.'

Jake had no words. They all smiled as he staggered to sit still, cradling the precious bundle. Already, he loved his daughter unconditionally, just as he did the other three. But really! Fate seemed determined to give him an apoplexy with yet another cruel joke at his expense.

'I am the father of *four* daughters.' He was doomed.

Jamie grinned and patted him on the back. 'And I'm the father of five. Between us we have ensured that the little girls now outnumber the little boys.' Jack and Joe had four sons each. All carbon copies of their fathers. Competition between the two sexes was fierce as each child was stubbornly competitive—just like their sires. 'I'm rather glad I lost that pound now. We have the bigger team.'

But Jamie didn't understand. He'd never been a rake like Jake and still slept the blissful, restful sleep of the ignorant. The man illustrated books, for pity's sake. He and Cassie had constructed a perfect, fairy-tale world in which good *always* triumphed over evil. But Jake lived in the real world. He'd played an active part in it. A very active part. He knew every single way a rake could waylay one of his precious daughters and worried about it constantly. He was already schooling the eldest two on what tricks to look out for. In a year or two, if he could keep it a secret from Fliss, he was going to teach them all how to shoot a gun and how to kill a man with their bare hands...

His wife squeezed his hand in understanding. She saw the way he tossed and turned at night when all the messy and complicated feelings intruded his dreams and his vivid imagination played with him. 'It will all be all right, Jake. You'll see. This one will be as feisty and fearless as her sisters.'

'And her mother.' He kissed her softly and they both gazed in adoration at the tiny miracle they had made. Yet another blessing in a life filled with them.

The lovely moment was interrupted by the heavy sound of an army stomping up the stairs as the children arrived back from the village. Jonathan and Serena had volunteered to take them all to the bakery to get them out from under the adults' feet, but the first Warriner to arrive was Edward, Joe's studious second son. His nose was bloodied and the wire rims of his spectacles were twisted out of shape.

He smiled at Bella, displaying the charming gap from where he had recently lost his two front teeth. 'Chivers says we have a new cousin!'

'Oh, good gracious! What happened to you!' His

mother began to fuss, then they all stared agog as the rest of their children filed in, in various states of dishevelment. Even the little ones clinging to Jonathan and Serena's near-adult hands sported scuffed knees and torn clothing. Sixteen battle-scarred next-generation Warriners with fire burning in their distinctive bright-blue eyes and steel in their spines.

'Have you all been fighting again?' Letty asked sternly. 'Could you not give it a rest on today of all days?'

Sixteen heads shook in consternation; all denying what they did noisily every single day.

'Not this time. That nasty blacksmith's son and his gang took Nick's toffee apple.' Edward grinned at his companions as he retrieved the sticky confection from his pocket and held it aloft in his grubby, grazed hand like a trophy. It was covered in twigs, leaves and enough grit to render it inedible. 'But *we* hunted them down and *we* got it back.'

'Of course we did.' Jonathan ruffled the younger boy's hair affectionately, as was his right as the leader of this new pack. The future. Their legacy. 'And that boy is an idiot as well as a bully.

Surely every nodcock with half a brain knows by now? When you mess with one Warriner, you mess with us all.'

* * * * *

LET'S TALK
Romance

For exclusive extracts, competitions
and special offers, find us online:

f facebook.com/millsandboon

⊙ @millsandboonuk

🐦 @millsandboon

Or get in touch on 0844 844 1351*

For all the latest titles coming soon,
visit millsandboon.co.uk/nextmonth

Want even more
ROMANCE?

Join our bookclub today!

'Mills & Boon books, the perfect way to escape for an hour or so.'

Miss W. Dyer

'Excellent service, promptly delivered and very good subscription choices.'

Miss A. Pearson

'You get fantastic special offers and the chance to get books before they hit the shops'

Mrs V. Hall

Visit millsandbook.co.uk/Bookclub and save on brand new books.

MILLS & BOON